DOT

Araminta Hall began her career in journalism as a staff writer on teen magazine *Bliss*, becoming Health and Beauty editor of *New Woman*. Her first novel *Everything and Nothing* received major critical acclaim. This is her second novel.

Also by Araminta Hall

Everything and Nothing

DOT

Araminta Hall

THE BOROUGH PRESS

The Borough Press
An imprint of HarperCollins*Publishers*
1 London Bridge Street
London SE1 9GF
www.harpercollins.co.uk

HarperCollins *Publishers*
1st Floor, Watermarque Building, Ringsend Road
Dublin 4, Ireland

This paperback edition 2014

First published in Great Britain by
HarperCollins*Publishers* 2013

A catalogue record for this book is
available from the British Library

ISBN: 978-0-00-748781-3

Set in Birka by Palimpsest Book Production Limited,
Falkirk, Stirlingshire

Printed and bound in Great Britain by
CPI Group (UK) Ltd, Croydon, CR0 4YY

MIX
Paper from
responsible sources
FSC **FSC™ C007454**
www.fsc.org

To Lindy & David, my Mum and Dad

To Linda & David, my Mum and Dad

'Wrong reasoning sometimes lands poor mortals in right conclusions: starting a long way off the true point, and proceeding by loops and zig-zags, we now and then arrive just where we ought to be.'

George Eliot, *Middlemarch*

Join-the-dots puzzle
noun (British): a puzzle requiring you to connect a series of dots by drawing lines between them. If the dots are correctly connected, the result is a picture.

Collins English Dictionary

1 . . . Discovery

They were playing a game of hide and seek, as they so often did. Some people might have seen it as a lack of imagination, but as both Dot and Mavis displayed so much imagination in later life, it seems more likely a fact of circumstance. Druith is after all miles from anywhere, sunk in a low, damp Welsh valley, and Dot's house suggested itself to hide and seek in a multitude of ways. Not that two ten-year-old girls were aware of any of this. They didn't even find Dot's house strange: it was still nothing more than a marker in their childhood landscape, and the fact that the floors tipped, cupboard doors opened into secret passages and a concealed turret sprouted out of the side of the house washed over them. The only thing they were beginning to find amusing were the plates which Dot's grandmother inexplicably chose to hang on the walls. 'What next?' they'd whisper to each other. 'Will we be eating off paintings?' Although one glance at the heavy oils of permanently displeased relatives and windswept landscapes made this seem very unlikely.

They never played hide and seek when they were at Mavis's house, not just because she lived in a perfectly proportioned box with no nooks and crannies, but also because her mother looked as if she might cry if you so much as walked on her permanently hoovered floors or breathed on her dustless possessions. Which was in direct contrast to Dot's mother, who seemed to float through life without noticing anything, and her grandmother, who unfathomably didn't care about dirt but about most other things. Out of two peculiar options, however, Dot's house always seemed the most appealing.

Mavis had annoyed Dot that day. She was a fastidious girl, given to huffing and puffing and slapping logic all over Dot's daydreams. Games of beautiful princesses or magic carpets were never allowed and sometimes Dot was bored by the shops where prices had to be accurate and bills added up precisely. That was usually when she suggested a game of hide and seek.

She left Mavis counting in her attic bedroom, nasally intoning the numbers up to one hundred, and raced down the stairs to the second-floor landing. Once there she weighed up her options and realised she'd used all her best places a dozen times already. Mavis would go straight to the bottom of the laundry basket, the jutting shelves in the larder, even behind the basement door which they both found so scary. The door to her mother's bedroom was open and the space below her mother's bed beckoned as invitingly as a pair of outstretched arms. Dot hesitated on the threshold, knowing that Mavis would never enter this room without permission and wondering if this meant she would be cheating. Mavis had already reached sixty-five; she didn't have much time. Dot glanced behind her but her grandmother's door was firmly closed, as it always was. Besides, her mother wouldn't care. It was only her grandma who was mortally offended if anyone entered her room without permission; a peculiar rule which had somehow permeated the consciousness of the house. Even Dot's mother knocked on her own ten-year-old daughter's door before coming in to kiss her goodnight. Dot decided that if she left the door open it wouldn't technically count as cheating.

Dot always felt depressed by her mother's room, although at that time she would never have used this word to describe what she felt whenever she went in there. She would have said that it made her feel empty, or sad, which is of course a childish way of saying the same thing. Nor would she have vocalised those emotions anyway as, even at the age of ten, she already understood enough about the human heart to know never to articulate feelings like those to her mother, who was so delicate even the slightest thing could disturb her for hours. Besides all of which, Dot couldn't have told you why it made her feel sad and empty. If pushed she might have said that it was because it lacked so much, which was true. No photos or pictures, no books, no ornaments, no mess; it looked like the spare rooms at the other end of the house and it made Dot worry that really her mother lived elsewhere.

Dot slid her body under her mother's bed, shimmying as far back as she could against the rear wall, where she was sure no one could casually glimpse her from the door. It was dusty under there, but it still smelt of her mother's favourite perfume, Rive Gauche, which sat next to her bed in a magical blue and silver bottle and was her only concession to luxury, or maybe even life. The springs which held her mother each night almost touched Dot's nose and she worried that her mother might come in for a rest and push the springs into her face. Dot would shout, of course, but she knew it would take her mother ages to figure out what was going on, by which time the springs could have dug into her skin.

Mavis was searching now. Dot could hear her in the bathroom next door looking in the laundry basket. She could probably roll out from under the bed before her mother lay down; in fact if she heard her coming upstairs she'd roll out just in case. This made Dot worry that she would scare her mother or not be able to make her understand what she was doing. Only the night before she'd been going up to her room and seen her mother sitting at her dressing table, staring so intently at her reflection that the woman in the mirror seemed more real than the one doing the looking. Dot wished that she hadn't hidden under her mother's bed; it had been a stupid idea and was bound to make Mavis cross. Nothing was ever simple. Why couldn't her mother be more like a proper mother? This mythical woman lived solely as an image in Dot's mind along with the ponies and princesses: proper mothers did things like bake and pick flowers and ask what had happened at school. A proper mother didn't drift off in the middle of sentences or rub her temples as if she would push her fingers into her brain if she could. She didn't cook the most indigestible and weird foods she could think of, she didn't still live with her own mother. Most of all, she didn't forget to mention who her child's father was.

The fact that Dot had never met a perfect mother was not the point. The only other mother she knew well enough to compare was Mavis's, who was as strange as her own, cleaning a pristine house every day, watching the world through smear-free windows and avoiding speaking to Mavis's father as if her life depended on it. There was her grandmother as well, who was of course her mother's mother, but it was almost impossible for her young mind to comprehend her as a mother and she was hardly what you might call normal anyway. Dot listed some of her grand-mother's beliefs as the dust itched her eyes and prickled her skin: do not sit on at least five of the chairs round the dining room table and three in the sitting room as they are too precious, never pick daffodils as they look common anywhere but in the ground,

4

under no circumstances say the words 'toilet' or 'pardon', stand up when anyone older comes into the room, never sit on the blue velvet chair by the fire or go into her bedroom or touch any of her china. Dot was still too young to decide what she thought about her grandma's rules, for all she knew they could have been right. And besides, they were related to Jesus, as proved by a family tree which some great-uncle had drawn and which now hung on her grandmother's bathroom wall. And that surely must give her grandmother some sort of right to preach.

Dot's arm had grown numb and was starting to buzz with pins and needles which felt like ants running through her blood. She pushed it upwards and her elbow brushed against the smooth surface of what she immediately knew to be a photograph. Unable to turn around she rubbed her elbow over the photograph again and felt that it was trapped against the wall by the head of her mother's bed. An excitement built inside her out of all proportion to the event: she knew she had to look at something so alien in her mother's bedroom. It was easy to dislodge and then she was able to pull herself out and reach back in to retrieve the photograph. Dot's eyes had been made lazy by the dark and it took a minute for them to adjust to the light, for them to focus on the face staring out at her. Then she saw him: a handsome man smiling out at whoever had taken the picture. His face took up most of the frame, but she could see enough blue sky to know that he was outside, as well as the fact that his mid-length brown hair was blowing across his good-looking face with his blue eyes sparkling out and straight into her. Dot felt her whole body tingle like it was Christmas morning. She staggered to her feet and ran to the landing where she shouted for Mavis.

Mavis had been downstairs and it took her ages to reach Dot, although any amount of time would have been too long.

5

'Where were you?' she asked. 'And why have you come out? I didn't call.'

'Under Mum's bed . . .'

'What? But that's not fair, you know I wouldn't go in there.'

Dot pulled Mavis into the bathroom and locked the door behind them. 'Look what I just found under there.' She handed over the photograph, which already felt like a precious possession to her. She watched Mavis look, studying her face intently, praying that she'd come to the same conclusion. Mavis sat on the side of the bath and Dot copied her so that they could both stare into the face of the handsome man.

'Where did you say you found this?'

'Under Mum's bed. It was sort of trapped against the wall by the bed.'

Mavis looked at Dot and her little face was so serious. 'Do you think it's him?'

'Who else could it be?'

'I think you'd know anyway,' said Mavis authoritatively. 'I mean, you must have some sort of bond.'

'I was really excited when I felt it. I knew it was a photograph straight away.'

'Well, you see.'

They both looked again until Dot felt she wasn't really sure what she was looking at any more, until the colours ran into each other and the background washed over the man's face.

Eventually Mavis handed the photograph back to Dot. 'He must be.'

Dot felt as if something was stuck in her throat, but the releasing tears refused to come. Instead she said, 'I think it definitely is him.'

2 ... Concealment

Mavis switched off her mobile because it was easier to ignore Dot when she didn't actually have to know that she was calling. The girl did not know when to let something go and if she had to tell her one more time that nothing had happened after the stupid sixth-form disco then she would scream. It had been six sodding weeks ago and still she was having to go through all the ridiculous details on an almost daily basis. Mavis had never lied to Dot about anything before and she wasn't enjoying it now, it was just that the whole thing with Clive was a lie and she didn't know how to make Dot understand any of it.

Clive was nothing more than a poster on a wall, a pathetic schoolgirl crush, which Dot in her naivety called love. Mavis wondered if Dot would ever speak to her again if she were ever to reveal that after they'd dropped Dot home she'd sucked his dick and then let him fuck her in the back of his car. Dot still thought Mavis was a virgin: until that night Mavis had been a virgin. Dot still thought that one day Clive would see the error of his ways, dump Debbie and declare undying love on a moonlit night to her. Yet the reality was that he didn't love anyone as much as himself and he hadn't spoken to Mavis once since that night.

Mavis was a clever girl, much brighter than her surroundings. She had lowered her sights and persuaded herself that she didn't really even want to try for Oxford and that Manchester suited her so much better, for no other reason than that was where Dot was headed. She couldn't wait to take Dot away from this dump, to show her that there were places where being clever didn't get you ignored for ten years, that there were people out there who would love them and listen to them.

She lay back on her bed now and curled herself into a ball, trying to erase the knowledge of the sickness that was relentlessly washing through her body. Her mother had complained the night before about the smell of vomit in the bathroom, if you could call meekly mentioning anything complaining. Any other mother might wonder why her teenage daughter had been sick every day for the past week or at least ask her if she felt OK. And if her mother didn't ask then maybe her dad might or even her best friend. Mavis thought that she had been surrounded by selfish people all her life and it made her want to punch a few walls.

She calmed herself with the thought that Dot wasn't really fundamentally selfish, she had been made that way. If you asked Mavis it wasn't Dot's lack of father that was the problem, more her lack of mother. You would never meet anyone who seemed more like a replica of a person than Alice Cartwright. She reminded Mavis of the last sheet you print out of an ink cartridge; pale and blotchy with missing words. Last Saturday night they'd all been at Dot's as per watching *X Factor*. Clarice had been groaning at everything that was said, which Dot found highly annoying, but which amused Mavis. Sometimes Clarice was the best person to watch reality TV with as she was the only other person Mavis had met who seemed to hold it in as much disdain as she did whilst being unable to look away. Eventually the adverts came on and Dot went to the loo and, just for something to say, Mavis had asked Alice whom she wanted to win.

She'd looked up at this and Mavis had been shocked all over again, as she so often was, at just how beautiful Dot's mother was. It was something about the fragility of her almost translucent skin which made you want to touch it to see if it was made of cream, or maybe her stupidly huge brown eyes or the long auburn hair that gave her the look of a fairy tale princess. Mavis thought she verged on a cliché; as if an illustrator had been asked to draw his perfect woman.

'Win what?' she'd said.

'*X Factor*,' Mavis had answered, but then felt the need to add: 'You know, the programme we're watching.'

Clarice had shifted in her seat and Mavis glanced at her, seeing a look of – what? – maybe embarrassment cross her usually impenetrable features.

Alice had glanced worriedly at the screen, seeming to see it for the first time. That is a television, Mavis had wanted to say, it projects moving pictures into our living rooms for our entertainment, although I think one day we'll discover it's the government's way of keeping us docile. We watch *X Factor* on it every Saturday, we've done it for years.

'The only one who can sing is that girl with the ridiculous hair,' said Clarice.

'Amber?'

'God, what a name.'

Mavis looked back at Alice but she was staring at her hands again, obviously relieved that nothing more was required of her. Not for the first time, Mavis wondered if she had something medically wrong with her. But then Dot came back into the room and the theme tune started and they had all let themselves be dulled by the blue box.

Not that any of that helped her now. Mavis left her bedroom for the first time that day to go to the kitchen to get a biscuit, knowing that the sweetness was the only thing that might subdue the sickness for a few minutes. Her mother was in there polishing the kettle.

'I was going to make some tea,' Mavis said, even though she hadn't been.

'I'll put it on for you.' It was obvious that her mother was only offering because she didn't want other hands to touch the sparkling chrome. Mavis opened a cupboard door and rustled around, feeling the tension at her back as she shifted tins of soup into tins of tomatoes, flour into sugar.

'Are you looking for something?' asked her mother.

'Biscuits.'

'They're in the tin. They're always in the tin.' There was a note of desperation in her voice so sharp Mavis wondered if she might cry. But instead of asking what the matter was Mavis walked to the tin and fished out a biscuit, eating it standing up leaning against the side, letting the crumbs drop on to her T-shirt before they hit the floor. Each one fell like a boulder into the silence; her mother watching their path. Mavis willed her mother to tell her to stop, to catch the crumbs, to get her a plate, anything apart from the awful twitching as she waited for her to leave the room so she could get out the dust devil.

A faulty scale sounded from the dining room. 'Dad got a pupil then,' Mavis said, pointlessly. Her mother nodded and Mavis knew she was too preoccupied with the crumbs to speak. She left the room, hoping that she was trailing crumbs behind her. She stopped outside the dining room door and listened for a minute to her father trying to sound important, trying to impress a primary-school kid with his musical knowledge. She was filled with an immense hatred for her family, her pathetic, tiny, fucked-up family.

And when you looked at it that way you had to feel sorry for Dot, didn't you, as her family were no better; sometimes they even seemed weirder than her own. At least on the face of it hers were semi-normal, she at least had the requisite number of parents and a mother with a fairly run-of-the-mill mental illness. Dot was stuck in that creepy house of hers with a grandmother who thought she was a cross between the Queen and God and a mother who lived her life as if she ingested industrial doses of Valium on a daily basis. Because what mother would never mention their daughter's father, never even tell her his name, pretend like she was an immaculate conception? 'Why don't you just ask her?' Mavis would ask Dot when she was still too young to understand the impossibility of the situation. Of course she'd understood for years now; she'd worked out long ago that families, unless they inhabit American TV shows, do not communicate when they speak. Now her hopes for redemption for both of them centred on late-night conversations in student digs illuminated only by fairy lights and candles in which they'd amuse their fellow students with tales about their lunatic mothers, making themselves sound so much more interesting in the process.

Mavis and Dot had often speculated whether they'd been drawn together because of this; they'd even made themselves blood sisters at some single-figured age and then had their noses pierced together in a shabby tattoo parlour in Cartertown when much too young. Dot's grandmother had been the only adult in their lives to comment on this and even she had limited

11

her disapproval to a shake of the head and a sharp intake of breath, something which had pleased them less than an observer might have thought. Two weird lonely little girls feeling their way through life without any real guidance. The thought was enough to make Mavis turn her phone back on, but as soon as she did it bleeped the arrival of a message. She pressed the screen and her heart flipped pathetically when she saw it was from Clive.

Yo! Debs n C r havin a hip hopping NYE party. Druith Cricket Club. 8 till late. Respect.

It was enough to make Mavis want to cry, although she never would have done. He thought so little of her he was happy to fuck her, not speak to her for six weeks and still invite her in a group text to his party. Why not shit on her doorstep while he was at it? Although probably she only had herself to blame. He'd been joined at the lips to Debra Paulson since year nine and she had the wardrobe of Kylie Minogue and the body of a porn star, as well as the reputation for never refusing anal sex. And Mavis had gagged. She'd been trying to block out the memory since it had happened but it refused to leave her alone, worrying her like a bad dream. She had been reassuring herself by repeating the mantra, 'It had only been for a second, maybe he hadn't noticed?' Mavis groaned and lay back heavily on to her bed; of course he'd noticed. He'd noticed and told all their friends; right now boys she had known since primary school were doubling over at the tale of that frigid freak Mavis. But it had been a shock. She'd read enough Anaïs Nin and Nabokov to expect his dick to taste salty and fishy like the sea, but it hadn't, it had tasted of sweat and even (faintly) of urine and she'd been overwhelmed by the thought that she might as well be licking a toilet seat, which had made her gag, just for a second.

Her phone rang and it was inevitably Dot.

'Hello.'

'Mave, did you just get a text?'

Her friend sounded so over-excited she wanted to put the phone down again, she even contemplated lying, but knew it was useless. 'You mean the one from Clive?'

'Like, hello? Of fucking course.' Mavis felt herself sink lower, as if her body was melting into the sheets. 'I mean I didn't even know he had our numbers.'

'Of course he's got our numbers. We've sat in small classrooms with him for most of our lives.'

'Yeah, but . . .'

'He's gotta fill the cricket club.'

'But still.'

'Yeah, well.'

There was a pause and then the question Mavis had been dreading. 'You are going, aren't you?'

'I sort of thought not.'

'But why?'

'Cos he's basically a dick.'

'Clive's a dick? When did this happen?'

'It didn't happen, he's always been a dick, I just hadn't noticed before.'

'Fuck.'

'Fuck what?'

'I mean, what's got into you, Mave? You've got so moody lately and now you're saying Clive's a dick when I've sat up with you on many nights discussing the fineness of his arse.'

'Yeah, well, you can be fit and still a dick, so.'

'Right.'

'I mean, fuck, we live in the middle of fucking nowhere and

13

he's having a hip hop night and in the fucking cricket club. I mean, please. He's probably never even been to London, it's so far on a fucking coach. And New Year's Eve. That's like ten weeks away or something. It's tragic.'

'OK, don't come then, I'll go on my own.'

'Come on, don't guilt trip me.'

'Whatever. Have you asked your dad yet?'

'Shit, I hoped you weren't serious.'

'Well I am.'

'OK, I'll do it tonight.'

'Great.'

'Great.'

Mavis and her parents' supper always took place in the kitchen, even though they had a dining room, and her mother always kept the main light shining down, as if daring either of them to spill a drop. Her father was smoking at the back door when Mavis went in and her mother was worrying herself into a frenzy.

'I think the ash is blowing in, Gerald,' she was saying as she tried to drain the beans without splashing any unnecessary water over the pristine sink.

'Well, if it is then I'll sweep it up,' he replied, raising his eyes at Mavis who pretended she hadn't seen, sitting heavily instead in her place. Her father stubbed his cigarette against the door and threw the butt in the bin.

'I wish you wouldn't,' said her mother.

'Wouldn't what?' he answered.

'It leaves marks, when you stub it on the paintwork.'

'You're joking, right? For Christ's sake, Sandra, I stubbed it on the outside of the door. No one's going to notice, except maybe a passing squirrel.'

14

Mavis was never going to hate anyone as much as her parents hated each other. She had to live here, but they actually chose this life. Her father pulled a bottle of wine from the rack and sat down. He was still wearing his tweed jacket, which he now shucked off, revealing another choice shirt/cardigan combo. He sniffed his wine before he drank it and Mavis hated him all the more for pretending that it wasn't really £3.99 from Tesco.

'Can I have a glass, Dad?' she asked instead of the bile she wished she could vent.

He looked surprised, but checked himself, not wanting to betray the role he played of the hip music teacher. I should have been in a band, he liked to say, nearly was before family life came calling. He poured out some of the dark red fluid into Mavis's glass but didn't bother to offer any to his wife, who had never drunk, to Mavis's knowledge.

The wine warmed her and so she said, 'Oh, before I forget, Dot wants to learn piano.'

Her father looked stupidly pleased, as if he knew that the desire to appreciate music would come to everyone in the end. 'Does she? That's fantastic news.'

'So, like, you'll give her lessons?'

'Of course. Hang on.' He fetched his diary from the sideboard and flicked through it. 'Mondays at five are good for me.'

'I'll text her.' Mavis jabbed the message into her phone before the wine wore off, spooning her food in with the other hand.

'You'll spill it,' said her mother.

'For goodness' sake, Sandra,' said her father.

The phone bleeped back.

'Looks like you're on,' said Mavis.

3 . . . Redemption

It began with the production of *Romeo and Juliet* at the village hall. Up until that moment Alice hadn't realised that she wanted to stand on a stage and say other people's words to a blacked-out audience. But she'd seen the poster when she was running an errand for her mother the Christmas after she'd left school and, really, what else was there to do? She'd gone straight round to Mr Jenkins's house, as it said on the poster, and knocked at the door and he'd let her in and she'd read for him and got the part of Juliet, all in the space of thirty minutes. You're a natural, Alice, he kept saying to her and she left with a lightness she'd never felt before because not only had she never been a natural at anything, but also because she knew he was right.

Somehow Alice knew not to tell her mother. She didn't know any other grown-ups properly, certainly nothing beyond polite hellos and isn't-the-weather-terrible conversations and so she had little to compare Clarice to, but she still knew her mother was odd. For a start she called her Clarice.

The other parts were soon allotted and they began daily rehearsals, either in the village hall or at Mr Jenkins's house. Everyone was at least twenty years older than Alice which did make her love scenes with Romeo rather odd, but still she had never felt more relaxed or at ease in her life. The bliss of knowing exactly what you should say from beginning to end, of being allowed to use up all your reserves of emotion on someone else's life . . . By the end of the first week she was already fantasising about the drama schools in London that Mr Jenkins said he would help her apply to.

'Is your mother coming to the first night?' Mr Jenkins asked her one evening, when they were washing up mugs in the village-hall kitchen. Alice had dreaded that question; everyone in Druith knew Clarice Cartwright, whose family had always owned the biggest house in the village, in which Alice and her mother still lived.

'I haven't told her I'm in the play yet,' said Alice. She'd never known how to lie but keeping quiet wasn't the same as lying. If her mother had ever asked her where she got to every afternoon she would have told her the truth in a heartbeat, but Clarice never had.

'Oh but, Alice, you've got to. You're amazing. She'd be so proud.'

'I am eighteen, you know,' she answered, as if she thought he was worried about permission.

'But everyone will be talking about you. You outshine the others by a mile. You'll definitely be written about in the local paper. And anyway, where will you tell your mother you're going every evening?'

Alice hadn't thought about this aspect of the whole performance yet, but as soon as Mr Jenkins said it she knew he was right. She finished drying the cups and went home and found Clarice in the garden, sitting under the apple tree drinking tea out of her china cup, set neatly back in its saucer after every sip.

Alice stood over her mother and said it all as quickly as she could. 'I have something to tell you. I got a part in the village play, *Romeo and Juliet*. I'm playing Juliet. That's the lead role, you know. Mr Jenkins the director says I'm a natural; he says I should go to drama school and become a proper actress. That's where I've been going every afternoon, to rehearse. The opening night is on Saturday and Mr Jenkins thinks you should come.'

Clarice hadn't betrayed any emotion during this speech, but Alice was used to that. Her mother took another sip of tea and set her cup back down. 'Does he now,' she said finally.

'Well, and of course I'd like you to come as well.'

'I'm surprised that you didn't tell me about all of this before, Alice.'

'I'm sorry.'

Her mother nodded at this. 'Have you enjoyed yourself?' Alice nodded. 'And you think you could be an actress? On the advice of one failed actor?'

'Failed actor?'

'Mr Jenkins. That's what he did in London before he came to Druith. Apparently he hardly ever worked until he accepted defeat and came to live here.'

'Oh.' Alice saw Mr Jenkins's flourishes and silk handkerchiefs and clapping hands and knew Clarice was right.

'So, you see, he probably doesn't know what he's talking about.'

'Oh but—'

'Of course I'll come and see you though. Should I buy a ticket or something?'

Alice felt as if someone had deflated a balloon in her stomach and she was filled with stale air. 'Don't worry, I'll get one for you.' She turned to walk away, but then stopped, her face flushing with the effort of staying calm. 'It's not just Mr Jenkins, you know, they all say I'm good. And I do love it and I think I'm quite good.'

Clarice smiled but Alice knew better than to trust it. 'Acting isn't a suitable profession, Alice. And besides, you'd never manage in London on your own.'

'But will you come and watch before you decide?'

'Of course,' said Clarice. 'I'm looking forward to it.'

The play went as well as it could have and Mr Jenkins was right: Alice completely outshone the others, everyone told her she was wonderful and the local paper ran a picture of her on their front page underneath the unimaginative heading of 'A Star is Born'. Not that Alice cared about any of that, she was so entranced by the sensation of stepping out on to that bright stage each night and looking into a deep, all-consuming blackness that she would have done it even if everyone hated her. The others talked of nerves and stage fright and some even took a shot of whisky before going on, but Alice couldn't understand that. To her it felt like diving into a cool swimming pool with the sun on her back; she felt her muscles unlock and her head drain of anxiety.

The play ran for four nights, but Clarice only came once on the first night. She hadn't come for a drink afterwards, but when Alice had arrived home she'd been sitting up in her chair by the fire and she'd said, 'Well done, you really were very good.'

After the last show Mr Jenkins produced two bottles of champagne, which the cast used to toast each other. Alice had never drunk alcohol before but she found it prolonged the floating, buzzing sensation she had so enjoyed on stage. After one glass she said her goodbyes and set off, but Mr Jenkins ran after her and took her arm and made her promise to come and see him the next day so he could tell her which drama schools to apply for and even help her make the calls. She promised that she would, her mother's words of encouragement ringing in her ears.

Clarice was in bed when she got home and so she made herself a sandwich and took it upstairs with her, where she spent the night dreaming about larger and larger stages and a deeper and deeper blackness. She woke up happier than she could ever remember feeling and tripped down to breakfast. Clarice was already sitting at the head of the table, buttering her toast.

'Morning, Alice.'

'Morning, Clarice.'

Alice set to work on her own toast, her legs itching to get to Mr Jenkins.

'So, now that's over then,' said Clarice, her gaze resting over Alice's head and travelling into the garden where Peter, the gardener, was already working.

'What's over?'

'Your little play.'

'Oh, well, yes.'

'I got you this.' Clarice slid a white sheet of paper over the table to Alice. It looked like an application form and for a moment Alice's heart contracted with the unexpectedness of life. Before this minute everything had been over in such short fleeting moments of time, tiny seconds which amounted to nothing, but here was a chance to live a life she understood. She joined the letters on the paper in front of her and saw the words 'Cartertown Secretarial College, Diploma in Typing'.

'But . . .' she started.

'I think it's for the best, don't you?' said Clarice and she really was smiling. She wasn't some wicked witch in a fairy tale, she genuinely believed that this was the best thing Alice could do. Alice saw all of that, she knew it and yet she also knew that she was wrong, wrong beyond measure. She opened her mouth to speak, but found that she wasn't in possession of the right words to make her mother understand any of this. 'I think we both know that being an actress is a bit of fantasy for someone like you. Not that you weren't brilliant, Alice, but it's such a tough world and you are so, so delicate. You would be gobbled up in a day by all those people. They run a summer course, it starts in three weeks.' Alice nodded, tears blocking her throat. 'And there'll be other village-hall productions. Mr Jenkins isn't going anywhere.'

And nor am I, thought Alice, as she took her pen and started to fill in her details.

Cartertown College of Further Education was as terrible as Alice had feared. None of the other girls spoke to her, as girls had never done. She knew that everything about her was wrong: she didn't listen to pop music or wear make-up or giggle about boys and, worst of all, she knew she was extremely pretty. She wasn't being big-headed; in fact if she'd had the choice she would have been plain: plain meant you could keep your head down and men didn't stare and women didn't sneer. Pretty was, in essence, nothing more than a genetic coincidence that had arranged itself in a pleasing way, which was totally baffling when you thought about it. Alice after all had the same features as everyone else and yet they appeared so much more appealing on her.

The time passed as slowly as she'd ever known it. She read

books written hundreds of years ago on the hour-long bus journey to and from Cartertown every day, she failed to place her fingers on the right keys in class and ate her lunch alone in a corner of the cafeteria. But it was only a twelve-week course and so she told her mother it was fine and devised plans about how she could get a secretarial job in London when it was over and pay her own way through drama school.

Then she met Tony. She left college at the same time every day, knowing that if she kept up a good pace she would make the 4.10 bus. She crossed the road in the same place as usual and just as she was about to step up onto the kerb, a heavy foot landed right in front of her, nearly tripping her up. She turned her head upwards and he was smiling down at her, his long hair blowing across his face. 'Sorry, love,' he said, 'I was just stubbing out my fag and you came out of nowhere.' He laughed.

She opened her mouth to speak but no words seemed adequate.

He laughed again. 'How about I buy you a drink to say sorry?'

Alice nodded without knowing what she was doing. She had never spoken to anyone outside of Druith before, apart from bus drivers and teachers. Dates had never been set, pubs never been entered, drinks never drunk. But this man had quite clearly been sent to save her. As if he had it written across his forehead, she knew that he was the real thing.

'Come on then,' he said, taking her hand, 'I know a great little place just up here.'

It was as if she was in a dream; nothing made sense as she was led up the streets of Cartertown by a man whose name she didn't know on the way to a pub. The sights of the journey were the same as every other day but her new circumstances distorted everything into an approximation of what she thought she knew. She imagined Clarice watching, from some omnipotent position and realised that she conducted most of her life this way, sure that her mother was watching. Relatively quickly they turned into a small smoky pub where Tony found them a tiny table covered with grimy mats, redolent with spilt beer and surrounded by authentic red velvet stools.

'So what can I get you?' he asked, standing over her.

'Oh, well, I think a gin and tonic.' The champagne she'd had with Mr Jenkins seemed like too much and it was the only other drink of whose existence she had any real confidence.

Tony smiled and she watched him glide his way easily to the bar where he made himself heard, waving a five-pound note between two fingers as if he was talking a hidden language. He brought their drinks back to the table and put them down, straddling his stool confidently.

'D'you want one?' he asked, proffering a packet of cigarettes. Alice shook her head as he lit one expertly, sucking deeply on the end. He smiled and extended his hand. 'Tony Marks.'

Alice blushed and giggled. 'Alice Cartwright.'

'Well, Alice Cartwright, what were you doing when I so rudely stepped on your foot?'

'Oh, just going home.'

He laughed. 'Just going home? From where, to where?'

She felt the flush on her face deepen and suspected her nervous rash was blooming on her neck. 'I'm at Cartertown College, doing a secretarial course. I live about an hour from here.'

'So you want to be a secretary?'

No one had ever asked Alice this many questions and she wasn't sure if her head was spinning from them or the gin. 'No, not really.'

'Why are you doing a secretarial course then?'

His voice had an accent which Alice couldn't place and she wanted to ask him about it, but didn't know if that would be rude. 'It's complicated.'

'Do you know what you do want to do?'

'I've just been in a play at the village hall.'

'Does that mean you want to be an actress then?' His voice had a hint of amusement in it.

'I don't know.'

'You're certainly pretty enough. Has anyone ever told you that you look like Cindy Crawford?' Alice shook her head. Tony looked at her a minute and then said, 'You do know who Cindy Crawford is, don't you?'

'She's a model, isn't she?'

'Not just a model, a supermodel. It's a big compliment.'

'Oh, OK.'

'Don't you read any of those women's mags?'

'No.'

He drained his beer and Alice suspected she was boring him. But his tone was more relieved when he said, 'I thought you were all addicted to *Cosmo* or whatever it's called. How about music then, who are you into?'

Alice felt herself sinking, it was no good. 'I'm sorry, I don't think . . .'

But Tony laughed again. 'Films?'

She blushed and shook her head, smiling despite her embarrassment.

'Shit, it's like you've been airlifted in from a different century. Where do you live?'

'Druith. It's a village in the middle of nowhere, really. We don't have a cinema or anything like that.'

'But you have been to the pictures before, right?'

'Oh yes.' Alice didn't think it would help matters to reveal that the one and only time she had been was to see *Bugsy Malone* with her father the year before he died. Of course she watched films on the telly, but she mainly loved the musicals with Marilyn Monroe and Doris Day and she knew she probably shouldn't admit to that either.

'Would you like to go again?'

'Yes.' Alice couldn't be sure if he was asking or teasing.

'How about I take your number then and maybe we could go at the weekend?'

Alice wrote her number on the receipt Tony found in his jeans pocket but knew he couldn't possibly ring her house. 'How about we arrange to meet now, instead of you calling,' she said, stumbling over her words.

He laughed again. 'But we don't know the times.'

'Well, we could just meet and then . . .' she trailed off. She was on such shaky ground it was impossible for her to continue.

'Don't you want me to call your house? Have you got a boyfriend or something?' But Tony said it so confidently Alice knew that he didn't see the mythical boyfriend as a threat.

'Oh no, it's just I'm not there much.'

He didn't look convinced, but let her off. 'OK, let's say we'll meet outside the multiplex at six and if we're early we can go for a drink.'

Alice knew her smile gave too much away, but she didn't know what else to do. 'Great.' She stood up. 'Anyway, thanks but I should be getting home now.'

Tony stood up as well. 'Really? I can't tempt you with another?'

'Oh, well, thanks, no. I live with my mother, she worries and, well, so.'

'Let me walk you to the bus at least.'

They left the pub together and the day was still bright and hot which seemed at odds with Alice's mood. As they walked Tony talked about how in his opinion town planners should be shot. How they'd torn down everything that had any soul in towns like Cartertown and replaced it with concrete monoliths which made the residents feel depressed. Alice nodded and murmured, hoping that Tony couldn't tell she had no idea what he was talking about. She didn't even know what a monolith was. By the time they arrived at the stop Alice's bus was pulling up. She turned to Tony, unsure of how to say goodbye.

'Nice to meet you, Alice Cartwright,' he said. 'I look forward to Saturday at six, when we know not what we might see or where we shall go.' There was a smile playing round his lips and Alice was filled with fear that he wouldn't turn up. She wanted to say something to ensure that he did, but she didn't know what that might be. Tony bent forward and pulled her towards him with a strong hand round her waist, pressing his mouth against hers, mashing her lips in a way she thought only existed in films, or on darkened stages. 'You'd better run,' he said, pointing at her bus. And so she did as she was told.

All the way home Alice was filled with the delicious thought that her mother was wrong. Clarice saw the world as a place of threat and violence and manners and rules. It was obvious now to Alice that she had simply never been in love and was quite possibly wrong about everything. Often when she had been younger she had fantasised that her real mother had died in childbirth and her lovely, kind father had remarried out of some sense of duty to her, his daughter. After he had died she thought this probably wasn't true, but – in a real sense – it might as well have been. Her father had become a mystical saint in death as is so often the way, and she felt sure he would have shown her the right way through the world, but left alone with Clarice what hope had there been for her? Tony, she thought, might be her one and only chance to escape a life that could very easily end up with her throwing herself off Conniton Hill in a few years' time. It was vital to her future that she got it right.

As it turned out Alice didn't need to do much more than be herself to impress Tony, which was one of the biggest revelations of her life. Being with Tony was like standing on stage, a leap in the dark in which she didn't even have to know the right lines. They drank in pubs, watched films, even ate a Chinese meal, and she made him laugh and he told her she was beautiful. But undeniably their time was snatched. Alice still hadn't told Clarice; all her excursions with Tony were hidden behind a fictitious group of friends she'd made at college who all lived in nice houses with parents who asked the right questions. Tony was very understanding and seemed to accept that Clarice was difficult without getting annoyed by it. Finally though he came up with a plan: why not tell her that Alice's course had been extended by a week. He would take the same week off work from the record shop where he worked while he waited to be discovered as the musical genius he so obviously was. And they could spend it together. There's a beach nearby, he'd said, I can borrow my mate Trevor's car, he owes me a favour and we could go there every day. The plan sounded delicious even though Alice was troubled by the mate she knew nothing about and the mysterious favour. She didn't want to be a bystander to Tony's life any more, she wanted to be part of it, which was enough to pull her through the lie to Clarice and get away with it.

Tony met her off the bus on the first day of their pretend holiday and held her hand all the way to the Ford Escort he'd parked a few streets away. They were unusually quiet, embarrassment radiating between them at what they were doing and all it said about how they felt. On the drive Tony wound down his window and turned Radio 1 up full blast, singing along to bands Alice didn't know. But it lightened the mood and made her laugh. Alice's hair whipped across her face and she let her head rest against the seat, drinking in the countryside around her, thinking that she would probably never feel happier. Briefly Alice thought about Clarice, either sitting in her chair under the apple tree, or maybe discussing the pruning of the roses with Peter, perhaps listening to the afternoon play on Radio 4, and she was filled suddenly by the sensation that she couldn't catch her breath, as if she was drowning. Fear of the future loomed over her, a complete knowledge that she could not submit to such a life, that eking out your days was not enough.

They parked in a dusty car park and walked over a hill to the beach, Tony carrying the picnic he'd brought along and Alice their towels. The sky was so blue it was as if you could look through it and Alice had to keep watching the horizon to stop herself from feeling giddy. The sun was hot and round and hard, as it so rarely was in the first week of October where they lived, so that by the time they reached the steps to the beach they had forgotten they were only half an hour from home and both were imagining Greek islands.

'Have you ever been here before?' Tony asked.

Alice laughed. 'Of course I haven't. It's so beautiful.'

They started their climb downwards. 'It's amazing, isn't it?'

Tony said. 'I've never been abroad, but people who have say it's better than any beach there.'

'How do you know about all these things?' asked Alice as she watched the top of Tony's head bobbing down the steps in front of her.

He turned back and smiled at her so that her stomach contracted into itself. 'I don't know. How do you not?'

They swam and they kissed and they lay in the hot sand and they were so beautiful and perfect and so complemented the beach that the weather rewarded them with a week of perfect sunshine. There was hardly ever anyone else on the beach and even when there was there were rocks and grasses to hide behind. Alice knew that she would lose her virginity to Tony, although the whole phrase seemed inadequate for the process. She was not losing anything and it did not belong to her. But Tony seemed strangely reluctant. She couldn't imagine that he was a virgin and she had imagined that he would lead her through this with the same confidence that accompanied everything else he did. She pushed her body into his, but still his hands seemed to stop at all the right moments.

By Thursday night Alice felt desperate. Desire had overtaken her body so that she tingled if a fly so much as landed on her. She showered when she got home, tasting the salt as it washed off her skin, and then stood for ages in front of the bathroom mirror, staring at her now brown face, wondering if perhaps she wasn't as pretty as she'd suspected. She rubbed at the freckles on her nose and worried that she looked like a child.

'You've changed colour,' Clarice said to her as they ate their incongruous supper of pork chops, sitting in their brown dining room, even though the evening was still warm and the air was as light as a kiss.

29

'Oh, I've been lying on the grass outside college at lunchtime with some of the other girls,' answered Alice, amazed at how easily lies now tripped off her tongue. Like everything else, lying seemed to be simply a matter of practice.

Clarice nodded. 'Have you thought about what you're going to do when you finish?'

'I suppose get a job in Cartertown.' Even the words tasted stale to Alice.

'It's funny', said Clarice, 'to see you growing up. There were times when you were younger that I thought it would never happen and now it's happened so suddenly.'

Alice had no idea what her mother was talking about and so she took a sip of water and the conversation stopped.

The next day was their last and Tony seemed as jittery as Alice. She felt him staring at her as she ran to the sea and his hands shook as he touched her body in the cool water.

'You really are so beautiful,' he said as they stood waist-deep in the ocean. 'Don't ever let anyone tell you otherwise.'

But there won't ever be anyone else, Alice wanted to shout, please don't say that.

After lunch they went to their favourite rock where Alice lay back into the sand but Tony stayed sitting, hugging his knees. 'Have you told your mother about me yet?' he asked, letting sand run idly between his fingers.

'No, she wouldn't understand.' Alice didn't want to talk, she just wanted him to lie next to her. But his next question shocked her.

'Is there someone else? You can tell me, you know, I wouldn't mind.'

'Wouldn't you?'

'I'd rather know.'

'Of course there isn't. Why, have you got a girlfriend or something?' Alice imagined a string of girls trailing Tony like confetti wherever he went.

He smiled over his shoulder at her. 'No, no. Only you.'

Alice sat up as well and wondered if they were stuck not because of her, but because of him. I have approached this whole encounter like a job interview, she realised, all the time worried that I wasn't good enough. Maybe he is feeling the exact same way. Maybe the fact that I haven't asked him anything about himself is troubling him, not soothing him. It was the first time that Alice had considered herself from the outside and this new perspective shamed her. She placed her hand on his bony back, curved and dotted by the ridges in his spine and he felt warm and sticky from the salt. 'Where are you from?' she asked simply.

'Manchester.'

'What are you doing here?'

He shrugged under her hand and the movement pained her in its loneliness. 'Just had to get away. My dad's a wanker and my mum's what you might call harassed. I'm the fourth boy and she never made any bones about the fact that she wanted a girl. Not that she didn't love us, but she was pretty spent by the time it got to me.'

'I'm sorry,' said Alice and she didn't think she'd ever spoken truer words.

'What about your dad? Why's it just you and your weird mother?'

'He died when I was nine. He had a boat and got caught in a storm. Swept overboard. They never found his body.'

Tony turned round at this. 'No, really? That's shit.'

And it was shit, shitter than Alice had perhaps realised

before. She saw herself standing next to her mother at her father's memorial, in her black dress and little white gloves, swallowing her tears, desperate for a shred of comfort from Clarice, who just looked forward, a veil over her eyes, her hands clasped in front of her.

'Don't cry,' Tony said and she felt the tears on her cheeks. 'Sorry.'

'No, I didn't mean that.' He leant forward and kissed the tracks they had made on her face. 'Look at the two of us,' he said. 'I'm never having kids. Parents just fuck you up.'

And as much to stop him from saying words that Alice could not bear to hear as anything else, she pulled him towards her and something about the way she kissed him or the pitch of the seagulls' screeches or maybe just the way the planets were moving round the earth gave Tony the courage to take the movement as far as they both wanted.

Sometimes you can feel summer ending in the whip of the wind or the coolness of a morning or a cloud passing over the sun. The news was filled with stories of their Indian summer, blown to them like a piece of magic from a mystical land, but still it happened two weeks after their holiday and, with the season's change, Alice felt a terror which she didn't know how to articulate. Sooner or later she would have to stop going into Cartertown for pretend interviews and actually get a job. In just a few weeks it would be too cold to meet on Conniton Hill and the boarding house Tony lived in didn't allow visitors. Their meetings would have to take place in pubs and cinemas, crowded with other people, and eventually he would lose interest and meet a girl who was less complicated and happy to introduce him to her parents.

By November it was as if the summer had never happened

and Tony shivered in the wind. Alice felt him slipping from her with every meeting until one day, on Conniton Hill, he wouldn't meet her eye and so she grabbed and thrashed with her conversation. 'I wish we could meet more often,' she said, longing for him to ask her to run away with him.

He lit a cigarette and she could see frown lines between his eyes. 'It's hard, what with your mother, my shitty room, no money, sodding life.'

'But maybe it doesn't have to be hard.'

Tony grunted. 'Life's always hard, Alice. Maybe not in your fairy tale castle, but for the rest of us it is.' His voice sounded gruff and something curdled in her stomach.

Besides, the insult had stung her and she felt tears popping at the side of her eyes, which she wiped furiously away. Somehow, somewhere, she'd always known that it could end this way and everything about the fact that she would die without him gave her courage. 'Come on,' she said, pulling him up and leading him into one of the many thickets on the east side of the hill. Once there she started to take off her clothes, pulling at his, standing on tiptoe to reach his mouth.

'Steady on!' Tony laughed. 'What's got into you?' But Alice didn't answer, kneeling before him instead and taking him into her mouth, feeling him harden against her tongue. 'Fuck,' he said from somewhere above her. Now she pulled him down so that he was on top of her, panting with the same desire that she felt. 'Wait a second,' he moaned, fishing a condom out of his pocket and every second that he wasn't inside her was too long so she pushed her hips towards him. But once he was she found that nothing was enough, he could not get far enough inside her so that she was almost crying with rage at the inadequacy of the human body's inability to turn itself inside out. She sucked him into her, pulling all of him, wanting part of him inside her for ever.

He came with a cry. 'Fuck,' he shouted, 'fuck, where did you learn to do that?' But he was laughing as well as he rolled off. He sat up and then he said it again and this time the word sounded different. Alice sat up and saw the condom shredded in his hands.

4 . . . Trying

I know I'm not perfect, my goodness no one needs tell me that. But I have tried my best, really I have, and yet all the evidence would suggest that I've failed pretty spectacularly. She should have told her years ago; in fact it never should have been something that needed telling, it should have simply been part of her knowledge, like the fact that I like marmalade for breakfast or that summer comes after spring. But I have known for years that my daughter is not going to; she's not going to do anything much more than function. I don't really blame her; I don't think I gave her much of a start in life or much to hang on to in the way of understanding about love and relationships. In my defence I would say I found it very hard after Howie died to be properly present in anything, which I do realise is a poor excuse, but is at least true. I know she hates me and thinks I'm ridiculous and stuffy and maybe she's right, but I do care, if only I could find the right words.

I decided to tell Dot this morning because it's her fourteenth birthday today. I don't know why it suddenly seems the right thing to do, but I think she's started wondering about things like who you are and where you're from and I don't want her to waste time wondering about things that should be obvious.

Goodness, we all have a hard enough time working the rest out, we don't need to start off on a losing foot. I sat on my bed, dressed and ready, waiting to hear her get up. When I heard her on the stairs I opened my door and asked her to come in for a minute. Of course she was surprised enough by this request not to question me. I know they both think I'm ridiculous about my things, but I have to keep them safe. Possessions are not just materials stuck together to make something, they hold time in their structure, meaning in their make-up. We are the guardians of their knowledge and without them we might as well all crumple up and accept the dust swirling around our feet. I appreciate this is an outdated concept in our disposable society, but I don't see life getting any easier by virtue of the fact that we can throw everything away. And besides, when you understand all of this, you realise that you are only a guardian in life, which somehow makes things easier, or at least it has for me. What you do and how you behave matters because that is what carries our history, we are what makes up the human race and that is a responsibility worth taking seriously.

Dot looked out of place in my room in her jeans and T-shirt, her hair tangled, so I smiled to put her at ease.

'Sit down,' I said, but then she went to my bed and was about to sit on the lace and I had to shout at her to stop and so we got off on the wrong foot. It's just that the lace was my mother's veil on her wedding day and her mother's before that and mine. I had hoped it would one day be Alice's but I think we all know that's never going to happen. So I'm keeping it for Dot, although chances are she'll never wear it either, even if she does get married.

I didn't know how to begin and so I launched straight in.

'It really should be your mother who tells you about all of this, but I can't see a day when she might and so I'm going to.' I hoped Dot understands that she must not repeat this conversation to Alice, she certainly nodded in a very serious way that made me want to sit next to her and soften the blow with a steady arm around her shoulders. But we are all made a certain way and I am too old to break my mould. 'Your father ran off with another woman, plain and simple.' I regretted the use of the words 'plain and simple' as they left my mouth, but I sat as still as I could, only allowing myself to adjust the brooch which always sits at my neck.

Dot looked at me for a while, her little face crumpling with the effort it was taking to absorb the information. 'Who,' she said finally.

'A woman called Silver Sharpe. She was the barmaid at the Hare and Hounds for a while. Frightfully common.'

'But . . .' She needed me to help her but my mind felt as if someone had whitewashed it. 'But why?'

I shrugged and then I said something stupid like, 'Men are very flighty, they pretty much always let you down.'

'Really?' asked Dot. 'Grandpa didn't.'

'Well, I suppose he did. If he hadn't been stupid enough to go out in that storm he wouldn't have been hit by the boom and, well . . .' I knew I had to stop even as I was saying the words because a strange rage was building in my chest when I hadn't even known that I was angry. 'Anyway, Dot, this isn't about Grandpa. I wanted you to know that your father left and there's no point fretting about him.'

'Did he love me?' she asked and the question was heartbreaking. I wish conversations were easier; I wish they were set in stone and there were rules and manners we had to follow like in the old days. I wish they didn't lead you into so many dangerous moments that make you want to run screaming in the other direction.

'Oh goodness, Dot, he certainly did. I used to watch him with you and he was always so proud. He used to carry you round the village on his shoulders.' At least I hope I said that – I'm sure I did.

'So why did he leave then?'

And that is a question I've often asked myself because I am not lying, he really did adore her. But by God it must have been hard to live with Alice. By the end I wanted to shake her myself. She was so bloody passive with him, so locked into her own world that it wasn't any wonder he looked for something elsewhere. Although I couldn't say any of that to Dot, so had to make do with a cop out along the lines of, 'I don't know. Really I don't.'

'How old was I?'

'He left on your second birthday. He said he was going out to buy some extra balloons and he never came back. We thought he might have had an accident or something, but in the end Charles Wheeler came round and told me what had happened.'

'Balloons?'

'I know, it was a poor excuse.' The whole conversation had become unbearable by then. It was reminding me of the terrible weeks after he left, when Alice stayed in bed and got so thin I became convinced that one day I would take Dot in for her visit and there would be nothing there. The doctor couldn't find anything wrong with her; where's the pain, he kept asking her like a stupid fool, when any idiot could have looked into her eyes and seen she was dying of a broken heart. If Sandra hadn't stepped in I don't know what might have happened.

'What did he look like?' she asked.

'Oh well, he was very handsome.' I was on safer ground then and I reasoned it might help to give her a sense of how her mother could have been so fooled by him. If she was fooled that is; with a sense of perspective I have come to regard their relationship more like a train in one of those old films chugging along down the track to the inevitability of the broken bridge. 'He had what I would describe as Roman features, if you know what I mean.' She shook her head. 'His nose was very straight and his lips were full, but he was often very pale. His hair was brown and he wore it long, to his shoulders. They made a very handsome pair, your mother and him.'

She sat quite still after this, looking not at me but at the carpet and I was filled with a sudden fear that actually I had been quite wrong about telling her. I know almost nothing about children really. It took Howie and me ten years to have Alice, in a time before tests and scans, just lots of silent tears and grim recriminations. Then when she finally came I found her too hard to love; it all just felt so bloody dangerous. So Howie did the important stuff, like cuddles and stories at bedtime and filling the Christmas stocking and I locked myself tighter and tighter. She was nine when he died and all I could do was pray that he'd done enough because it was too late by then for me to start.

But while I was thinking all of this Dot stood up. 'Well, thanks, Grandma, are you coming down to breakfast?'

'In a minute, dear,' I answered and only when she'd left the room did I realise that I hadn't even told her his name. I wanted to run after her, but it felt too late by then.

After Tony left and Alice had got up again I would stand at my bedroom window and watch them in the garden sometimes and my heart would pump with pride at my daughter. She loved Dot so completely and purely; I could stare at them for hours making daisy chains or playing hide and seek, reading books, painting. Of course I hadn't realised then that this was the easy part for Alice, that she was capable of love but not of all the responsibility that went with it.

Which is funny because I think I'm the other way around. I never found it hard to feed Alice correctly or brush the knots out of her hair or teach her times tables. It was all the other things that stuck so in my throat. I have looked for answers in my own past and found it too bleak to really make sense of. I have no clear picture of my parents; in fact the predominant memory that I have of my mother is the back of her head. She was a great beauty, just like Alice, who looks so like her I sometimes travel back through time when I catch sight of my daughter unexpectedly. She was always entertaining and we would be brought in to say goodnight to her, in this very house, by a succession of nannies. My brother Jack and I would stand there, meek and quiet, until she turned her dazzling gaze on to us. Then she would make a great fuss, drawing us on to her lap and asking the assembled company if they had ever seen more perfect children and of course everyone would agree with her because she was one of those people whom others wanted to please. She would kiss the tops of our heads and tell us to run along now and we would be taken out of the room and it was like shutting the door on Christmas, every night.

After Jack died there were of course no more parties, not that I saw much more than the back of Mother's head still. Except then it was in bed, with her face turned to the wall and the curtains perpetually drawn. I would glimpse her from the

40

door as I tiptoed past being shushed by whoever was with me. I don't think I was surprised when Father told me that she'd died, she'd been desperate to join Jack for the whole of the six months that she'd been without him. Which was quite a shock in the end, that she'd cared that much about either of us. Well, I suppose she really only cared that much about Jack, because if she'd cared as much about me she never would have left me alone.

Was I right to tell Dot that story? I am so confused by this world I find it hard to remember who I am sometimes. It would be impossible to make Dot, or even Alice, appreciate the changes I have witnessed. I was born into a world of manners and rules at the end of a great war in which brave men fought against a clearly defined evil. Now ideas whip around the world at the touch of a button so that information has become so scrambled it is often hard to know who is right or wrong. Men still fight, but our wars seem remote and unfathomable. Governments appear corrupt and the press is laughable. Sometimes I feel so alone and adrift I fear I may fall over.

When Alice was much younger and it was just the two of us alone in this house I would lie awake every night with my heart pounding as if it was running a marathon, imagining dying and leaving Alice all alone. I was filled with terrors of her shouting for me, of eventually coming to find me and my body being cold and unresponsive. Of her having to negotiate her way out of the house and to our nearest neighbours. Because I knew that if she didn't leave no one would miss us and come looking.

About the only thing that could comfort me on those long night-time voyages was the thought that one day she would grow up and get married and fill this house with children.

I actually looked forward to arguments over furnishings and eventually moving into the turret and getting annoyed by noise. But that has never happened; it wouldn't even have happened if she had created another family instead of just having Dot. Her surroundings are yet another thing that she fails to notice; if I asked her to describe this house she might find it hard, even though she rarely leaves it from day to day. We occupy our generations singly. We are all single.

5 ... Fear

When Alice told Tony that she was pregnant his first feeling was that of defeat. In the time since their fake holiday he'd known that he had to break it off. But, Christ, she was gorgeous and she quite clearly adored him and, well, he didn't think he loved her as such, but she was funny and sweet and far from the worst person to spend time with. In the end though she had become like all women, full of questions and need and such desperation to be loved you sometimes hated them. You can never give women enough, his older brother Matt had told him once as they'd sat on their back step coughing on their father's purloined fags, they're like sodding oceans, there's always more. Tony hadn't known what he'd meant at the time, but he did now.

Tony was not going to be like his old man, who was nothing more than a drunk and a waster. He'd grown up watching his mother work two jobs, one to bring in the money and one to take care of them all. They'd all known that she'd longed for a daughter, presumably as her anchor against the sea of testosterone which surrounded her, or maybe simply not to see her husband's face everywhere she looked. She had loved her sons, probably still did, but she was always tired and often she found it easier to pretend she hadn't heard than to answer. Now Tony was going to be a dad and he was going to do it right. So he got down on one knee and asked Alice to marry him and she was so happy he felt sure that he'd done the right thing, he thought he probably did love her, he thought everything would be OK.

Alice said they could live on love, she'd eat cheese on toast for the rest of her life and never want anything ever again, but that was just irritating. You could not live on love because love, in Tony's experience, rarely survived poverty and Tony was poor. Besides, the thought of Alice on the Cartertown estate or even in some shitty studio flat was absurd. She basically had no idea what she was talking about, which made him feel as if he couldn't breathe properly. We have to talk to your mother, he said finally, when he realised that she was never going to come to the right conclusion on her own. She's not going to be involved in this, Alice had answered. For God's sake, Alice, he'd said, we're getting married and having a baby, you're going to have to introduce us sometime. He knew he was probably a disappointment to most parents, but still it hurt that Alice should feel this so keenly.

On the day of the introduction it felt ridiculous to Tony that at his first meeting with the mythical Clarice he was going to be telling her that he was marrying her daughter and she would be a grandmother in six short months. It was the first time he'd been to Alice's house and he even had to bloody write down directions, standing in a cold phone box with the phone wedged under one ear as he scribbled the route on to an old receipt. It all felt wrong.

Alice of course hadn't warned him that she lived in a castle. He'd known she outclassed him and presumed that she came from a bit of money, but not the huge house that towered over the village and had a turret tacked on to its side, for Christ's sake. He'd recently bought a shitty three-hundred-pound Renault 5, which smelt of petrol so you had to drive with the window down, even in the cold February air, which obviously wasn't going to work for a baby, but was the best he could manage right now. He parked down the road and fortified himself with a fag before going in, wishing he had something stronger. A strange need to see himself overtook him and so he flicked down his sun visor and looked into the mirror, which was tiny and cracked but still showed the sweaty, white face looking back at him.

Eventually there was nothing to be done other than get out of the car and ring on the baronial bell. It was self-evident that this afternoon would put paid to his dreams, pathetic as they were. He'd have to get a proper job, probably cut his hair, start wearing a suit. He'd come home to his tea cooked and, if they were lucky, look forward all year to two weeks on the Cornish coast. His money would go on nappies and milk and Alice would never work because it was simply impossible to imagine her doing so. His hand hovered over the bell. It could be easy to forget this had ever happened. The baby wasn't even real yet. Alice might miscarry. But his father's red, bloated face swam before his eyes and so he pressed hard on the brass ball.

Alice opened the door so quickly he wondered if she had been standing behind it. Her eyes were shining and she pulled him into the house, which seemed dark and cold.

'Bloody hell,' he whispered, 'you didn't tell me you lived in a mansion.'

She looked around her and it seemed to Tony that she was seeing it for the first time, which made him feel even colder. She shrugged. 'Mum's in the drawing room. We've got the fire lit.'

At least that sounded nice and friendly, so Tony let himself relax slightly. He touched her arm to hold her back for a second. 'What was she like when you told her?'

'Told her?'

'Yes, you know, about us, the baby.' Very occasionally Tony wondered if Alice was simple, because even when she said very clever things she didn't seem to know what she was talking about.

'Oh, I haven't said anything yet,' she answered, smiling brightly, as if it was completely normal to get him to come here with their news without preparing her mother in advance.

'You're joking, right?'

She looked puzzled. 'No. I thought that's why you were coming.'

'Christ, Alice.' He really wished he'd had a drink now.

'Come on,' she said, taking him by the hand and leading him into one of the rooms off the hall.

The drawing room – or lounge as he would have called it, although he could immediately see why the word was all wrong to describe such a room – was not nice and friendly. It was too big for a start, with a massive fireplace surrounded by what looked like marble, supporting a huge gold mirror. And the paintings, Christ, he'd never seen so many paintings, all worth a fair packet in Tony's estimation and all of such peculiar subjects, like dogs and old women sitting by fires and country paths leading nowhere. The walls were the deep red of blood that has been exposed to the air for a while and the carpet was lush, folding over his feet. Disconcertingly there were also things everywhere; a multitude of silver and china perched like butterflies on little tables so that his head spun with all the reflected light.

Then there was Clarice Cartwright herself, the woman who was going to become Tony's mother-in-law and grandmother to his child. The thought ran into his feet and he wondered if he was going to faint. She was sitting very straight in a high-backed blue velvet chair, with a china cup and saucer on her lap. Tony hadn't known that people actually used them outside of the TV costume dramas his mother had favoured; he couldn't imagine drinking tea out of anything other than a mug. And the expression on her face was so – what was the word? – unforgiving, as if nothing he could say or do was of any consequence to her.

'Clarice,' said Alice, 'this is Tony.'

Tony jerked his gaze away from Mrs Cartwright for a moment. Surely he'd misheard? Surely she'd said Mum or Mother or Mama even?

'Hello, Tony,' said Mrs Cartwright. 'And to what do I owe this pleasure?'

Tony held out his hand. 'Pleasure to meet you, Mrs Cartwright. I've heard lots about you from Alice.' He knew he was getting everything wrong because her smile was too small and flat.

'Please sit down.'

Alice put her arm out to stop him. 'No thanks. We won't be long.'

They wouldn't be long? Tony looked at Alice again and saw a broad smile on her face, as though she was going to burst with the excitement of a child. He looked at his hands to give himself a sense of perspective, he couldn't be sure that he wasn't in the middle of an episode of *The Twilight Zone*. He looked

47

back at Alice's mother and she didn't seem to find this behaviour strange, she simply sat waiting, twirling the expensive-looking brooch at her neck.

Alice ploughed on. 'We've just come to tell you that we're getting married.'

At least this seemed to ruffle Mrs Cartwright. Her hand clasped the brooch now and Tony estimated that it was probably worth more than he got paid in a year. 'Don't be ridiculous.'

'Why would that be ridiculous?'

The absurdity of their words washed over him and he realised that he barely needed to be there. He felt Alice's enjoyment of the situation radiating out of her like heat. All of this was some sick game to both of them, one they'd probably been playing for ever and Tony recognised himself as nothing more than the hand which would win Alice this round.

'It would be ridiculous because I've never met this man before. And you're only nineteen.'

'But we love each other.'

'Oh come on, Alice. You don't know what love is.'

'And you do, I suppose.'

'Tony,' said Mrs Cartwright, shocking him out of his thoughts. 'Do you love my daughter?'

'Yes, I do.' It was the only possible answer, apart from also being close to the truth, but he would have liked to add that of course he knew she was right and they were too young, but that they had a reason to get married. Somehow though he knew that would be denying Alice something.

'And how long have you known each other?'

'About six months.' His mouth was dry and he heard his tongue click as he talked.

'Where did you meet?'

'In Cartertown.'

'Yes, but where?'

'On the street. We sort of bumped into each other.'

Clarice sighed and Tony hated himself for wanting to impress her.

'Alice,' she said, 'you are not getting married.'

Tony wished she was right, but he heard Alice draw in her breath, he heard her say, 'Oh, but we are, Clarice. You see, I'm pregnant.'

Tony saw Clarice shrink from the news, her head actually rocked slightly on her neck. 'You silly girl,' she said. 'How far gone?'

'Twelve weeks and I'm not getting rid of it so don't bother suggesting that.'

Clarice stood up – Tony imagined she wanted to be on the same level as them – and walked over to the window. Her eyes looked moist.

'We don't want anything from you,' Alice was saying. 'Tony's got a room, we'll live there and we'll be fine.'

Tony stepped forward at this: he had to stop the madness. 'Actually, we can't live in my room, Alice, I've told you that. I'm going to get a job, Mrs Cartwright. I've already started looking. I mean, I do work now, but it's just in a record shop and I know I could do better than that. I think Alice should stay here for now, I don't think she'd do very well in Cartertown.'

'Well, at least one of you has an iota of sense,' said Clarice. She motioned to some chairs. 'Please, let's sit down and discuss this.'

Tony moved forward even though Alice had put her hand on his arm. He turned to her and she shook her head. 'Come on, Alice. If we're going to do this we need help.' And Alice looked so upset he wondered if really he had just lost her this round.

Later, as he sat in a pub in which he knew he wouldn't meet anyone, Tony thought he had to give Mrs Cartwright some credit. If his parents had had a daughter and some bloke had turned up with the news that he'd got her pregnant, his dad would have flattened him. But Alice's mother had mostly seemed concerned that they made as little mess as possible out of a situation she clearly understood to be catastrophic. They'd agreed to live with her. Or, to be accurate, he had agreed they would live with her, while Alice sat and fumed like a baby next to him. Do you think I want to live in this freak show of a house? he'd wanted to shout at her. I'm doing this for you, everything is for you.

He was going to move in after the wedding, which Clarice wanted to happen as soon as possible. Alice was going to get on to the Register Office the next day. No one, him included, wanted to invite anyone, so it was hardly going to be an organisational task.

'What about your parents?' Clarice had asked.

Tony had shaken his head. 'I don't talk to them any more. Honestly, there's no one.' And the words had sounded so desperate and lonely he'd almost stopped at a phone box on the drive home to call his mum. But he hadn't because that would mean admitting something to his dad, something he didn't yet understand, but felt sure he soon would.

Three weeks later Tony woke up on his wedding day and couldn't tell himself how he'd got there. He even felt nostalgic shutting the door of his pokey room and saying his final goodbyes to his landlady, whom he'd never even liked. Good luck, lad, she'd said as he was walking out of the door and he wanted to cry on her shoulder and ask her what he should do. Not that there were any choices, he knew that.

When he arrived, hot from the bus in his charity shop suit which smelt of death, Alice and Clarice were waiting outside the municipal council building, even though Tony had made sure he was early. Alice looked absurdly beautiful. She was in a white silk dress with flowers in her hair and a tiny bump, which you would never know was a baby, rounding her stomach. His heart lurched involuntarily at the sight of her, at the knowledge that the girl everyone was looking at wanted to be joined to him. He'd never seen the dress before and he wondered if she'd bought it especially for the occasion, which touched him, until he checked the ridiculousness of his thoughts. What bride didn't buy a dress especially for her wedding?

Tony and Alice stood side by side in a room which was much nicer than he'd feared, despite its fake wood panelling and formulaic flower arrangements. The registrar had to get two members of staff to come in to witness their vows. Clarice stood behind them and Tony could feel her poker straight even though he couldn't see her. The witnesses smiled at them, probably thinking they were so romantic and young and full of hope. Tony stole a look at Alice and she smiled at him, spots of colour high on her cheeks. He smiled back and took her hand and a flash of what felt like love shot through him. The sun was out and they were going to be fine.

It was only words after all and Tony had said enough words in his life that he didn't mean. Not that he didn't mean this. No, it wasn't that, it was more that it was hard to take completely seriously. Laughter bubbled up inside him, puffing out his cheeks and the registrar nodded at him because she'd no doubt seen many men overcome in the same way. 'I do' were hardly even words. Three letters, that was all.

They left the room at the same time as the couple next door, whose room was overflowing with guests, all dressed in their finery. Women in parrot-bright colours tottering on high heels and rosy-cheeked men with flowers in their buttonholes, slapping each other on the back. And a bride and groom with their arms around each other, the woman too fat for her dress which strained at the sides, but still beautiful in her happiness. All of Tony's meagre party stopped and stared at this marital vision as they tripped down the white marble stairs, built no doubt for a duchess hundreds of years ago. The photographer at the bottom was waiting for them, moving them around to look their best. Give her a kiss, mate, he was shouting and the crowd surged, excitement on their lips, bubbling over everything. Tony realised he'd forgotten to buy a camera, even though that had been on his list of things to do. He looked at his tiny, impersonal party and saw that even the witnesses were leaning over the balcony, wanting to be part of these strangers' happiness for as long as they could.

Tony suggested a drink because it seemed too tragic for them to go straight home. All his money from his new job at the call centre had to be saved for the baby and Alice hadn't even mentioned a honeymoon. She was amazing like that – unlike any woman he'd ever met – in her lack of desire for anything material. Clarice politely declined the offer of a drink and hailed a taxi, wishing them goodnight. So he sat with Alice in the garden of a wine bar with a bottle of champagne they couldn't afford as the sun set over their wedding day. Tony wondered what they must look like to the other people in there, a group he had been part of but now felt so separated from. He looked at the men in their shiny suits and the women with their big shoulders and permed hair, he saw their mouths moving in conversation, saw them laughing and wondered how many of them would be going home together that night. He knew the mind-cleansing pleasure of a warm body you could forget in the morning and a great longing welled up in him that felt like a sadness, but he pushed it down and stared at his new wife, who was easily the prettiest person there.

They were home by eleven and in bed, across the hallway from Clarice. Alice rolled into him and he knew it would be wrong for them not to have sex on their wedding night. But it took an act of concentration on his part, not because he didn't find Alice attractive – you'd have to be blind for that to be true – but because he felt so strange it was as if he was removed from himself. Their love-making was silent as he supposed it would have to be until they had enough money to move out, which in his estimation would be in at least five years. Afterwards Alice cried and said she had never been happier and Tony put his hand on her stomach and imagined the part of him already in there, swimming in its own dreams. The thought was magical and surprising and made him smile like a fool in the dark.

6 . . . Consumption

Mavis didn't know how Dot had managed to persuade her to go shopping for a dress she didn't want to wear to a party she wished she didn't have to go to. But maybe it would be a good opportunity to say sorry for how she'd been behaving, perhaps even to explain. She longed for her friend's advice in a way she'd never felt before and yet she'd never felt further away from asking for it.

They met at the bus stop, aiming to catch the 11.06 into Cartertown. Dot was late and Mavis stood in the cold, stamping her feet and slapping her arms around herself. She looked at the timetable for something to do and thought how only a town planner who drove a four-by-four and talked too loudly on his BlackBerry would devise a route which turned the bus the wrong way down the Cartertown Road in order to take in three other villages before heading towards the mecca of the town.

Mavis sometimes wondered what people a hundred years ago would think of their cities. Had they stood on the cusp of the modern world and thrown their minds forward into a future of shiny chrome and marble and structures which reached into a sparkling sky? She wondered why, despite all the evidence, they now in turn imagined their own future filled with alien domes and cars that whizzed through the air. In reality nothing changed and it was maybe time to accept that.

Dot arrived just as the bus was drawing up and they silently made their way to the top deck as they always had done, although Mavis felt heavier now, less like pulling herself up the stairs.

'I think we should start in Topshop,' Dot said, pulling out a copy of *Grazia* in which she'd marked a page depicting an impossibly beautiful girl wearing a dress that their Topshop would never stock. Mavis groaned.

'Any other ideas then?' Dot asked, turning to her friend.

Mavis shook her head. 'I'm not buying anything so it's your call.'

'Seriously?'

'Seriously.'

The bus puttered onwards or backwards, depending on how you looked at it. Cows and horses were eating grass, birds were flying in the sky, cars were overtaking them; Mavis had to swallow back her tears.

'You are still coming though, right?' asked Dot and Mavis hated the whine in her voice. She had to pinch the inside of her hand to stop herself from screaming.

'I said I would, didn't I?'

'I don't want to force you.'

'For fuck's sake, Dot, I'm coming, don't ask me to be happy about it as well.'

'Mave, what's wrong?' Dot's tone was tender and concerned, so that without planning it, Mavis turned to her friend to tell her. This was the perfect moment, this was the point that could make it all better. Dot might even have a solution.

But the words slipped and slid around her head; saying them out loud would make it real and she didn't know if she was ready for that yet – ever. She chickened out. 'What colour's the sky?'

'What?'

Mavis knew she was starting to piss Dot off and who could blame her. 'What colour's the sky?'

'Blue? Are you on something?'

'Ha! Why d'you say blue?'

'Mave, you're scaring me.'

'Because the sky's always blue, right? Because that's what all the fairy stories tell you, because you painted it blue with your mum.'

'What?'

'Look, just answer the question.'

'OK.' Dot looked out of the window. 'Right, it's completely grey. So?'

Mavis sat back, pleased with herself but lost as to how she might go on now.

'Are you trying to say something?' Dot asked and the question made Mavis want to punch her.

'We don't all spew our feelings everywhere you know, Dot.'

'Are you talking about me and my dad?'

'Fuck, no! Not everything's about him. He left, Dot, and you need to get over it.' Mavis knew she'd gone too far, could feel the tension radiating off her best friend like electricity. 'Sorry, ignore me, I'm a bitch. But I mean, what do you want from him now anyway?'

Dot shrugged. 'I dunno. I wonder that myself sometimes. Like, it's probably too late, right?'

Mavis wanted to put her arm round her friend because they were both alone, really. 'I'm sure it's not.'

'I wouldn't mind asking him why he called me Dot.'

'What?'

'Come on, it's such a crap name. A dot is the smallest, most insignificant thing there is. And it's a full stop, so an ending. I mean, who on earth would call their child Dot?'

'How d'you know it was him? Maybe your mum thought of it.'

Dot snorted at this. 'Come on, Mave, can you imagine my mother doing anything as definite as choosing a name?'

'Fair point, but at least you're not called Mavis after your dead gran.' Dot laughed and for a moment they could have been anywhere, but the thought scared Mavis in its possibilities and she shook her head, trying to shake the tears away from the corners of her eyes. Her fear mutated into a desire to sabotage her life. 'Look, I've been meaning to tell you. I'm not going to go to Manchester.'

'I said you should go for Oxford. I don't mind, really.'

'No, no. I'm not going, to university at all.' Mavis fixed her eyes on her hands; she could feel her face reddening under Dot's persistent gaze.

'What are you talking about? We've only just applied and you'll easily get in. I'm the one who should be worried.'

'I'm not worried. I'm just not going.'

'Even if you get in?'

'Yeah.'

They sat quietly now, all the intimacy gone, the rough seats of the bus vibrating gently beneath them.

'I don't get it,' Dot said finally.

'There's nothing to get.'

'So what're you going to do? Go to Cartertown College of Further Ed with Debbie?'

'Maybe I won't do anything.'

'Are you depressed or something?'

'Probably.' Mavis felt something bubbling, as if her insides were itching, as if there was no way out any more. 'Look, I'm not depressed like that. I don't need Prozac or anything. I just think it's all a bit pointless. Three more years studying when I could be . . .'

They both waited for what Mavis could be doing, but her mind was blank. In the end Dot said, 'You're not making any sense.'

It was raining now, the drops streaking the window like grease, the road looking sleek in front of them. If you would only ask the right question, Mavis said, but not out loud. She was struck by a vision of herself in ten years' time, bumping into Dot on the street in Druith when she came back for a visit, because of course by then Dot would be living in London or Paris or New York. She'd be glowing and tanned and well dressed, her hand lazily holding an equally attractive man. Mavis would try to hurry on past them, but Dot would stop her, wanting to reminisce because the past is fun if your present is great. Finally Mavis would be able to get away and she would hear the man asking Dot who she was and Dot would say, Oh we used to be friends once, a long time ago. And Mavis was suddenly filled with the knowledge that life is only moments, that the thing we are doing now is past as soon as it is done, that nothing is real, nothing guides us, nothing holds us. Her heart pumped with the fear of the knowledge.

The bus stopped on the high street, which was a new development, born out of the fact that this was the only reason anyone went to Cartertown any more. The industries were long gone and factories and offices lay abandoned on stretches of concrete wasteland where disaffected youths went at night to sniff glue, drink cider and break windows. They raced stolen cars in the weed-infested car parks, played music too loudly and fucked in cold rooms if they were lucky. In another time, when Mavis had still been interested in the news outside of herself, she had read in the *Cartertown Gazette* how residents from the nearby estates, both private and council, formed groups and lobbied the police, but nothing was ever done. The police simply didn't have enough officers to approach these children who roamed in packs like animals and were so emboldened by their mass that they were capable of any wrongdoing. Instead the police resorted to responding as quickly as they could to the muggings and burglaries and intimidation that found its way out of this feral environment, as if acting after the event was as good as preventing it in the first place. Mavis suspected that this was a more accurate vision of the city of the future.

Topshop had always reminded Mavis of a joke, if that was the right word, one which she had heard being played on Primrose Duncan in the first week of secondary school. Primrose Duncan who was so badly bullied that her father found a new job, sold their house and moved her hundreds of miles away to a school with a great reputation. Primrose Duncan, who Mavis had read about in the *Guardian* last year, was the youngest solo cellist to play at the Royal Albert Hall. Two year nines had approached Primrose and told her a complicated story about a fish riding a bicycle, and then they'd started to laugh. Primrose had obviously copied them and they'd stopped as suddenly as if she'd slapped them and asked her what was funny, a question she'd been unable to answer because nothing was and so they'd started laughing again, but this time most definitely at her. Dot and Mavis had watched them walk away and Primrose cry and they had assured each other they'd never have fallen for such an obvious prank, but now Mavis wondered who they had been kidding. She imagined Primrose telling this story to an interviewer in years to come; she imagined turning on the television to find her laughing over it with Graham Norton or Alan Carr. Now that's what you called revenge.

The clothes on the rails wilted under Mavis's touch and she found herself simply following Dot, sucked into an ennui so deep she feared she might never have another useful thought again. Of course the *Grazia* dress was nowhere to be seen, the shop assistant didn't even recognise it and Mavis thought it probably only existed on the pages of magazines. Dot ploughed on until she found another, infinitely inferior version of the dress which she held in front of her, held away from her, wondered at, rubbed between her fingers, squinted at.

'Just try it on,' said Mavis wearily.

'You really not going to try anything?'

'No.' The changing rooms were being guarded by Stacey Young from their class and Mavis felt the last vestiges of energy drain from her body.

Stacey lazily handed Dot a tag, her expression doubting the wisdom of trying on the dress, of them even being in the shop. 'You can't go in without something to try on,' she said to Mavis.

'Seriously?'

'It's policy.'

'Don't be ridiculous.' Mavis grabbed the nearest thing to hand, a pair of lime-green hot pants, and held out her hand for a tag.

Stacey laughed. 'You're never trying those on.'

'Give me the fucking ticket, Stacey. Or shall I call your manager and tell her you won't let me try on any clothes?'

Stacey slapped the numbered plastic circle into Mavis's hand and mimicked a Jamaican gangsta accent to say, 'It's not my fault you is mingin'.'

'And it's not my fault you're too thick to even speak properly,' answered Mavis.

'There are some parts of the new you I could get used to,' said Dot as they made their way inside. But Mavis didn't agree. Dealing with people made her feel sad now.

The changing room was bright and there didn't seem to be any other option than to take your clothes off in full view of everyone, so Mavis slumped on to the floor by the mirror as Dot struggled out of her jeans and into the dress. She looked quite pretty in it really and Mavis was moved by the slight rounding of her stomach and the curve of her unblemished upper arms. But at the same time none of it seemed real. Dot looked like one of those cardboard dolls Mavis had played with as a child, with the cardboard clothes that never stayed on however hard you pressed on the ineffectual tabs which were meant to hold them on to the body. You would try a dress, then a skirt and shirt, move on to a pair of jeans, try in vain to get any footwear to stick, end up with a hat. The memory of dressing up simply for its own sake made Mavis laugh.

Dot looked down at her. 'Problem?'

Mavis shook her head, but the laughter was rumbling inside her, as though it was riding a rollercoaster in her body. She held her hand to her mouth but the sound bubbled out, escaping like a naughty child. The other occupants of the changing room were looking round and Dot had gone red.

'What the hell's your problem now, Mave?'

'It's not you,' she managed to spit out before the laughter erupted, unbidden, inappropriate.

'Thanks a bunch,' said Dot, struggling out of the dress so quickly that it stuck, exposing her mismatched bra and pants, until she emerged sweaty and fuming.

Mavis stood up, composing herself. 'Dot, it looked great. It wasn't you. I was remembering something.'

Dot was dressed now and she marched out, pushing the dress at Stacey who shouted after them for the hot pants. They didn't stop to answer and were outside in minutes with Dot walking fast so that Mavis had to run to catch up with her. She pulled on her friend's arm and Dot turned round, anger flickering in her eyes.

'Dot, I'm sorry, really it wasn't you.'

'I don't know if I care any more.'

'Please.'

'What?'

'Look, I'm starving. I really fancy a Maccy D's.'

'You hate McDonald's.' But they started to walk towards it anyway. 'You went on that protest in year eleven, remember? You stood outside this very McDonald's and handed out leaflets about how they were ruining our environment and our health.'

'Yeah, I know.' They walked through the doors and the smell of reheated grease assaulted their nasal passages.

'So, what's changed?'

'Nothing I expect, I just want a Big Mac.' Mavis heard Dot sighing. 'Look, who am I to change anything? Me not eating a Big Mac isn't going to change the world. I was a prat for thinking it would.' Mavis recognised this argument as dangerous and was shocked to hear it coming from her own lips.

They stood in the queue behind a girl their age with a crying toddler and a gaggle of spotty young boys. 'If we all thought like that nothing would ever change,' said Dot.

'Nothing ever does change, Dot, or hadn't you noticed?'

'Nothing will change if you don't go to university and stay here all your life, that's for sure.'

'Look, it's not possible.'

'Not possible? What are you talking about?'

They reached the front and Mavis ordered a Big Mac meal with Coke, knowing that Dot would refuse to eat anything. She leant against the plastic counter. 'Just drop it, OK?'

'Not really. But guess I don't have a choice as you don't tell me anything any more.'

Mavis's meal was put on to the counter way too quickly for any proper cooking to have occurred and they went to sit at a sad table for two by the wall. The toddler was eating chips and his mother chicken nuggets as she stared out of the window. Mavis wished she'd thought to sit with her back to them. She bit into the foamy bun, her teeth connecting with air and cattle innards, sugar-sweet condiments and limp lettuce. Her desire faded as suddenly as it had arrived, her stomach repulsed by what she was asking of it. She imagined the factory, the meat-recovery process, the chemicals, the lack of air, the underpaid workers and then Dot was swimming in front of her, her vision shaky and disconnected. She stood up.

'Are you OK?' Dot was saying from the other side of the room. 'You've gone white.'

Vomit was travelling up her gullet and all Mavis could do was stumble to the loo where she retched into the toilet, its rim dotted with someone else's piss. Her body contracted, sending heat pulsating through her in waves again and again until she thought she was finished and leant weakly against the wall of the cubicle. Dot was on the other side of the door, knocking and asking if she was OK. Mavis flushed the loo and emerged into the dingy bathroom. She splashed some water onto her face and then drank some but it tasted of the sweetness of sickness.

Dot rubbed her back. 'Hey, are you OK? Is this what's wrong?'

Mavis looked at herself in the mirror and was surprised by how pitted and pale her skin was, how deep the black circles under her eyes, how greasy her hair, how chapped her lips. 'I've been feeling shit for a while now.'

'Maybe you should see a doctor.'

'Maybe.'

'Come on, let's get you home.'

'But your dress?'

'It's fine.'

They had only been in Cartertown for just over an hour and Mavis couldn't shake the feeling they were somehow leaving in disgrace as they waited on the opposite side of the road for their bus home.

'I could call my mum if you can't face the bus. Or your dad,' said Dot.

'No, I'll be fine.' Mavis's head was too tight, as if her skin had shrunk or her bones had grown. But Dot was being so nice when she had no reason to even like her any more. She wanted to be nice back. 'How're the lessons going with Dad?'

'OK. You don't have to go out every time I come, you know. In fact, I wish you wouldn't.'

'He's so fucking embarrassing though.'

'He's not too bad to me.'

'Come on, they're freaks, my parents.'

The bus came and they got back on, climbing the stairs

again. For all Mavis knew it could have been the very same bus in reverse. 'D'you think your mum's OK?' Dot asked when they were sitting down.

All Mavis wanted to do was sleep and so she laid her head against the window, which felt wonderfully cool. 'I don't think she's ever been OK. Imagine living like that. So scared and meek and so . . . so fucking nothing.'

'Our mums would probably like each other.'

'We've been down that road, Dot. One of them would have to leave the house for more than a trip to pick up industrial amounts of cleaning products for that to happen. I don't know what Dad sees in her. And as you well know, he's nothing special.'

'Our mums are both so weird. D'you think they realise it?' Dot was drawing hearts into the condensation of the windows, which annoyed Mavis unduly.

'No, how could they? I don't think you set out in life trying to be weird. We won't ever understand them, Dot, we might as well accept it.'

'So why're you staying around here then?'

The question hung in the air.

Dot snorted, probably annoyed but wanting to prolong the old familiarity which had surfaced between them like a drowning man: 'What on earth do you think's made them both like that?'

But Mavis's brain felt as mushed as her insides and she couldn't do anything more than shut her eyes.

There are plenty of things, she wanted to say to Dot, countless scenarios in which you could become a shell of a person, eaten up with regret and longing for a life you couldn't have. And mostly it was your own fault, the place you found yourself was made by your path, by the way you dealt with shit. Because we all have shit in our lives. Maybe that was the lesson Dot still had to learn, Mavis thought as the bus took them home in the wrong direction. Her friend was like a child, always convinced she had it worst, that nobody else ever had to live through the things she did. Which was absurd when you thought about it; about her big house and her mother and grandmother, who might be weird and not exactly what you'd choose, but who loved her. The rage Mavis had felt so often recently tightened around her stomach again and the nausea rose inside her. Dot had fallen silent herself and Mavis pushed her fingers into her eyes, trying to blot out her view of her friend's complacent profile set against the frame of the bus window. Dot didn't understand anything.

Mavis must have slept because the next thing she knew Dot was shaking her awake and they had to stand up quickly so that the blood rushed from her head and she banged her arm on the rail as they went downstairs. It was cold and unforgiving when they got off, the sky a dark slate grey and the trees bending against a bitter wind. It was a day to be inside next to a fire, with someone cooking you tea and toast, except that her mother would never light their fire because of the dust and no one was ever allowed to eat or drink in the lounge. They set off on the same road together.

'D'you feel any better?' Dot asked.

Mavis grunted. The anger seemed to have been solidified by her sleep, thickened like a good stock. She knew that she needed to be on her own.

'D'you wanna come back to mine?' Dot tried.

'No.'

'OK.'

They came to the place where they had to part, Dot going up the hill and Mavis down. Mavis half lifted her hand, not even meeting her friend's eye. But she heard Dot following her, felt her hand on her arm.

'Mave, have I done something to upset you?'

Mavis kept her eyes on her feet. 'No.' But it felt as though she had.

'So what is this then?' The wind was whipping Dot's words away.

'Please, Dot, nothing, I just wanna go home.'

'I'm sick of your bloody nothing.' Her friend's voice was harsh.

Mavis looked up at this and saw the pink on Dot's nose, her bright lips, a sanctimonious glint in her eye. It made her speak. 'You're not the only one who has it hard, you know, Dot. You are so unbelievably selfish.'

Dot threw her hands up at this and turned to walk away. But then she turned back. 'I can't take this any more, Mave. You obviously hate me for some reason you're not prepared to divulge. And fine. But I'm bored of banging my head against a brick wall.'

Mavis set off down the hill. She wasn't crying, it was the wind working its way into her eyes. Her limbs felt so heavy, she wondered if she'd make it home. She tried to see herself from above, to get some perspective as to why she was pushing away the one person who could help her. She had no understanding of herself any more, was unsure what she was going to do next, worried she was turning into someone she didn't recognise. Maybe she was going mad. Her mind certainly felt disconnected from her body, as if she was watching herself on TV, as if reality could jar out of place at any moment. Anxiety rushed around her unbidden and for none of the usual reasons. It prickled inside her veins until the sweat seeped onto her skin and dried, leaving her smelly and greasy.

She sat on the bench on the green. She didn't want to go home but she couldn't stay out in this cold. Her toes felt like ice even through her boots and socks and her hands ached. She took out her phone and bashed out a text to Dot.

Sorry, don't know what's up with me at mo.

She set off again but her phone beeped in her pocket almost instantly.

It's OK. I'm here if you wanna talk xxxx.

7 . . . Friendship

Sandra Loveridge, née Powell, felt that she had been born to be a mother. Which is an odd thing to think about a baby: that their sole purpose in this world could already be simple procreation. But Sandra not only consistently failed to think of herself as anything other than the person she was now, she also didn't think there was anything simple in growing a whole other person inside you and then being the best mother you could be so that they became confident, kind people. Besides, she couldn't find meaning in anything much else and the first time she held Mavis she fell so deeply in love the rest of the world had fallen away. She wished that her parents had been alive to see her baby, but made do with giving the little girl her mother's name.

Of course Sandra had known about Gerry's reputation when they met. Most people thought he was too big for his boots, and he'd had to leave his job at Cartertown Secondary after an 'inappropriate relationship' with a pupil. But they were so young themselves, it hardly seemed that much of crime to Sandra. Then he got the job at the music college in Darlington, which was an hour in the other direction from Cartertown, where nobody she knew ever went and Sandra could almost pretend didn't exist. And besides, he'd loved her so completely, everyone had commented on it, how he couldn't take his eyes off her and how he laughed at all her jokes. And best of all, he was completely happy for her not to work and to go on producing babies year after year. They'd had Mavis when they were young, both only twenty-three, and even as she'd lain in her hospital bed, her face still red and blotchy from pushing their baby out, she'd told him that she wanted one every two years until they had at least six. And he'd laughed and kissed the top of her head and said, Why stop at six, why not make our very own football team.

Sandra hadn't been wrong about her natural abilities either. She not only loved being a mother, but she was undeniably great at it as well. She had the patience of a saint, as her mother would have said, and she took unbridled pleasure in watching Mavis sail through all the various developmental stages. She kept a little book by her bed in which she wrote down everything Mavis did, always dated and sometimes with a photograph taken with the Polaroid camera Gerry had proudly brought home one night.

When Mavis was eight months old she started taking her to the mother-and-baby group at the church hall, where she met other mothers, some like-minded and others who found parenting hard and relentless. They were fun women and the group extended its remit into coffee mornings at each other's houses and picnics on the village green. Relatively quickly, as easily its most capable member, Sandra took to running the group herself, welcoming new mothers, devising art activities and leading the end of session sing-a-long. She was aware of how she looked to the other women and liked it, so capable and serene, so that often she would lock up the hall with a feeling of contentment not unlike an old, fat cat stretched out on tiles warmed through by the sun.

She had seen the very pretty young girl with the red-haired

daughter around in the village for a while, but she'd never spoken to her or seen her at the mother-and-baby group. Sandra liked to keep things neat and she didn't like the thought of another mother missing out on being sucked into her orbit. So, when she saw her pushing her daughter on the swings on the green one morning, she stepped off the pavement and made her way over with Mavis.

Sandra lifted Mavis into the neighbouring swing and started pushing, until the two little girls fell into line.

'Don't they look sweet,' she said, 'both with their red hair.' Sandra felt the woman next to her tense slightly. 'How old's yours?'

'Nearly two.'

'Oh, so's Mavis. What's her name?'

'Dot.'

They pushed on in silence. Sandra hadn't yet met a mother who didn't want to talk.

'How's her sleeping?' she asked, deploying the standard mother question.

'Oh, OK.'

But the woman still sounded guarded.

Sandra looked at the woman's amazing profile, at the smoothness of her skin. 'Really? Lucky you, Mavis is a nightmare. Up every couple of hours.'

This got her attention. 'Really? So's Dot actually. I thought I was doing something wrong.'

Sandra laughed, on much firmer ground now. 'Of course you're not. None of them sleep. Don't you talk to other mothers?' The girl blushed. 'You live in Druith, don't you? I've seen you around.'

'Yes.'

'But I've never seen you at the mother-and baby-group.'

'The what?'

71

Sandra wondered if she was for real. 'I run a mother-and-baby group at the church hall. We meet every Tuesday at ten. Just a group of mothers, we talk, the kids play. Many biscuits are eaten!'

'There are other mothers in Druith?'

Sandra laughed. 'Of course there are. There are mothers everywhere.'

'Tony, my husband, said he thought there'd be something like that going on. We were only talking about it the other night.'

'Well, he's right. You should come along.'

'Thank you, yes.'

'My name's Sandra, I run it so I'm always there, I can introduce you to everyone.'

'Thanks.' The girl blushed. 'Alice.'

The swings started to slow. 'Do you mind me asking how old you are?' Sandra asked. 'It's just you look so young. I mean, you could be sixteen or something.'

Alice laughed. 'Not quite. I'm twenty-one.'

'Oh, right. I think it's your skin, it's so smooth and you haven't got any bags. Not like me, I could carry the weekly shop in mine.'

Dot was squalling to get out and Alice lifted her up, kissing the top of her head, resting her on her hip. Sandra did the same with Mavis, who immediately wriggled free and toddled across the grass. 'Anyway, nice to meet you, Alice. Hopefully we'll see you and Dot next Tuesday.'

'And you.' Alice smiled. 'We'll be there.'

Sandra was confident they would be, and of course they came, the next Tuesday and all the following ones. The other mothers were wary of Alice at first, as Sandra knew they would be; she watched them pulling T-shirts down over their still flabby stomachs or smoothing their hair whenever she walked in. They soon learnt, like Sandra had, that Alice was not a woman to play on her beauty, in fact if anything Sandra would have laid money on her not liking it.

There was something charmingly vulnerable in Alice that made Sandra want to protect her, like an older sister. So when she turned up to Alice's house for coffee one morning and saw her eyes rimmed in red she felt her heart lurch with worry.

'Hello, Mrs Cartwright,' she sang to Alice's mother as brightly as possible as they followed the little girls through the back door into the garden. Sandra had grown used to Alice's house by then, and even to Mrs Cartwright, who seemed to belong to another time altogether; she prided herself on the fact that the other mothers would be intimidated by it, but Sandra suspected that Alice barely noticed its grandeur.

Sandra also knew her friend well enough to know that you couldn't rush things with her, suddenness made her nervous. The girls were running round the lawn and showing Mrs Cartwright a worm they'd found, which was making her laugh.

'Everything OK then?' asked Sandra.

Alice nodded, picking at the lawn as a child might.

'Come on, you look upset.'

'It's just Tony.'

Sandra sighed. Of course it was Tony, she knew that without being told. Gerry saw him sometimes in the Hare and said he was a jumped-up so and so, always sitting at the bar on his own. She'd seen him at weekends carrying Dot around on his shoulders and he definitely had an air of someone who felt they were too good for their surroundings.

'He's always at the pub,' said Alice. 'He used to come home straight from work every night, but now he's never in before ten.'

'Men like the pub,' said Sandra simply. 'They like to feel they're still free.' Alice looked up and her face was so puzzled Sandra wondered how far back she was going to have to go in her explanation. 'Have you spoken to him about it?'

'Oh, no.'

'So you mean he comes in smelling of beer and missing supper every night and you haven't asked him where he's been?'

'I didn't, I mean, I couldn't . . .'

Sandra felt annoyed, with both of them. 'Oh come on, Alice. You have to lay down a few ground rules with men. They're like kids, they like it that way.'

Alice was close to tears. 'But how do you do that?'

'Imagine Dot was doing something she shouldn't, like, I don't know, picking your mum's roses. You wouldn't just stand there watching, you'd explain to her why it was wrong and then you'd maybe say something like she could pick them sometimes, but only when you said. It's the same with men. Gerry goes to the pub on Thursday evenings. I don't complain when he comes home drunk and he doesn't expect to go any other night.'

'Really? Do you think that would work?'

'Of course it will.' Sandra rubbed Alice's arm. 'Come on, cheer up. You're hardly the first woman who's had to fight the pub.' Alice laughed. 'Anyway, I've got some news I've been dying to tell you.'

Alice looked up, all expectation. 'What?'

'I'm pregnant.'

'Oh my goodness, that's amazing.'

Sandra put her fingers to her lips. 'Shh, it's still a secret, especially from Madam over there. I mean, I'm only a few weeks, but, well, I don't mind you knowing.'

Alice put her arms round her friend's neck and kissed her on the cheek and Sandra thought it was perhaps the gentlest kiss anyone had ever given her.

There is a friendship that often exists between women that is the most perfect of relationships. In its best form they feel no rivalry, they love purely, they anticipate and complement each other. Alice and Sandra reached that point quite quickly, when the beginning of a friendship often feels like the beginning of falling in love, except without the sexual tension that makes falling in love so dangerous.

So when Alice turned up at playgroup the next Tuesday Sandra could immediately tell that she was lighter and happier.

'Did you talk to him then?' Sandra asked as they moulded play dough into shapes for a table of toddlers.

'No, but he didn't go to the pub at all this weekend. And he seems much happier. I don't know, maybe I was making a fuss over nothing.'

Sandra sucked back her innate worries, she would never trust any man completely. But why rain on Alice's parade?

'I've decided to have a party for Dot's second birthday,' Alice was saying. 'I've got Mavis's invite in my bag and I thought I'd ask a few of the others from here.'

'Great idea. When is it?'

'Two weeks. We'll just have it at home, hopefully the weather will be good and they can all play in the garden.'

When Gerry got home that night and he'd poured them both a glass of wine which they drank in front of the TV after dinner, Sandra asked him if he'd seen anything of Tony recently.

'He wasn't in the pub on Thursday,' said Gerry, 'but I've heard a stupid rumour that he's got the hots for the new barmaid.'

'Really? What's she like?' Sandra couldn't imagine anyone

matching up to Alice, but then men were odd, they rarely did what was expected of them.

Gerry shrugged. 'I don't think she's up to much. Bit over-weight, peroxide hair, wears her skirts too short, you know the type.'

'Typical barmaid then?'

'Well, yeah, sort of. But when you talk to her she's not like she looks. She's got this, I don't know, vulnerability, I suppose. Like she's always about to cry or something.'

Sandra looked across at her husband. 'Sounds like you've been studying her.'

He laughed. 'Don't be silly. You're the only woman for me.' And with that he drew her towards him with his strong arm, nuzzling into her neck and making her put down her wine glass and giggle with the pleasure of being desired by a man about whom she felt the same way.

Sandra did think about what Gerry had said the next morning as she walked to the green to meet Alice, but the baby was making her stomach churn so that the only real thing on her mind was a need to know where she could be sick at all times. Besides, it was only a stupid rumour and there was something about interfering in someone's marriage, even when one half of that couple was your best friend, that seemed horribly wrong. She snuggled instead into the knowledge that her Gerry didn't find the barmaid attractive.

Of course Sandra lived to regret this decision. She comforted herself with the thought that all her warnings would have probably gone unheeded, but still she felt pretty shitty about herself whenever she thought about it in the weeks that followed.

Tony was quite clearly absent from Dot's party, which

was strange, considering that it had been held on a Sunday especially so he could attend. And besides, he had always seemed very connected to Dot, as if they understood each other. Alice was also decidedly distracted and Clarice had a look of grim determination on her face. The other mothers were as impressed with Alice's house as Sandra had always known they would be, but she couldn't get any enjoyment out of this, couldn't parade her best friend as she would have liked to have done. There was something weary and stale in the air that Sandra couldn't place, something which made her want to leave, as if the house was haunted.

'Where's Tony?' she asked Alice as they were peeling cling film off plates of sandwiches in the kitchen and the children screeched in the garden.

'He went to buy some balloons,' answered Alice.

'Balloons?'

Alice stopped her unwrapping and Sandra saw her hands were shaking. 'Yes. He came into the kitchen half an hour before the party was due to start and said he didn't think there were enough balloons. It was so strange. I didn't know what to say. I wanted to stop him, but I didn't say anything.'

Sandra put her firm hand over Alice's trembling one. 'It's OK, he'll be back.' But the words sounded hollow. Sandra thought the best-case scenario would be that he'd been run over or something, but surely they'd have heard the ambulance.

'Where could he have gone?' said Alice, the tears now dropping out of her eyes. 'I mean, who misses their daughter's second birthday? How do I forgive this?'

You should have talked to him, Sandra found herself thinking, didn't I tell you that men need ground rules? But instead she said, 'I'm sure there's a good explanation. Something you haven't thought of. He'll be back later and you can have a good chat.'

'He said something else strange. He told me that I'm an amazing mother. I was icing those stupid fairy cakes and he said, Dot's so lucky to have you, Alice, you're an amazing mother and you mustn't ever forget it. What do you think he meant by that?'

The baby was turning Sandra's stomach again. He was telling you goodbye, she thought, but only said, 'Nothing. He was being nice, see. And you are amazing. I mean, look at this party. Dot is lucky. That's all.'

Sandra wasn't surprised that she didn't hear from Alice over the weekend, but she felt uneasy when there was no phone call on Monday. This only turned to proper worry though when she didn't turn up to playgroup on Tuesday. Sandra allowed the memory of Alice by the end of the party to dominate her thoughts; she had looked as awful as it was ever going to be possible for her to look, with deep dark circles shrouding her eyes and her skin as pale as paper. Sandra had offered to stay and help clear up but Clarice had ushered her out, telling her they would be fine. Sandra had walked away from the house with a mixture of relief and deep worry and she'd felt ashamed of both emotions. But now she knew she couldn't avoid it any longer. She walked back home from playgroup via Alice's house, telling herself all the way that she was being stupid and of course there would be a perfectly rational explanation for everything. Mavis was tired and dragged her feet, whining to be picked up, which made Sandra's back ache.

Clarice answered the door and even though she was dressed in her usual silk shirt and smart skirt something looked awry. Dot was clutching on to her leg and there was an air of desolation that rushed out of the house like smoke.

78

'Oh, I'm sorry,' said Sandra, without knowing what she was apologising for. 'I just wanted to check that Alice is OK. She didn't come to playgroup this morning.'

Clarice looked tired, that's what it was, Sandra realised. Her skin was drawn on her bones, almost as if she'd aged. 'She's come down with a bug. Since the party, actually. I'd ask you in, but she's in bed.'

Sandra took an involuntary step backwards. Mavis was pulling at her hair and the sun was hot on her head. 'Oh no, that's fine. I was just worried – silly really.'

'Not at all.'

'Well, tell her I said hello. Maybe she could call when she feels better?'

'Thank you,' said Clarice, but she was already shutting the door and Sandra couldn't wait to leave; she even wondered if maybe the house was haunted.

Gerry came home early from the pub on Thursday. Sandra was reading in bed and she heard him come in and run straight up the stairs. He fell on to the bed, still in his jacket and shoes, lying next to her on his stomach, his eyes twinkling. 'You will never guess what I heard tonight,' he said.

'What?'

'Charles told me that Tony has run off with the barmaid I was telling you about.'

Sandra sat up at this. 'You're joking.'

Gerry rolled on to his back. She knew he was enjoying this and sure enough he started to laugh. 'I know, bloody priceless. You live with a supermodel and you run off with Bet Lynch.'

Sandra hit him on the shoulder. 'That's my friend you're talking about.'

'I told you he was weird,' said Gerry.

'How sure are you?'

'Charles said Tony came storming in at around half one last Sunday and Silver followed him outside and they had this really deep-looking conversation on the green and then walked off together. Neither of them has been seen since and apparently he used to come in most nights and sit at the bar and whenever she wasn't serving they'd be chatting and laughing. And once, when Charles was going home, he saw them talking down the back of the pub.'

'There's no law against talking.'

'Oh come on, San, you'd be OK to find me talking to some woman in the middle of the night, would you?'

'Oh shit,' said Sandra, 'poor Alice.'

There was nothing for it but to go back to Alice's house the next day. Clarice answered the door again.

'I know what's happened,' Sandra said simply.

Clarice opened the door wider. 'Come in.'

The house felt cold even though the August sunshine was warm. Dot and Mavis were pleased to see each other and ran off into the garden. Clarice led Sandra into the kitchen. 'Would you like some coffee?'

'Oh no, thanks. I just wanted to see how Alice is.'

'How did you hear?' asked Clarice and Sandra thought she looked relieved that someone else finally knew.

'My husband told me. He heard it from some men in the pub.'

'Yes. Charles Wheeler's mother, Lillian, is a friend of mine. He came round and told me.'

Sandra looked out of the window at the girls playing in the beautiful garden. Everything felt very illusory. 'How's Alice?'

Clarice sighed and Sandra could see how hard all of this was for her. 'Not good. To tell the truth, I don't know what to do with her. She went to bed after the party and she hasn't got up since. I've had the doctor round, but he says there's nothing physically wrong with her.'

'She's not getting up at all? Is she eating?'

'Barely.'

'How about Dot?'

'I've been keeping her away. I didn't want to scare the child.'

Which of course was a mistake, in Sandra's estimation. A child was a reason for any mother to get up, if you asked her. 'Would it be all right if I went up to see her?'

Clarice shrugged as if she was so out of her depth she might as well be underwater. 'Be my guest. You can't do any worse than me.'

The house was creepy when you had to walk up the wide wooden staircase on your own, looked down on by generations of Clarice's bloodline who had no interest in you and your petty problems. Sandra knocked on the door of Alice's room, but there was no reply so she turned the handle and let herself in. Alice was lying in bed, just as Clarice had said, but still it seemed shocking to Sandra. Her body made a neat lump under the white sheet and her eyes were open but fixed on the ceiling. Her skin was more than white, it was the absence of colour, as if it had forgotten to be alive. Sandra walked over to the bed, but Alice only seemed to notice her when she sat down next to it. Her friend's eyes were raw, but still more tears fell when she focused.

Sandra put her hand on Alice's cheek. 'Oh sweetheart. What's he gone and done?'

Alice's face folded in on itself. 'He's left me, Sandra. He's gone.'

'Well, he's a prize bloody fool then.'

'He's left with the barmaid from the Hare. Her name's Silver Sharpe. Isn't that perfect? I can just picture her, I bet she's amazing. I bet she's like a film star. I can almost understand why he went.'

Sandra swallowed down her knowledge of Silver. 'Don't be ridiculous. You're like a film star. He wants his head read, the wanker.'

'God, San, it was so awful. We thought he was dead or something. We called all the hospitals.'

'You mean he didn't tell you or leave you a note or anything?' Alice shook her head and tears sprayed off her face. 'He's been in touch since though?'

'No. He never came back after the party, he's not called or anything.'

'Oh my God. What a bastard.'

'I think I'm going to die, San. The doctor keeps asking me where it hurts and I want to scream: Everywhere, you moron, it feels like demons are ripping off my skin but I know you can't do anything about it.'

Sandra felt her body filling with a terrible rage. Worse than when she'd caught Gerry with Tracey Finch when they were engaged. Or maybe not worse, maybe the feeling was connected, maybe her anger was with all of them. All of those bastard, wanker men who thought it was their right to do as they pleased, to take women as if they were nothing more than a commodity, as if they didn't have hearts which were so easy to break. 'Stop it,' she said, her voice harder than she'd intended. 'You are not going to let him beat you.'

Alice was still snivelling. 'I don't think I can go on without him. What will I do? Stay stuck in this house with my mother?'

'There are worse places, Alice. Some women are left with nothing. They have to go and live in some crappy B and B with their kids. You're not the first woman who's been shat on from a great height.'

'But he was my last chance, San. You don't understand.'

'Oh, for goodness' sake, don't talk soft. You were a baby when you met him. You're gorgeous and men will be queuing round the block for you.'

'I don't want anyone else.'

Sandra had to resist an urge to take her friend by the shoulders and shake her. 'Alice, please. What about Dot?'

At least this seemed to register. 'Is she OK? Clarice says she's fine.'

'She is. But she needs you. You have to get up.'

Alice turned on to her side at this and sobbed, although Sandra knew she'd heard and thought she could maybe see a slight reinflation in her friend's body. 'Alice, you can't let him win like that. God, I'd like to cut his dick off.'

At least Alice stopped crying at that, but her eyes looked blank. 'I feel so alone. I don't know if I can do all of this without knowing he's coming home every night.'

'You're not alone, Alice. You've got me and your mum and Dot.' Sandra felt the community of women so strongly, but she wasn't sure that Alice did. Maybe it was because she was still young, or maybe she didn't want to.

'D'you know what Clarice gave me a few nights ago?' Alice said by way of reply. Sandra shook her head. Alice reached over to the drawer in her bedside table and took out a small piece of paper, which she handed to Sandra. On it were written the words: *I'm sorry, Clarry. I thought I was prepared for Jack's death, the doctors told us it would happen.*

But since it has the world has spun too fast and I have to get off. Mamma.

'What is this?'

'My grandmother's suicide note.'

'What!'

'I didn't even know she killed herself.' Alice half laughed.

Sandra felt she needed to get a handle on the situation. 'Why on earth did your mother show you this?' She put it back into the drawer, not wanting it to contaminate the atmosphere any more.

'I asked her that. I said, Are you suggesting something? I didn't mean it literally, but she got really agitated and went on about how wrong her mother had been. Don't you see how stupid it is to give everything up for one person, she said, to leave people who love you. Because there are always people who love you.'

Sandra sat in silence; she found Alice's world baffling. But then Alice rolled on to her side and said, 'I feel so weak. Like my legs are pieces of string or something. I can't imagine ever getting up and making food and taking Dot out and getting through to the end of the day, ever again.'

'Well, you need to eat for a start,' said Sandra. Sometimes she felt as if the whole world needed to be mothered. 'In fact, I'm going to go and get you something now.'

Sandra went to the kitchen where she made her friend some tea and toast with butter and honey. She could see Clarice sitting in the chair under the apple tree with Dot and Mavis at her feet. She was very still, but Sandra thought she could see agitation running through her veins. She carried the food back upstairs and when she opened the door didn't think that Alice had moved at all. She might not have even blinked. Sandra bustled as much as she could, trying to make waves in the dead air.

'Come on, Alice, I'm not leaving till I see you eat this,' she said, pulling a chair up so she could sit next to the bed.

'My throat feels like sand.'

Sandra pushed the plate closer so Alice had to sit up and take a small bite. She was like an invalid: it took twenty minutes for her to get through the tea and toast and by the end she was crying, but it was the same as getting Mavis to take medicine when she was ill, you couldn't turn your back because it made life easier.

'I'm sorry,' said Alice finally. 'I'm being pathetic. You're so kind.'

'Don't be silly. I'm doing what anyone would. We'll get you up and about in no time.' Alice nodded. 'And you know he will be in touch. He's not just going to walk out of your life. I mean, there's Dot apart from anything else.'

'I keep thinking about that.' Alice swallowed hard. 'I know he loved her. Oh God, San, he must have found me disgusting to walk away from her.'

'He hasn't walked away. He's made a stupid mistake and he'll probably be back. Not that I would ever let you take him back. I just mean, he'll be back.'

Alice shook her head. 'You don't know him. He's already walked away from his parents. I think this is it.'

'Alice, apart from anything else, if he really wants to split up you'll have to get divorced. This Silver woman sounds like a sort of breakdown, if you ask me.'

'Do you think so, really?' Alice looked like a beautiful child and Sandra was shocked both at Tony's ability to leave her and the certain knowledge that she would take him back if he so much as waved through the door.

'I think the important thing is to get you better,' she said by way of an answer.

Before Sandra left she sat with Clarice and told her that she would come every day and when she was there she would take Dot in to see Alice, but that Clarice should insist she ate and let Dot go in as much as possible. Clarice nodded and thanked her and Sandra was amazed at how people who seemed to know a lot really often knew nothing at all about the things that mattered.

Sandra was as good as her word and within a week she arrived to find Alice sitting in Clarice's chair under the apple tree with Dot on her knee, reading her a story. Dot was twirling a lock of her mother's hair round her little fingers and smiling. Alice still seemed weak and fragile, but Sandra thought that over time things would fall back into place. She was amazed that Tony still hadn't been in touch, but for some reason Clarice seemed as certain as Alice that he wouldn't be. Clarice didn't even seem that surprised that he'd left. Sandra knew she'd never properly work these people out, but she also knew that this had bound them together and that they now would be friends for ever.

It was on the way back to her house one afternoon that Sandra saw the poster for the Russian circus in Cartertown, just before Christmas. She wrote the number on a receipt that she found at the bottom of her perpetually messy bag. She decided to buy tickets for her, Gerry, Mavis, Alice and Dot. It was exactly what they all needed.

8 . . . Confession

In defence of Dot Cartwright
16 April 2005
(To be used as my defence if I do get arrested as I don't think I'll be capable of actually explaining any of this in words)

(Also, please note the date – I am not eighteen for another four months (6 August) and so am still legally a child, I presume)

The first point that I'd like to make is that I absolutely did not think I was committing incest when I slept with him. You might find that hard to believe, but I think I'm a bit slow emotionally and it really and truly was only afterwards that I figured it out. I don't know if this makes any difference; it certainly isn't giving me much comfort.

OK, I think I need to explain something about my family to give you some idea as to how I got here – I believe they call it mitigating circumstances. My mother has never, and I really do mean never, told me anything about my father. I don't even know his name. My grandmother did tell me a weird story about him running off with a barmaid called Silver on the day of my second birthday after saying he was going out to buy some extra balloons. But I mean, come on. Only a woman who has never been inside a pub would actually think that barmaids are called Silver, it's like a boxer called Butch, and what sort of wanker would leave on his daughter's second birthday anyway?

If you knew my gran you'd get why she said it. She hates mess and chaos and anything resembling emotion. Her and my mum have the freakiest relationship you've ever seen. I mean, Mum calls her Clarice and if they accidently touch they sort of shiver, like they've given each other an electric shock. But sometimes I've wondered if they communicate telepathically or something because Mum's never shown any desire to move out and they do seem to anticipate each other in quite a weird way.

Gran has all these rules about life which took me years to figure out were bogus. Our house is like some giant shrine to her past and so everything she owns is, by her estimation, priceless. There are loads of chairs you can't sit on in our house, some even round the dining room table. Almost all the china is only to be looked at and her room is completely sacrosanct. Daffodils are common, as are the words 'pardon' and 'toilet', which was pretty confusing as a child as if you say 'what' and 'loo' at school you tend to get told off for being rude. Most people outside of our family are 'ghastly' or 'common', although strangely ones she gets to know like Mavis then almost become family. Oh and (I am not making this up, check her bathroom wall) she thinks we're related to God, thanks to some ridiculous family tree that an obviously mad uncle of hers had made that traces us right back to Jesus and Mary Magdalene, a theory which would probably still get you burnt at the stake in some countries.

Then there's my mum. Where to start with her? She's one of those women who looks like she should be fantastic. I mean, she is really beautiful and I'm not seeing her through rose-tinted glasses because those came off many, many years ago – if they were ever on, that is. She was nineteen when she had me and the other day I realised that she is still younger than all those women on the pages of *Hello* and *Heat* who get described as yummy mummies and do the school run in leather trousers. She could be so cool my mum, but of course she isn't. She has completely no idea of the effect she has on men, although I do, as I have not inherited her looks (we'll come to this later as it's an important part of this story). So I have to stand there as delivery boys stand open-mouthed or shopkeepers get tongue-tied as she glides past. Although maybe there's a price to pay for the beauty because sometimes I think if they got to know her they might not be so impressed because she's not actually real. I don't know how to describe her any better than this. I know she loves me and would probably do anything for me, but it is so far from enough it's a joke.

Mavis, my best friend, used to tell me to just ask her who my father is, but she stopped years ago. And I know you'll find that hard to believe. You'll come and look at our large house and our beautiful possessions and listen to my grandmother's cut-glass accent and you'll think, Oh come on, this is a nice middle-class family, there can't be any secrets here. But I can assure you there are. In fact, I'm starting to think that if you scratch the surface of any family you'll probably find a teeming mess of shit. Sometimes I walk around our pathetically small village on winters' evenings at the time when people have turned on their lights but not yet drawn their curtains. I stare into the windows and watch people turning on TVs or doing their exercises or chatting to their children or whatever. It used to make me feel cosy, but now it leaves me a bit cold. Instead of seeing happy lives I wonder at secret porn stashes or murder victims in freezers or just plain general misery. It's the same as how I used to look at my classmates and envy what I saw as their easy lives: you know, with a mum and a dad and maybe a brother or sister, perhaps a pet, grandparents who visited with bags of sweets, relatives to go and stay with at Christmas. But now I'm beginning to wonder if more people just means more shit?

So, anyway. When I was about ten I found a photo of a man stuck behind my mum's bed and Mavis and I immediately decided that he must be my dad. I mean, what other explanation could there be to our immature minds than this? And sometimes when you believe something when you're very young it sticks like toffee on your teeth and becomes a fact without any proof. I've always kept this photo in the drawer of my bedside table, stuck inside a copy of *Great Expectations* (and yes, I do get the irony, it's why I chose the book). When I was younger I looked at this photo a lot and my dad went through loads of incarnations. As I grew so he was a fireman, other times a lawyer, a celebrity agent and for a good year an actor, when I became convinced that the man explaining the Theory of Relativity on a physics video bore more than a passing resemblance to the man in the photo. Even Mavis agreed with me and so we'd sit up late on Friday and Saturday nights watching made-for-TV films and bad Spanish soap operas. Mum never even asked us what we were doing, but Gran started to sit with us and get as sucked in as we did so that even now you can have a great conversation with her about the relative merits of Sylvester Stallone and Jean-Claude Van Damme, which is pretty cool, I have to admit.

Sorry, you might think I'm rambling, but all of this is relevant. The man in the photo could be a rock star and my mum could be his supermodel girlfriend. And then there is me. I am not that tall, I wear size twelve clothes, my legs and bottom are decidedly dumpy and, the real clincher, I've got ginger hair, when they are both sleek brunettes. You might wonder why it took me seven years to figure this out, but like I said, this man simply was my father. Besides all of which, I hadn't looked much at the photo for a good eighteen months before the fatal time. But then Mavis was being super moody and refusing to tell me what happened with her and Clive after they dropped me after that disco (which is a whole different story that has nothing to do with this one) and Mum and Gran were being mega annoying. So I got the photo out for old times' sake, I suppose like some sick comforter or something. And it suddenly hit me. Wham! How the hell did I think that I could possibly be the product of such an outrageously gorgeous couple as my mum and this man would make? I felt like I'd been sleep walking, like I was a complete idiot. Of course my dad hadn't walked out on my second birthday to buy some balloons, of course my mum hadn't got rid of all his possessions and her photos of him because she found them too painful a reminder as I'd always presumed. No, no, the much more likely truth was that my father had never really been ours in the first place, that he belonged to another family.

Which is when I got my second little revelation that had been far too long coming. Sitting on my bedside table is a photo of Mavis and me, which she had framed for my last birthday. It was taken when we were about two or three, on the one and only 'family' outing we ever went on together. The story goes that a famous Russian circus came to Cartertown and Mavis's mother got us all tickets, but then on the day she was ill, so Mum and I went with Mavis and her dad. The photo jogged some deep memory in me; a hot car, a huge tent, the smells of sawdust and sweat, sparkling ladies and men on stilts towering into the sky. But what the photo failed to do until that day was show me the obvious similarity between the two girls, who occupy it. They could be sisters, what with their chubby red cheeks and long ginger hair. And if you then look at Mavis's dad, Gerald Loveridge, with his dumpy legs and short stature and ginger hair you would be forgiven for thinking that he was a father to both of them.

Naturally the person I would have gone to with this theory was Mavis, who has listened diligently to all my father theories over the years. Even a few months ago I might have done, but like I said she's changed so much recently I knew I wouldn't get a sympathetic reception. Which is a shame really as it'd explain a lot to both of us; namely why our parents never speak and why both our mums are such freaks.

After my little revelation I felt so shocked I went downstairs with the intention of confronting my mother and grandmother, who had quite obviously kept all of this a secret from me for ever. But there they were, sitting at our ridiculous dining room table with the shit-brown walls that Gran thinks are sophisticated but are really totally depressing and I felt like someone had punched me.

'Didn't you hear me calling?' asked Mum, ladling some

foul-smelling stew out of a pot in front of her. Did I mention that she is a completely disastrous cook? Of course she is, because food cooked without emotion is inedible. Who knows, maybe that's where all the men in our family have gone, into the pot. Maybe we ate them all?

I didn't answer but instead went to stand by the fireplace, which has a mantelpiece laden with photos of my mother's father, all in their individually polished silver frames. Not by either Mum or Gran, I hasten to add, but by Mary who's cleaned our house twice a week for as long as I can remember. I picked up one of my grandfather bouncing my mother on his knee, a look of pure concentration on his face.

'What on earth are you doing?' asked Gran.

'Just looking,' I answered, willing one of them to make the connection.

'Come and sit down,' said Gran, 'it's getting cold.' As if that would make any difference.

So we sat and they ate and I fumed. 'I'm going to learn the piano,' I said finally, forming the idea as the words were leaving my mouth. 'I'm going to ask Mr Loveridge to teach me.'

Even my mother seemed to have heard this. 'Why?'

'Why? Because I want to learn.'

'You've never said anything about that before,' observed Gran.

'Well, no, but I do. Seems silly to waste the opportunity of having a best friend with a piano teacher for a dad, wouldn't you say?'

My mother hummed something and my grandmother pushed her stew around her plate.

'It's quite odd, wouldn't you say, Mum,' I tried, 'how Mavis and I are practically sisters but you and Sandra hardly speak.'

Mum looked as though she might cry so Gran spoke for her. 'For goodness' sake, Dot, why on earth would anyone be friends with a drip like Sandra?'

It was obvious that the information would have to come from Gerry Loveridge himself and, quite frankly, piano lessons seemed as good a way as any.

It took Mavis about two weeks to remember to ask him as, like I've said already, she seems to have had her personality sucked out of her by aliens or something (you'll have to take my word for this although I guess you could ask my mum), so that by the time she finally did I was feeling pretty wound up and desperate. The lessons were always disastrous, let me make that very clear. If Gerry is my dad (which I hope to God he isn't) then he hasn't passed on his musical talent to me. But we ploughed on for months, all through the winter, past Christmas. Me sitting there sweating, him taking more and more fag breaks and a build-up of tension rushing between us like a catastrophic tsunami. Of course I, like the idiot I am, thought that he was building up the courage to declare his parental claim on me, whilst God only knows what he thought I was building up to. Well, we do know; I'm just trying to make the point that I didn't get it.

Gran sighed every time I went for a lesson and even Mum said there were better ways to spend precious study time than learning the piano, which is about the only opinion I've ever heard her utter. Mavis got more and more surly with me, so that by the end whenever I turned up she'd just push past me in the horrid huge black jumper she's taken to wearing every day, like I'd asked her to go out, when I'd have far preferred her to stay in anyway.

So we wound our sad, pathetic way around to last Monday, when I turned up as usual to squeak my way through scales I should have learnt months ago. Gerry, as he'd asked me to call him, seemed especially nervous; I could certainly smell the smoke on him. Mavis was long gone.

'Do you know what's wrong with her?' he asked, rather desperately I felt, as we sat next to each other on the too-small piano teacher's stool.

'No,' I answered truthfully, but relieved to hear it wasn't only me she'd gone off.

We started on a faulty C scale, but my brain felt like a sieve, totally unable to contain any of the information he was imparting. In the end Gerry sat back and sighed. 'What are you really doing here, Dot?' he asked.

I couldn't look at his face and so kept my eyes fixed on his hands, which were resting on the white keys. For the first time I noticed that his fingernails are long and filed, which is surely all wrong for a piano teacher. (Not sure why this is relevant, but it feels like it is.)

'I think I know,' he went on. 'And I can't pretend that I'm not flattered, but very surprised, I suppose.'

To say that my heart was galloping is too much of a cliché, it was more gambolling like a little fawn on a warm spring day, which might not be a cliché but is certainly a very naff metaphor. This is it, I was thinking, oh my God, he's going to tell me the news I've been waiting to hear all my life. He's going to tell me how hard it's been, how he's been watching me all these years, how he couldn't ever say anything because Mavis and I were born only a month apart and Sandra is obviously very delicate.

'Why don't we go upstairs,' he said.

I followed him up the staircase. He led me into his bedroom, which I did find a bit strange, but thought maybe he had some memento of my birth hidden in a secret place close to his heart.

The bedroom itself was a bit of an assault on my senses as well, if I'm being honest. As I stood there looking at the sunflowers on the walls and the doilies on the dressing table and the swirling carpet at my feet I was so distracted by the thought of Gerry and Sandra standing in a shop and actually choosing this stuff that I hardly noticed when he started to slip my cardi off my shoulders. I think I even wondered if this was some strange father/daughter ritual that I didn't know about.

But then his breath was hot on my neck and he started gyrating against me so I could feel his erection like a rat in his pants. And let me make this very clear: I absolutely know that I could have said no at any time. I remember not making one sound, not even trying to push him off or anything. I didn't encourage him, but I also didn't try to stop him. I can't tell you why I didn't. The closest I can come to an explanation is, you know that feeling when you are so scared you can't move (I get it when I'm watching horror films)? Well, I wasn't scared, but I felt paralysed in the same way. This was a man I'd known all my life, father of my best friend and until a few minutes before presumed father of myself. AND THIS IS VERY IMPORTANT AS WELL. As soon as Gerry started breathing all over me and putting his hand up my skirt and shoving his tongue down my throat I took it that he obviously wasn't my father. I clearly remember thinking that all of this palaver had been another bloody blind alley, like the stupid TV-watching or bogus photograph and that Gran had been right and if I don't do as well as expected in my A Levels I can always blame my real dad. I thought about my mother a lot during the actual sex, which I know doesn't sound right, especially when I'm trying to form a defence against incest, but I don't mean it like that. I just kept thinking: Look what you've driven me to, you mad, stupid woman, are you happy now? Is this what you wanted?

The sex was over so quickly I'm not sure we could be prosecuted anyway, and it hurt, like someone rubbing sandpaper inside me. I certainly derived no pleasure from it, if that makes it better. Afterwards Gerry seemed amazingly pleased with himself.

'I hope you enjoyed that, Dot,' he said. 'I'm sorry it was a bit quick. But I can't really get over all this. I mean I had no idea you felt this way.'

The whole situation could have been funny if it hadn't really been completely bloody tragic and disgusting. I wanted to get away from him as soon as possible, but I didn't know what to do or say, so I stayed quiet.

'I take it you're not really interested in the piano,' he said. 'But I'd love it if you still want to come on Mondays. Sandra always goes to Asda on a Monday afternoon. She goes by bus so it takes her hours.'

'Why don't you drive her?' I asked, for something to say as much as anything else.

He looked shocked by this suggestion. 'I have to work. And anyway she doesn't do anything else. I think it's pretty much the only time she leaves the house all week.'

Life is strange. Probably I don't need to tell you that as if you're prosecuting me no doubt you've lived a bit. But I'm starting to realise this more and more and it makes me wonder if I do want to grow up and have a relationship and all that stuff. Even when you think you know people you don't, probably even the person you share a bed with for fifty years could be a stranger. I wondered why people don't move on more often like my dad. And I wonder why when they do it's always so devastating.

I stood up and straightened my clothes. He hadn't even removed my knickers and there was an odd metallic smell coming from them. I think I said something moronic like, 'Well, I'd better be going.'

Gerry stood up as well, zipping his horrid pink penis into his trousers. He followed me downstairs and I willed him not to touch me again in case I was sick.

'So,' he said at the front door, 'will I see you next Monday then?'

The door was open and my exit was clear. 'Ah, well, probably not.'

'Probably not?'

'It's all a bit too weird for me, so . . . . But thanks, anyway.' I really said that.

'You weren't a virgin, were you?' asked Gerry, suddenly looking all concerned.

'God, no. No, not at all.' This, I had decided, would never count and so, by that reckoning, I am still a virgin.

'Oh, right, well – good.' He laughed lasciviously. 'I know what all you girls are like nowadays.'

I left after that and went straight to the Co-op that serves us all even though they've known us since we were babies and must be able to work out our ages and bought two WKDs and ten Marlboro Lights. (Della served me if you want to verify

98

this and she remembers everything as she has no life and likes to gossip.) I cut back down past Mavis's estate to the bluebell wood. I hadn't been there for years although I know most of our class go there every weekend to smoke and rut like animals. I used to go with Mum when I was little to pick bluebells. I was always struck by how beautiful they are, but also couldn't believe how short their life was. They're only here for two weeks, I used to repeat as we walked and picked and she would nod and laugh at me. But now I think two weeks of glory sounds like quite a good deal, especially if you can lie dormant for the rest of the year.

Of course I'd missed their short slot and the air was putrid. If you haven't smelt a forest of rotting bluebells then don't bother, you're not missing out. And it's not only the smell, they also look so sad, falling over like dying soldiers. But still I trudged through them because it was the one place I could be sure not to run into Mavis or anyone else I knew.

I was a bottle of WKD and five fags down when I was hit by the reality of the situation. My mother has never told me who my father is, ergo she is highly unlikely to have told my father about me. Which leads us to one conclusion: Gerry Loveridge is still the most likely candidate for 'person who supplied half my genes'. And I had just slept with him. I was sick immediately after this thought.

I stayed in the forest for as long as I could, but in the end I realised that I was going to have to go home. I was almost enjoying the smell coming from between my legs by then, it seemed disgustingly fitting.

By the time I got home I was hot and angry and went straight upstairs to run myself a bath. I like hot baths, but this one was scalding. I lay in it for ages, watching my skin turn pink and wondering if I might pass out and save everyone the bother of explaining anything to me.

In the end I had to get out because, really, what else is there ever to do but carry on like you did before? There was no way I was going to tell anyone about what had happened and anyway, I know hardly anyone, which was another thing I realised as I lay simmering in that bath. I wrapped a towel round my body, picked up my clothes filled with my misdemeanour and opened the door. Grandma was sitting in the wicker chair that we have on the landing, looking strangely at me.

'Do you know what time it is?' she asked pointedly.

I didn't but realised it must be past nine-thirty, which is when she takes her bath, at the same time every night, and woe betide anyone who gets in her way. There are two more bathrooms in our house, I'd just like to point out, but for some reason the landing bathroom is Grandma's. 'No.'

'It's my bath time.'

'I'm sorry, I forgot.'

'I don't ask for much in this house, Dot. I don't make many demands, when by God I could. But I do take my bath at the same time every night and have done for so long I'm quite surprised you've never noticed.'

'Of course I've noticed. It was a mistake.'

'A mistake? Oh, so that's OK then, as you might say.'

I felt like something was falling through my body, like a lift plummeting through floors. 'Gran, I'm not feeling great, I'm really not in the mood for this.'

She stood up at this and for a second I thought she was going to say something important. 'What are you in the mood

for then, Dot, because you don't seem very well at the moment?'
I tried to detect something caring in her voice but couldn't.
Wasn't it obvious anyway?

At that moment Mum came silently up the stairs, surprising
both of us. 'What's going on?' she asked.

'Dot decided to have a bath when it's my bath time and now
she's not in the mood to talk about it.'

'My God,' I said, 'why is it such a big deal?'

'It's not a big deal in itself,' said Gran. 'It's the principle.'

'What principle?' I shouted.

'Dot, please,' said Mum and we both looked at her but she
didn't seem inclined to elucidate.

'God,' I shouted, 'look at us. What's wrong with us? There's
a whole world out there you know, getting on with life, having
fun.' Then I stamped upstairs to bed where I cried myself to
sleep and woke up this morning in my towel with my hair like
a scarecrow's round my head.

I got that feeling when you wake up where you feel OK for
a minute and then you remember and you want to put your
head under the pillow and go back to sleep. I had never been
rude to my grandmother before and I couldn't imagine what
was waiting for me downstairs. I lay in bed for a while but
then decided that I either had to face them now or later and
so I might as well get it over with.

Mum was in the kitchen washing up when I got down and
she looked jittery and nervous when I came in.

'Sorry, for last night,' I said.

She turned round at this, letting her soapy hands drip all
down her skirt and on to the floor. 'I do get it you know, Dot,'
she said. 'I mean, Druith is very small. There was a time I
wanted to leave, you know.'

This was news to me and I wanted to know more. 'There was? When?'

She turned back to the sink. 'It doesn't matter. I just mean I know it can be frustrating. But you'll be leaving soon, going off to university. You don't have to put up with it for much longer.'

There were, I realised, many unsaid words circling in the air, but I didn't know how to access them. 'Is Grandma really angry?'

'She's under the apple tree.'

I knew Mum wasn't going to help any more than that so I went out, walking across the lawn as if I was going to the gallows. Gran was in her chair, sipping tea. She watched me approach.

'I'm sorry, Gran. I didn't mean those things I said last night.'

She replaced her cup in its saucer and looked up at me. 'It's all right, Dot, you don't have to apologise,' she said and I was more shocked by this than if she'd shouted. 'I know it's hard for you. It's probably always been hard and I'm sorry.'

I didn't know what to say to that and so I smiled and walked away. I walked across the grass and wondered how long we would all go on not saying his name. I wondered if I would reach my mother's age and my mother my grandmother's and whether we still wouldn't have talked about him. I wondered if I'll make it to university without that knowledge. If I'll be able to hold down a relationship or a job without the knowledge of half of myself. If you can function in this world without knowing where you come from.

But, sorry, you're not interested in any of that. I only

mentioned my grandmother because it was such an unusual interlude in our lives, which means she'll remember it and vouch for the fact that I was behaving very strangely that day. And I was behaving strangely because . . . well, you know the rest.

9 . . . Nothing

What do you actually do with a day? Physically, that is? There are enough thoughts in any mind to keep it spinning for the whole twenty-four hours, but the body needs something as well. It needs to feel useful or it starts to tell the mind that there's no point, that it might as well scramble and trip and turn and flip and bounce.

Dot and Mavis were good at inertia. It is after all the natural preserve of the teenager to lie immobile on a bed thinking deep thoughts they are yet to understand. Besides, they had just finished school, which still seemed like the hardest point of their lives: they knew that they were waiting, that something new was around the corner, whether they wanted it or not.

Tony had learnt to fill his days by taking the short walk to Ron's shop after the school drop-off every morning. He knew that bringing up children is lonely and solitary and that we live in a cold, damp country where there is often a cloud overhead and that the washing up can take all morning if you let it. So, his nothing was to sit in the back of a small shop with an old man whom he'd grown to love, one either side of a thick wooden table, pockmarked with years of good honest work. A bright bulb without a shade hung over the table illuminating all they did, discouraging shadow. Pieces of clocks, toasters, vacuum cleaners, beloved toys and sentimental radios rested in neat piles. Each man had his tools and magnifying glass. Radio 4 droned on comfortingly in the corner and if someone came into the shop one of them would stand up to see what they needed. People thanked them when a much-loved item was restored, small amounts of money changed hands and tea was always being offered between them. Sometimes they barely spoke and at other times they didn't stop all day. On more than one occasion Ron had stopped what he was doing to put a friendly arm round Tony's shoulders as they heaved with his tears. This was his nothing, and yet it was so much more than something.

Alice was now bound to the house. For a while after Tony had left and Dot was still small she'd flirted with the idea of moving away, to London or even further. But that was long gone now. She had even got used to Dot getting up and fixing her own breakfast and leaving for school on her own. She didn't ask her daughter any more what time she might be home or what she'd like for supper. Dot was nearly an adult and she was developing adult sensibilities. Once a week Alice drove to the big supermarket in Cartertown to stock up on tins and loo roll and pasta and packets. Otherwise she'd walk into the village when they needed things and patronise the butcher or the greengrocer, and sometimes the newsagent. She knew that other people had interests; her mother for example loved the garden as if it was a person and spent hours planning the planting. But since the village play all those years ago, which had come to nothing, nothing more had ever come to Alice. She quite liked reading although sometimes weeks could elapse between her finishing one book and starting another; she was an adequate seamstress; she fed them all; but nothing grabbed her and made her want to investigate it until she'd mastered it. Ideas turned to dust in her head, or at least that's what it felt like. She would think about making a cushion or looking up a recipe or going to see the bluebells and be immediately struck by how pointless it all was. Everything would be over in less time than it took to do. One day they would all be dead anyway and then who would care that the roses had a colour theme or that chocolate tasted good or that the curtains matched the duvet cover? She had become good at sitting still, at resting her hands peacefully in her lap while she sat at the kitchen table. At lying in bed when she had no intention of sleeping. At walking through the village as if she had some-where to go. At watching a film as if she was interested in the ending. She waited for Dot to be around and tell her things in the way she used to wait for the phone to ring. In another life she liked to think that she'd have made a good Buddhist.

Clarice employed order. There was a relentless routine to her life which she followed every day. Same time to rise, same time to bed, with everything she needed to know in between. She rarely left the house and garden any more, finding nothing more fascinating than what occurred within her small realm. Not that she wasn't interested in the world. She watched Channel 4 news every night and read the *Daily Mail* every day. She did the crossword and Sudoku to keep her mind active and loved it when Dot came home with a film or stayed in on a Saturday night to watch terrible game shows. She had breakfast and lunch at the kitchen table and dinner in the dining room. She had a cup of tea by the fire in winter and under the apple tree in summer at four o'clock precisely. She walked the garden in the mornings and spoke to Peter about the planting or the weeds or the vegetables. On Tuesdays and Thursdays she told Mary what needed to be done and had a cup of coffee with her at eleven, listening to Mary's children and now grandchildren grow up. On Wednesday afternoons she put on her wellies and walked on Conniton Hill with Lillian and her dreadful dogs and on Sundays she went to church, not because she believed but because it was expected of her. And once a month on a Thursday evening she drove to Stella Baycliff's house just outside Druith where a group of them played bridge and drank one or two sherries and exchanged news. She slept well each night, her mind untroubled by too many dreams, her body tired out enough not to let her stay awake.

Sandra spent most of her time looking down. You had to keep your eyes down if you were going to spot all the dirt. There was no point in doing the washing up and staring out of the window or polishing a table and looking at the wall. And there was always more dirt; it was as if the others didn't notice that everything they did disturbed something which caught a piece of dust or brought in a speck of mud. Sandra could remember Gerry saying to her a few years before, 'What do you want us to do? Move out and seal you into the house so that it's always perfect?' She hadn't answered but she had kept the thought neatly in a part of her mind so that she could always get it out and admire it like the china cats on the mantelpiece. She only had to shut her eyes to see her house wrapped in a giant roll of cling film, its insides gleaming and sparkling. She started upstairs every day, believing that the dirt would flow downwards. She made their bed and cleaned the bathroom. She put away any washing and tidied up clothes that Gerry might have left lying around. Mavis had put a lock on her door and so she couldn't go in there, but as the door was always shut she could also pretend that the room didn't exist. Next she did the sitting room, plumping cushions and dusting all the objects. She followed this with the dining room, polishing the table and chairs and again dusting anything on any surface. The kitchen always seemed to take the longest as there were so many chrome surfaces which needed washing and then rubbing down with oil and even when you'd finished there was always another streak. The dishwasher had to be emptied the second it was finished, as did the washing machine, and the ironing had to be tackled every day. The windows also needed washing every third day and the bed sheets had to be changed twice a week, on Mondays and Thursdays. The last thing she did was to hoover the house from top to bottom, changing heads to get into every corner. This alone could take up to an hour every day and often made her shake and sweat with the exertion. Finally she would wash the kitchen floor, emptying the dirty water down the loo so she could immediately replace the mop and bucket in the cupboard under the stairs. Sandra didn't listen to the radio but worked in silence, often forgetting to eat and making do with a mug of instant coffee, which had to be washed as it was finished. Her hands were red and raw and her hair hung loosely round her face. And then Gerry or Mavis would come home and the mess started all over again.

Over the years Gerry had found a nothingness in sex. Not with his wife, of course, whom he had last made love to sixteen years before, but with a succession of faceless women whom he barely registered as human. Since the Alice debacle and right up until Dot he'd kept these encounters professional. He was a regular at lap-dancing clubs and massage parlours in towns like Paddockbridge and Woolley, a good hour and a half's drive from his home. Occasionally he would simply go to a pub in one of those industrial towns where he could still pull a woman who expected as little as him, although he'd noticed that these encounters were becoming steadily seedier and more depressing with each passing year. He always wore a condom and he never kissed any of them because he still held out hope that one day Sandra would let him kiss her again, even if only on the cheek. Bodies were good at giving absolution; they were warm and giving, tender and fragile and a good reminder that you were alive. And then there was the rush of the orgasm, which flowed through his body like a drug, washing over his frayed nerves and calming his whirling brain. It was one of the few times when Gerry stopped seeing the destruction he'd caused in his life. He would lie still for a few minutes afterwards, anaesthetised to the world, a great silence inside him. A cigarette could prolong the sensation, so that on the drive home he might even smile. But then he would walk through his spotless front door and neither his wife nor his daughter would acknowledge him and he knew that everything he did disturbed Sandra's order and the tension would flood back so that his eyes burnt with the effort it took not to cry. He'd grabbed at the chance Dot offered him, but along with everything else he'd got that wrong too: it had been yet more nothing and the realisation that only his wife offered him a something was starting to make him feel desperate.

10 . . . Bewilderment

So, Tony has just left and I probably should go and find Alice in whatever corner of the house she is hiding, but, truth be told, I can't face it. I have received the third truly shocking news of my life; first my mother, second Howie and now Alice. I suppose you could say Jack's death was shocking, but I was too young and besides he'd been ill for about a year before he died. And after Mother I was always waiting for the news about Father. Really I shouldn't lump Alice's news in with all this death, but that's what it feels like: the end of her life, except she doesn't even realise it. The people l love always seem to let me down one way or another; or maybe I should look at it from a different viewpoint, maybe there's some intrinsic fault in me that makes them want to let me down.

I saw Alice's face when she was telling me and I am sure I am not wrong to say that she enjoyed hurting me. Not the way that young girls so often come up against their mothers, because we never do any of the usual screaming and shouting and door slamming. More that it gave her a ghastly pleasure to cause me pain. That's almost the worst of it, actually: that I could have done such a terrible job of being her mother as I have so obviously done. Of course I know that I've been far from perfect, but I do love her and I obviously haven't managed to convey that at all. How did Howie do it? That's what I'd like to know. How did he make it always look so easy? How did he have the courage to kiss her and bounce her and tell her he loved her? How did it not terrify him to his very bowels to give so much of himself to someone else, to invest all his happiness in another fragile human being?

I went to stand by the window when they were telling me as I needed to see a marker, like the rose bushes, to make sense of it all. The light was on the window, but I swear I saw myself skipping down the path at the bottom of the garden. I was even wearing my favourite blue dress from when I was, what, twelve, and my hair was streaming behind me. I had to dance when Father told me about Mother, there didn't seem to be any other appropriate reaction. I went into the garden and danced under her window, trying to feel my way around the thought that I was never going to see her again. Of course it seemed impossible; I always presumed it was too big a concept for my young mind, until the police told me about Howie and I realised it had nothing to do with being a child. Because trying to understand that particular thought is the worst thing about death, the desperate scrabble the brain makes of trying to fit the pieces together, as if you could dip your hand into time like it was a pond and fish out the bits you need to make a whole. People talk about waking up after someone they love has died and forgetting for a second, and then the awful business of remembering, but I don't think I ever forgot, I think I awoke with the desperate impression that I could change it.

Her hair was still in her brush when I was allowed into her room after the body had been removed. I took it and held it as though it was the most precious thing I would ever own, but of course hair is dead even when it is on your head and nothing to

111

get excited about. Alice looks so like Mother. She looked like her the moment she was born. I never told Howie that, it seemed too dangerous to say out loud, but I wish I had now, I wish I had shared some of the things I know with at least one other person. Because what if looks signify more than genetic alignment? What if my mother's character has seeped through the generations as well? What if I am no more than a conduit of her, sandwiched between two women unable to love me as I love them? Certainly Alice has my mother's distance, that disconcerting way of looking through you, as if there's always someone more interesting over your shoulder. They both have the same icy blue eyes that stare when they don't understand something, as if ordinary life is too banal for goddesses like them. They are dangerous women.

To think that when they first walked in I presumed she was parading an unsuitable boyfriend before me and I felt a stab of excitement as I thought we might be moving on to a more normal footing. I allowed myself whole minutes of fantasy in which we raised our voices and came to agreements and learnt how to live with each other. But of course Alice had done something spectacular, how could I ever have imagined otherwise?

I can't remember much of our conversation, I lost all sense of myself when she told me that she was pregnant. She wanted to leave me though, I do remember that, as distinctly as I know every word on Howie's grave. She thought they could go and live in Cartertown in one room and live off – what? – love, I suppose. You know nothing about love, she said to me and she is quite possibly right.

At least Tony seems to have his head screwed on. I can see what she likes about him. He is obviously good-looking, although I don't like his long hair or his tight jeans, but that is nothing. He also seems to be more than the sum of his parts. When he sat opposite me and said that Alice could not live in some room in Cartertown, I saw that he understood her. And more than that, he cared for her. He had weighed up the situation and made a choice, the right choice if you ask me. Of course they must live here and, who knows, maybe it will all turn out fine. Maybe a baby will be the making of Alice. I was having a hard time imagining what she might do with her life and maybe this is a good solution. We do not live in a world of nannies and entertaining like when my mother had me and so Alice will have to take on these responsibilities and maybe she'll be good at it?

The problem is that he is scared. I saw his eyes flicking over everything when he walked in; I heard the stammer in his voice when he spoke to me. And scared is not the best way to enter a marriage. It is hard enough to get right when you are as in love as Howie and I were, but when you are scared and bemused and feeling inferior it stands little to no chance.

Howie used to laugh at me when I insisted on things being right, as I so stupidly called the traditions we pass down through the generations. But he understood what I meant. He could find me amusing because his mother had been almost the same person as me and so I was easy to love. But Tony will be lost in Alice and she in him. They will speak words in the same language and yet their meaning will be obscured by their experience.

It's strange because when I couldn't get pregnant I don't think Howie was really that bothered. He worried for me because I was so desperate, but if it had turned out that we never had children I don't think he would have been heartbroken. But then when Alice came along he fell in love with her so easily and readily. I think with men it is always the actuality, whereas women prefer ideas. Women can live whole lives in ideas, create realities out of nothing. Oh Howie, what would you make of

113

this? The best, I imagine, although if you were still here, no doubt she wouldn't have got pregnant in the first place.

You know, Howie, sometimes I hate you for leaving me. Often I hate you, Mother. Someone, I forget who, once said that love and hate are very similar emotions and they are so, so right. Why did you go out in that storm? The coastguard at the inquest said that it had been fine when you left, but you must have seen the storm approaching. You used to tell me how that was one of your favourite aspects of sailing, how you could look across the sea and see the weather approaching, like different seasons in the same day. If you saw that storm, why did you carry on? Or maybe you didn't, maybe you turned back, that's what the coastguard said was most likely. Of course your boat was so broken up it was impossible to tell what you had been doing, but I'm sure you headed for home. I'm sure you tutted at the wind in your pragmatic way. I hope to God you never even saw the boom coming, never felt a thing. You were there one minute and not the next; that's all there is, that's all there is for anyone. A ceaseless journey from one breath to the next, until it stops and we become nothing more than blood, flesh and bone. Except we were denied even that of you. Oh God, Howie, please come home. Please don't leave me alone any more.

Everything changes and yet it stays the same. I am not shocked any more by the poll tax riots on the television or striking miners with starving children or continents baking in a relentless heat that deprives the land of food and water. I have realised that the only truly shocking things to me concern the people I love. If I was an African mother or a miner's child, I would feel shock for these things, but they would look at me and feel nothing. This world we fight our way through is only personal and I think maybe I have realised that too late.

11 . . . Acting

Clive Buzzard liked to think he knew things. And one of the things of which he was most sure was the accrued worth of him and Debbie in Druith. He and Debbie made a fine couple, they were like the Posh and Becks of their moment, except cooler and more relevant.

Clive liked to say that he was all about rap music. His father was Druith's parish priest and his mother ran the Sunday school and battered women's shelter in Cartertown, but Clive liked to dream that he had been born in downtown Harlem and that if only Public Enemy could meet him they'd embrace him as a true brother. His family lacked imagination, that was their problem. His sister liked to please, doing well at school, getting into university, never staying out past twelve and seemingly had little or no interest in boys. Clive wanted to keep it real, hardly understanding that real is whatever you deem it to be and that Public Enemy's reality was irrelevant to him.

Clive dreamt of being a rapper and moving to London and making millions like Eminem. It didn't matter that he hadn't grown up in a trailer park with a drug-addled mother, married too young and lost everything he had to gambling. He could still feel their pain and reckoned he could still be a cultural marker of his generation. So he wore his trousers low, his baseball cap backwards and walked as if one leg had been shot and had to be propelled round his body as a stiff entity. Debbie followed suit, pushing her breasts up to her chin, bleaching her hair, shortening her skirts and exaggerating her make-up. They'd even had matching tattoos, which hovered above the crack of their bottoms, predictably a decorated D for him and a C for her. And they spoke in a gangsta slang, sucking on their teeth and using words they sometimes barely understood.

It wasn't only their words that confused them, but also often the ideas they attempted to express which were as mixed and murky as a sludgy pond. He had an intense desire to 'be someone' and to have lots of money, although both ambitions were as flimsy as the miniscule lace underwear Debbie wore. Life, to Clive, was all about what you had and what people thought of you and it didn't matter how you got there, as long as you didn't have to work too hard. Open any of the magazines that littered the floor of Debbie's pink bedroom and you'd see people exactly like him or her whose lives were followed in minute detail from year to year without any real reason. But reasons had ceased to matter a long time ago; for Clive and his people everything was about the here and now, the immediacy of existence.

Occasionally Clive would watch the news with his parents and see pictures of boys his age who had died fighting in a country he would be hard pressed to find on a map. Suckers, he would think to himself, as his father offered up silent prayers that you only knew he was making because his lips were moving. It wasn't even as if soldiers got paid much and the only way they got their faces in the papers was once they'd died and what the hell was the point of that? His father often talked about the value of money and the pleasure of a good day's work or a job well done but Clive would only roll his eyes into his head. It's all bullshit, was one of his favourite phrases, something he and his friends would say to each other about any and everything. They were against the system, but never even considered that when something is knocked down something else has to be put in its place. A sense of righteousness and being owed pervaded them like the cheap aftershave they had recently taken to wearing.

Clive's sister, Natalie, made no attempt to hide her disdain for her brother and his girlfriend, but his parents were annoyingly tolerant. They liked to talk about things like self-expression and individuality and respect for teenage boundaries, which made Clive bubble over with rage at the lack of things he had to fight against in his life. Not that he fully understood that this was the reason for the rage which seemed to overtake him so frequently. He could only identify his malaise in the simplest terms, by looking at those of his classmates who lived on the Cartertown estate or had only had one parent; a few had even been arrested. Clive found it stomach-churningly unfair that they should be given the opportunity of a life worth exploiting in song, whilst he had to put up with a vicarage, of all places, as well as understanding parents.

His parents' understanding, however, crashed into a brick wall when they came back from the last parents' evening of the lower sixth to be told that he was probably on course to fail maths A Level. Clive never should have taken maths, but his father had balked at politics, saying it wasn't a proper subject, and Clive had relented and now it looked as though he'd only be getting two A Levels, which wouldn't even get him into an ex-poly. We'll have to get you a tutor, said his father, but Clive had stood up at this, twisting his baseball cap on his head; No man, he'd said, I'll sort it, promise I will. And no more MTV Base or Xbox till your exams are over, his father had shouted as he'd stormed out of the room. Even Clive thought maybe he should cut down on the incessant porn he watched on the laptop in his bedroom if he was going to stand any chance of passing his exams.

Mavis Loveridge was easily the cleverest person in their year and maths was her specialist subject. Plus she was a geek, which meant she didn't speak to any of his friends and so wouldn't tell, and no doubt was in love with him, so would lick the gob off his shoe if he asked her to. Clive knew he had been right in his estimation when he cornered her in the playing fields one lunchtime and the look of exhilaration on her face had been impossible for her to hide in time. Of course she agreed to give him a few lessons, at her house, for free, no questions asked and telling no one.

Clive had gone to her house once a week and found her to be a great teacher. She talked about numbers in a way which almost made him wish he'd paid a bit more attention over the last six or so years. After a few weeks he realised that Mavis didn't see numbers as boring stretches of problems, but as puzzles that were as intricate as some of his favourite lyrics. And she was pretty if you looked at her while she spoke and ignored her dreadful old school DMs and long skirts and ginger hair. She was also so accommodating, studiously avoiding him at school and not even glancing his way when Debbie shouted 'Ginga' after her as she waited for a bus.

So when she turned up to the sixth-form disco looking so unexpected Clive felt as if he didn't have a choice. He wanted to tell her that she should always wear her hair up and that

118

using an oversized man's T-shirt as a dress was far sexier than all the other girls' bum-skimming skirts and high heels that looked as if they might snap off their ankles. Besides, Debbie was being a prize pain that night, sulking because he'd gone to Taj's house first to help with the tunes; generally dissing him and giving him the bum's rush. No doubt it was her time of the month, he thought.

Initially he'd only started talking to Mavis and Dot because of all of that, but soon he found they were funny and before long an hour had passed and then Trev and Ketch had joined in the conversation because where he went others soon followed. Debbie flounced off around twelve, but Clive knew it was nothing he couldn't solve in the morning, knew that she knew that her stock would plummet without him. His head was groggy from the vodka they'd smuggled in and, as he stood leaning against the wall of their school gym, he thought that if you took away the make-up and the hair and the pushed-up breasts and skin-tight dresses, maybe Debbie wasn't really as fit as a page-three honey. Or maybe it was that page-three honeys weren't that hot after all. And he found himself wishing harder than he had done since he was a child that he'd do well. Not that he thought any of those things for very long: his brain was too used to seeking out pleasure and easy routes and so starved of real ideas that it sucked any up like a sponge, not letting anything settle. Instead it fixed itself on Mavis, chatting brightly to Kai across the room, and knew what needed to happen.

Clive only had to ask Mavis once if she needed a lift home for her to accept. But then, annoyingly, she remembered her strange ginger friend as they were leaving and so Clive said he'd drop her off first. Dot was really drunk, staggering and swaying and Clive told her not to puke in his car or he'd go fucking mental and she seemed to agree. By then though there was no going back anyway. The desire to possess Mavis had lodged itself in every part of him because if you want lots of things you can't have and if you live in a world of immediacy, it sometimes works to have something you don't particularly want but can have.

Snoop Dogg spat out his bile as soon as Clive turned on the ignition, shouting about the things he'd do to his bitch in his private plane. The video started to play in Clive's head as it did for almost every song he ever listened to: images of women in bikinis, their impossible bodies oiled and ready, lollipops stuck in their open mouths, whilst fully clothed men mouthed the words to their songs, as in control as they had ever been. Clive didn't know that what he was feeling was sexual tension; maybe he hadn't even heard of Marvin Gaye and all the forerunners to the music he thought he owned. He didn't imagine making love to Mavis; he imagined fucking her senseless like the porn stars and rappers in his head. He didn't imagine any other scenario other than that she would love it, opening herself up to him like a flower.

He had a hard-on by the time they reached Dot's house and he drummed his fingers on the steering wheel as he waited impatiently for Mavis to see her friend to the front door. He rolled a steadying joint to avoid the premature ejaculation he was in danger of experiencing. When Mavis got back in she smiled and he offered her a toke, which she sucked deep into her lungs. The sweet Sensi, as he liked to call it as if he spent his days on a Jamaican beach rather than a windswept Welsh village, was having its desired effect, as if someone was spreading a warm blanket through his veins, and so he smiled back.

'Where to now then?'

She shrugged. 'I live on Bateman's Road.'

'I know,' he lied. 'D'you wanna go home then?'

She giggled and blushed. 'I don't mind. Do you?'

Clive put his hand on to Mavis's leg and brushed it up under her T-shirt/dress thing. 'Nah, man. You look well hot.'

'We can't go to my house.'

'Nor mine. How 'bout Sayers Common.' It had been one of those unusually warm Septembers and being naked outside wasn't unappealing.

'OK.'

Clive restarted the car, praising the weed now swirling round his blood, giving him time to get somewhere and show Mavis a thing or two. They left Druith behind in minutes, the lights from his headlights bouncing off the road so that he kept on having to remind himself that he wasn't playing Need for Speed, which always happened when he drove at night. Clive turned off about halfway through the common. He couldn't see any other cars but there were bound to be other people fucking nearby. He found the thought warmly erotic, being a young man as he was who lived in a world without sexual boundaries. He had learnt years ago that men, women, animals, dwarves and shit you'd never even dreamt of was no more than a mouse click away.

He shut off the car and the silence enveloped them, making him immediately turn the music back on. The moon was full and Mavis looked pale; he wondered if the skunk was too strong for her and hoped she wasn't going to puke before she'd sucked him off. Clive stroked some hair off her face in an embarrassingly clichéd move, but which he felt safe with as he presumed he was the first person ever to have done this to

Mavis. His skin prickled and he felt an urgency. He wished he could skip all this shit.

'Do you come here with Debbie?' she asked and Clive had to force himself not to shout at her because, man, what the fuck was the point of that question? He wasn't going to stop but he didn't need his girlfriend in his head.

'Nah. Her mum's cool, she lets me stay over whenever.'

'Oh, right.'

He felt her tense beneath his touch. Don't give me this shit, bitch, he imagined shouting, although of course he never would. For a second he even felt sorry for her, realised she was a nice girl who didn't deserve to be treated like a ho. But then again, come on, he was Clive Buzzard, she was lucky to be about to be fucked by him. 'You know what this is, right?'

Mavis looked at him and her eyeliner had smudged so he had to look away. 'Are you saying you're not going to leave Debbie and start going out with me?' Then she laughed. 'Of course I know that. It just feels weird.'

Clive responded to this in the only way he knew how; by pulling her towards him and kissing her hard on her mouth, sticking his tongue down her throat, feeling her breasts and eventually pushing her head towards his lap. By the time they were properly fucking Dr Dre was blasting out of the stereo and he felt righteous and perfect and on top of the fucking world, man.

Mavis didn't grind into him the way Debbie did, nor did she moan or whisper in his ear that he was too big for her. But she seemed to have enjoyed it, she was certainly flushed and smiling when he dropped her off at her front door forty minutes later.

'Thanks, yeah,' he said as she got out of the car.

She turned round, looking puzzled, and he realised she'd misunderstood; he turned the music down so he could be clear. 'I mean for all the maths shit. You're a good teacher.'

She smiled at this. 'Oh right, that's fine.'

'So, see ya at school then.'

'Yeah. Thanks for the lift.'

Clive didn't think about Mavis much after that. There was no need; he'd got what he wanted from her in all respects and life floated on as it was intended. Of course Debbie was fine with him the next day. In fact they were fucking in her bed less than twelve hours later. When he finished Clive rolled over to light a fag and wondered whether he'd had a shower between women. He didn't think he had and the thought filled him with a great warmth, a real sense of achievement. Sometimes he regretted being Debbie's friend on Facebook, a story like that was made to be shared.

Still, however, a residue of guilt must have been swirling somewhere in his body because Debbie had been dogging him out about having a joint birthday party for ages and he'd been knocking her back, but when she brought it up again that afternoon he agreed much too readily. Besides their birthdays were months away and so he put it to the back of his mind.

Time, however, is not stable, a lesson which Clive was learning with increasing regularity. Dates that seemed far away loomed up pretty quickly, ambushing you like a mugger. Like exams, when you worked out that you didn't have enough hours to study every topic that you needed in order to pass. Although Clive did work much harder than he had expected; something played on in the back of his mind, which he never realised was a tiny memory of that night with Mavis, urging him to knuckle down and make sure he didn't regret wasting his opportunity. And maybe he didn't recognise the phrase for what it was because it so permeated the airwaves, usually when some dumb kid was wasting theirs on a reality TV show. Sucker, Clive would shout at the screen, using the same word for the desperate singers as the dead soldiers. But then again, what did it matter, none of it was real when you flicked that off switch.

Debbie wanted them to have their party in the Christmas holidays, which soon became a New Year's Eve party. When he started protesting, she cried and in the end he threw his hands into the air and told her to go ahead and organise it, although obviously she was to have nothing to do with the music.

The next time he thought about Mavis was when he was sending out his text invites and he saw her name flashing out at him. Something tightened in his stomach and he included her in his send-out, deciding as he did so to ask her friend Dot so he wouldn't have to actually speak to her on the night. He clicked the button and then it was gone, along with all his reasoning and thoughts.

Years later Clive would become the sort of person who thought intensely about other people's reactions and responses. After university he decided that he wanted to work for more than money and retrained as a psychotherapist, taking a course on which he met his wife, a pretty brunette with short hair who had never even heard of Eminem. They moved back to Kelsey, not far from Druith, both running their practices from home and his parents have their two children three days a week so that Clive often finds himself grateful that they are such a solid good presence and that he has never lived on a trailer park. And they are great friends with Mavis and her family, in one of those ways that life twists and turns and, sometimes, lands you in the place you were meant to be. They meet for lunch in country pubs and their younger children play.

But all of that is yet to come; for now it doesn't exist. It is as unreal as the future in which he becomes a rapper and marries a porn star. The Clive who sent out those invites never thought beyond the moment, couldn't possibly follow his electronic communication down the wires and into the homes and lives of those he'd sent them to. He never considered how it might make Mavis feel, never felt embarrassed at the crudity of his own behaviour.

He wasn't surprised that Mavis and Dot turned up to his party; it hadn't occurred to him that anyone would refuse their invitation. He imagined a woman with a clipboard standing on the door of a club, framed by two burly minders, having to refuse all the legions of gatecrashers. The fact that they were actually in the cricket club made no real difference, it was going to be a banging night and everyone was going to be talking about it for weeks afterwards. He was momentarily surprised though by how Mavis looked. No T-shirt/dress combo tonight, just jeans and a baggy jumper, and she looked surly and angry and as if she hadn't washed her hair in weeks. Then Debbie asked who the fuck had invited those two no-marks, pointing at them, and Clive wondered what the fuck he'd been thinking of, on all counts, and was about to say something, but then a banging tune connected with the MDMA in his system and he turned away to dance.

Clive woke the next day in Debbie's bed, a thick hard pain lodged across his shoulders and up his neck. He knew that when he moved it would explode into his brain so his bones would feel hollow and shattered. His breath tasted of shit, not in a metaphorical way but literally, as though he'd licked the inside of a rodent's cage. His back ached and his throat was swollen and sore; his lungs felt useless, as if he'd got them cheap in the Primark sale. He reached on to the bedside table to see the time on his phone: two-thirty. He had to get some water. He sat up delicately, but his brain still crashed into his skull, making him groan. Debbie moaned in reply; she was lying on her stomach, one arm over her face, her bra still on and her hair in livid clumps round her head. There was a smell of vomit, he realised, and when he stood up he saw that a neat pile of puke lay on the floor next to her side of the bed.

'Shit,' he said out loud.

Debbie raised herself and rubbed her hands over her face. 'Shit,' she repeated.

'You've puked on the floor, man.'

'Oh God.'

Clive left the room to use the bathroom. His piss came out a dark and menacing yellow and felt hotter than usual. He splashed cold water on his face and drank greedily from the tap, then he used Debbie's toothbrush to rid himself of the sensation that someone had shovelled shit into his mouth as he slept. He remembered very little of the night before, just odd flashes like being outside in a thunderstorm. His head rocked on his shoulders and a nausea that he knew wouldn't leave for hours formed in the pit of his stomach. He opened the cabinet doors next to the sink and found some Nurofen, swallowing two and contemplating a third.

The smell in the room hit him afresh when he went back in. Debbie had fallen back down, her mouth hanging open so that dribble was escaping on to the pillow. He shook her shoulder. 'Come on, man, it stinks in here.'

'I can't move.'

'Shit.' Clive scanned the room and decided that a few copies of *Heat* would do the job as well as anything else. He scooped the sick off the floor, releasing more of the acrid smell, which made him retch until his eyes filled with tears. He wrapped the disgusting bundle up a few times and then stuffed it into her bin, which he put outside the door. He couldn't hear any noises from downstairs, but he didn't want to risk running into Debbie's mother and all her jolly questions about the party.

He was sweating and every time he bent over it felt as if his brain was going to roll out of his stinging eyes, so he opened the window and lay back down on the bed. Debbie's eyes were open now, red and streaked in black. Her pillow was brown, smeared by her foundation. She smiled.

'Good night anyway.'

'Can't really remember.'

'You were pretty wasted.'

'Unlike you, right?'

'Nah, just, you know.'

They lay in silence for a while. Clive didn't think he could let his body go through this now, all his limbs felt like glass and his heart was heaving uncomfortably. He toyed with the idea of another drink to put the hangover off by a few hours.

'Did you see Kai and Tash?' Debbie asked.

'No.'

'They were going for it. Went back to hers.'

Debbie always talked about other people; sometimes it made Clive feel dizzy, her ability to be so involved in lives other than her own. He reached for his BlackBerry and flicked on to

127

Facebook: already a couple of people had written about the party, one of their friends had even uploaded some photos. It was hard sometimes to remember that he hadn't yet become as famous as he knew he would be one day; especially when he was tired or hungover like now he forgot he wasn't who he thought he was, forgot that he was reading about his own life.

'Oh yeah,' Debbie said, breaking into his thoughts. 'Who the fuck invited Mavis and Dot?'

Clive put his phone back down, looking at the small screen was hurting his eyes. 'Dunno.'

'How come they came then?'

'I dunno, babe.' He wished he was asleep.

She sat up and he could feel the air prickle around them. If he'd been capable of it he'd have stood up and left. 'It's just Tash and I bumped into them in the toilet and she said you did.'

'Who?'

'Mavis said you invited them.'

'Shit, Debs. What are you going on about?' Clive felt too ill to decide what the best approach was to any of this.

'They pissed me off. Standing by the wall all night like the losers they are. And she was so drunk, Mavis. She was caning it and, like, I just thought why the fuck should she drink all our booze and so when they went to the toilet I followed her and asked her what the fuck she was doing there and she looked at me, bold as fucking brass, and says, Oh, didn't you know, Clive invited us. Made me look like a prize wanker.'

Clive groaned. 'Are you seriously gonna do this now?'

'Just answer the fucking question.'

'What fucking question?'

'Did you invite her?'

'No. I mean – maybe. I dunno. I invited everyone in my mobile, maybe I did by accident.'

Debbie lay back down at this. 'I hate her and her stupid ginger friend. They think they're so much better than the rest of us, just because they're clever.'

Clive wondered what being clever did mean, but the thought was too much for his addled brain. 'Don't sweat it, babe.'

'But Dot was really rude to me. I just commented on how much weight Mavis was carrying and she told me I had a net-curtained future or some shit like that. What d'you think that means?'

'Shit, how should I know, they're freaks.' But Clive had to suppress a smile, his head suddenly filled with an image of Debbie peering out of a window from behind net curtains, worried by what people were doing, worried by what others thought of her. He knew he didn't want to be in the room behind her.

Then it clicked into place: that was what had been different about Mavis; she'd piled it on. A shiver went through Clive, he hated fat birds. They had no respect for themselves and if you didn't respect yourself then who the hell was going to respect you? Rappers were all big on respect and so Clive was big on respect as well. Fat men were all right, obviously, lots of rappers were fat, but fat birds were plain wrong. It was a shame, as Mavis had been pretty tidy when he'd got up close and personal with her. He tried to remember when that had been, end of the summer or some time like that. But his head hurt too much and the light was already fading on the day. He thought clouds were gathering outside; the wind coming in through the open window was bitter and he hoped it would snow. He hoped it would snow for days on end, piling up outside so that no one could get in or out. He wanted to lie in this warm bed for ever. To turn on the TV, chat to his mates on Facebook, fuck his girlfriend, eat the food he hadn't bought in the fridge downstairs and sleep. The thought of the New Year seemed wearisome: 2005. It was a neat number and surely required neat actions. He rolled on to his side. Most of all Clive wanted to sleep.

12 . . . Speech

There was a tatty stack of papers, yellowed and brittle, forged with creases from years of resisting their folds, sitting neatly in a small drawer in the middle of Clarice's dressing table. The drawer wasn't locked and anyone could have opened it at any time, but no one else ever had. She took them out to read from time to time, treating them as if they were made of gold and not wood pulp. Clarice knew it was ridiculous to think it, but of course they were more precious to her than gold, more precious than anything else she possessed. Sometimes the words on the paper made her smile, other times cry. She never knew which to expect until she started to read.

Clarice had only found the papers about ten years before, tucked inside a book of Howie's which had sat, along with all his other books, on the shelves of his study since he'd moved into the house just after their marriage all those decades ago. Before Howie the study had belonged so resolutely to her father that she would never have been able to imagine Howie occupying it so completely. Sometimes she tried to remember her grandfather occupying the space and at others she worried that it belonged to no one now which meant that there was no one to continue its history into the future. The thought of

131

the house being sold after her death caused her physical pain, a tightness across her throat and chest, so that she had to shut her mind to the young couples she'd seen with skips outside some of the older houses in the village.

Clarice would never know what had made her so restless the night she found the papers. Never know why her legs twitched as she sat by the fire, never understand why she stood up and opened a door which had been closed for so long the air smelt musty and walking across the room was like swimming through time. Or what drew her to the bookcase, what made her take down that particular book, showering dust as she'd pulled it towards her like fairy powder, tickling her nose, stinging her eyes. The book had opened naturally where it held the papers, as of course it would do, but Clarice swore she heard it sigh as it gave up its ghost, as if it had been waiting a very long time for this moment.

She had sat at Howie's desk then, which of course was no longer really his but also waiting for someone else to lay claim to it, and unfolded the papers, her heart stopping and then racing, so unprepared was she to see the familiar handwriting again, so out of context and time. She had felt as if he had reached out to her across the years, as if he'd put his arms around her from far away. She'd had to stop for a moment before she read, resting her head on her hands and taking gulps of air into her lungs as she was hit again by a jarring pain, which she recognised all too keenly, as she realised all over again that she was never going to see him again. That Howie was as truly gone as if he'd never existed. Her stomach had felt as empty as if she'd fasted for a month.

When they told Clarice that Howie was missing she under- stood her mother for the first time. She felt so alone she ached.

But as his absence meant that it was only her and Alice from that moment onwards she also knew that she could not indulge in the luxury of death. Her father was long dead by then and her only living relative was an aunt in Yorkshire who didn't even come to the memorial service. For much of the first year she wondered if he had felt anything, if he had known that he was going to die as the boom hit or if all of that was pure supposition. Sometimes she imagined his body as it must have looked after a few days, swollen with water and nibbled by fishes. He would come to her in dreams like that; in fact he still did, all those thousands of nights down the line. She wished she had been nicer so that he hadn't felt the need to sail whenever he wasn't at work, wished she'd created one of those warm homes which men rush back to, bathing themselves in a golden glow of security. They say there are stages of grief and that one is anger, but the only anger Clarice ever felt was towards herself. She still believed that Howie was the kindest, most gentle person she'd ever met.

It was, however, also true to say that over the years the words on the papers had come to comfort her. They catapulted her right back to the time they enshrined, so that for all the minutes it took her to read them she was a giddy bride again, hearing her new husband's firm voice. She knew those words and they encased her heart just as they had done on the night he'd really said them.

The papers were slightly stained by marks which looked like grease, but Clarice suspected were champagne. They were also worn away at one corner and she shut her eyes and saw him standing in front of her, holding the papers, worrying them at the edges. She imagined him putting the papers into the book, maybe on the night itself, and she wondered if he'd always meant to leave them there, or if he'd randomly placed them inside, meaning to move them another day. Maybe he'd always known, not consciously but in some deep recess of his soul? Maybe nothing we do is truly random? Maybe he'd always meant to speak to her from afar, to come back when he was needed? It made her remember the feeling she'd had on her wedding day, the bliss of feeling linked to another human being for the first time since her mother died. Over time this was the version she'd decided to believe in.

Start with thanks etc. Remember to say bridesmaids pretty, thanks to vicar, Percy, mother, C's father, Patsy & Lou for the food. What an amazing house and how excited I am that we're going to live here, how generous of Charles, how beautiful it looks with the marquees. (Maybe something here about C's mother missing it all and how she would have loved it - keep that bit brief, don't want to upset C today, judge it on night.)

Clarry and I met at a dance, which is so commonplace I almost didn't mention it. I wanted to make something up. Some exciting adventure, maybe an African safari or a romantic cruise or a daring rescue, because that seemed like a more fitting way for something so momentous to have started occurred. I spent ages wondering about the best way to have met her, even wrote a few down, but then I threw them away because I realised it didn't matter how we had met, but how we now live our lives. I also realised that I

could stand here for ever telling you how perfect
our love is and how happy we are today, but that
I will sound like every other bridegroom at all
the other weddings you've no doubt been to this
year. The important thing is that Clarry and I
know it is true and intend to live the rest of our
lives making each other happy.
As all of you who know Clarry well can testify
she can be a touch ~~difficult~~ obstinate. When I
asked her to dance at our first meeting she
didn't ~~reply and asked~~ give me an answer, but
instead asked me my name. When I told her she
looked rather put out, so I said, 'When I say
Howard Cartwright, of course I mean Sir Howard
Cartwright.' Her mouth set for a moment, like
it does when she isn't sure of what she thinks, but
then she laughed and said, 'Sir Howard Cartwright,
I would love to dance.' We danced all night: her
card had of course been marked, but she refused
everyone else and was so polite in her apologies.
I think I fell in love with her right there and
then.
    ~~Clarry is like a fine wine, she improves with
time.~~ Clarry is wise, she doesn't give away her
emotions lightly. Nor does she judge people
immediately. She takes her time, watching and
waiting and weighing up not just whether you are
~~worth investing time~~ in her cup of tea, but also
whether you are going to return her feelings.
Luckily for me she deemed me worthy on both
counts. And once you have felt the warmth of her

135

love you couldn't do anything else than love her back.

So, enough sentiment. I'm not a man given to outpourings of emotion and I expect I am puce in the face right now. I just want to end by saying that today I am marrying the woman of my dreams. I cannot wait for our life together to start, to raise a family and tackle all the hurdles life puts in all our paths. I hope to see you all in 50 (check this, is it 60?) years' time at our golden wedding party.

13 ... Revelation

Dot had turned into her grandmother's apple tree. At first the sensation was peculiarly pleasant: the gnarly bark encasing her limbs, the sense of permanence and strength, the birds in her branches. But then the wind started, pulling at her frame, wheedling its way underground in a way she couldn't understand, prising her roots from the earth, laughing at her as she wobbled and toppled and fell to the ground. Faces appeared over her: her mother, her grandmother, Mavis, Clive, Mr Loveridge; and Dot realised they didn't know that she was now the tree. Their mouths were moving, but she couldn't make out what they were saying; Clive and Mavis turned away, laughing about something. Then Miss Benson, her history teacher, leant close over her. 'History is all about roots,' she said. 'You can't possibly understand anything unless you find out where people came from. Decisions are not made in a vacuum, you know.' A siren sounded and Dot presumed someone had called the fire brigade.

When Dot opened her eyes it was light, but she knew it was early. For a moment she still felt as stiff as the tree, was still straining for the fire engine, but then life exploded around her in its uncompromising intensity and she understood that her mobile was ringing on her bedside table. She reached for it and saw the name flashing up at her: freak. Gerry Loveridge had been sending her texts since she'd made it clear that she wouldn't be making Mondays a regular visit and she didn't want to hear whatever madness he was proposing now. But her clock told her that it was 6.12 a.m. and she felt worried by the strangeness of it all.

'Hello.'

'Dot. Did you know?'

Dot rubbed her face, wondering if she was having one of those double dreams that you see in films. 'What?'

'Did you know about Mavis?'

'What's happened to her? Is she all right?'

His tone calmed a bit. 'You didn't know, did you?'

'What are you talking about, Gerry? What's going on?'

He half laughed. 'She's had a baby.'

It was much too early for this. 'She what?'

'Last night – well, a few hours ago. She had a little girl.'

'Oh my God.'

'Precisely. She didn't say anything to you?'

'No.' The realisation smacked at Dot like a harsh wind.

'So you don't know the name of the little shit who got her pregnant?'

'No.' It was obvious now, of course. Dot longed desperately to go backwards, to ask Mavis what was wrong properly. She remembered with shame the time she'd forced her to go to Cartertown to buy a dress for Clive and Debbie's disastrous New Year's Eve party. She remembered standing in Topshop with Mavis pretending that she didn't care, refusing to try anything on. She remembered shouting at Mavis at the bus stop, asking her why she was being so moody, what her problem was. She remembered Mavis telling her that she wouldn't understand, that Dot still lived in a world of easily solvable problems, like equations and essays. Mostly she remembered the outrage she'd felt at this because of her dad. Her dad who obscured everything else.

'I'm going to kill him, whoever he is,' Gerry was repeating on a loop in her ear.

'Where are you?' Dot asked.

'Cartertown General.'

Dot hung up and got dressed. The bus to Cartertown ran from seven and she could make it if she hurried. As soon as she was dressed she crept down the stairs, but as she reached her mother's landing she stopped and listened at her door. The day was so surreal she had an urge to put a marker on it, to take something tangible with her on the odd journey she was about to make. She thought she was just going to look at her, take in a familiar view, but as she peered round the door she saw that her mother was wide awake, lying very still on her back, staring at the ceiling.

'Dot?' she said, half sitting up. 'What is it?'

Dot came into the room, the day dissolving into weirdness around her. How often did her mother lie awake at six-thirty in the morning? How often did she sleep? Dot sat on the edge of her mother's bed. 'Mavis's dad just rang. She's had a baby.'

Her mother sat up completely at this. 'A baby? Did you know she was pregnant?'

'No.' Then Dot was crying. 'I can't believe she didn't tell me.'

Her mother stroked her hair. 'I expect she wanted to, Dot. Some things are very hard to say.'

'What sort of friend am I? Too wrapped up in myself to even notice.'

'It explains why she's been acting strangely. Why she said she wasn't going to university.' Dot nodded, tears flicking round her face like fireflies. Her mother got out of bed, an air of purposefulness invading the air. 'Come on, I'll drive you.' Dot looked up at her quizzically. 'I take it that's why you're dressed, to go and see her. I'll drive you.'

Dot thought it was a beautiful day to be born: 12 June 2005. The air was soft and warm, with neither the suffocating heat of summer nor the bite of spring. The sun was shining out of a clear blue sky and the ground seemed to be pulsating with the presence of life. The roads were quiet, curtains were still drawn across windows and only industrious dog walkers watched them drive away. Her mother opened the car window and turned the radio on, Dot presumed to drown out the questioning silence between them. It was as if, now they found themselves in this unusually intimate situation, they didn't know how to act. *What was the weather like on the day I was born?* Dot wanted to ask, but the words held too much weight to force them out of her mouth. *What was my father like? Was he a nice man? Is he standing right now in Cartertown General taking a first look at his new granddaughter?*

They drew into the car park just before eight and Dot's mum told her she'd wait in the car, to take as long as she needed. Even though the hospital obviously never slept, it still retained an early-morning atmosphere as Dot followed the signs towards maternity. The air felt still and close, expectant almost, as if it was trapped, marking time until someone opened a window. Two nurses in navy-blue uniforms, clipboards under their arms and smiles on their faces, were chatting by the reception desk.

'Can I help you?' one of them asked as Dot approached.

'I've come to see my friend, Mavis Loveridge. She just had a baby.' The words felt too unlikely, too real.

'Oh yes,' said the nurse. 'But I'm afraid it's not visiting time till eleven.'

'But . . .' Dot's eyes misted with tears; she had to get a hold of herself.

'Are you family?'

'Yes. No, but nearly. Her dad just called me.'

'What's your name?'

'Dot Cartwright.'

'Hang on a sec,' she said and disappeared through the double doors. Dot heard babies crying and women screaming, but the other nurse just smiled at her and looked down at her clipboard. Things were changing all around her, whole new worlds opening up, but to these women it was all nothing more than a working day. One person's life is another's pay packet, after all. The first nurse came back a few minutes later. 'I really shouldn't let you go through. She's not even been moved to a ward yet. But she does want to see you. Ten minutes, OK?'

Dot nodded, her head bobbing like a waving cat in the window of a Chinese takeaway. The nurse held open the door for her. 'Second on the right.'

All she had to do was walk. It was easy and yet her legs refused to move. It was preposterous to imagine that she was a few steps away from meeting Mavis's baby, from seeing her friend so altered, for this newest of beginnings. Mr and Mrs Loveridge came out of the room and started to walk towards her so she had to do the same.

'We thought we'd go and get a coffee, give you girls a minute,' said Sandra and Dot was amazed by her. She looked as if she was shining, like someone had come in the night and polished her skin. In contrast Gerry looked grey, his mouth set in a downturn, his eyes ringed in angry black.

The room containing Mavis and her baby was bright and much larger than Dot had anticipated. A wall of windows looked over the hills behind Cartertown and a strange-looking mini swimming pool stood in the centre of the room, filled with what looked to Dot more like blood than water. The bed stuck out of a wall and Mavis was lying on it, pale and blotchy, her face stained with something that Dot thought might be effort, a tiny white bundle in her arms. She looked up as Dot approached, her face breaking into the smile of her old friend.

'Oh my God, Mave,' said Dot, sitting down on the chair which had been pulled up next to the bed. The bundle stirred and Dot realised that Mavis was feeding the baby, that the sucking sounds were not a machine, but a contented baby nursing. The world rushed around her, air sucking to and fro through her head. She didn't feel strong enough to look directly at the baby yet. 'Why didn't you tell me?'

'I don't know. I wanted to. I tried. I just couldn't.'

'But you must have been so scared. I can't believe you did this on your own.'

'It was stupid really.'

'What did your parents say? What happened?'

'I started getting contractions at about midnight last night.' Mavis grimaced. 'Ow, shit it hurts.'

'What does?'

'Feeding. It's a bit like squeezing pins out of your tits.' Dot laughed. 'Anyway, I knew what was happening, I'd read it all up on the Internet and I knew I was due around now.'

'Hadn't you been to the doctor at all?'

'No. I'm an idiot – what can I say? I had this crazy plan to

142

call a cab but I wasn't prepared for how quickly they happened or how much they hurt and I didn't want to be alone. So I woke Mum and it was weird. It was almost like she'd guessed or something, like she was prepared. She got straight up and told me to get in the car and I thought she'd appear with Dad and we'd row all the way to the hospital, but she got into the driver's seat and drove us here.'

'I thought she couldn't drive?'

'Yeah, that's what I said to her. But she said it wasn't that she couldn't, it was just that she hadn't done it in years and it was time she started again. Then when we got here she was amazing. All taking charge and rubbing my back and telling them I wanted to get in the pool, when I hadn't even thought about that. And when I felt like I was dying and was shouting for them to cut me open, she was the one who held my hand and looked into my eyes and told me I could do it.'

'Maybe I should have a baby.'

'She was like a different woman. I can't explain it. And she is so happy now, she doesn't even seem to care that Dad's got the serious arse.'

The baby jerked her head back and Mavis started cooing, lifting her on to her shoulder and rubbing her back. Her breasts were huge, lined with thick blue veins and dark brown nipples that looked almost grotesque. It all looked more natural than Dot could allow herself to believe, yet here it was, this wasn't a film, it was real life, raw and ready.

'Can I see her face?'

Mavis smiled and turned the baby around, holding her gently in the crook of her arm, a part of the body without meaning before this moment. The only visible part of the baby was her head, a tiny circle of red, flaky flesh with eyes shut tight like a kitten, nostrils but no discernible nose and a perfect pair of pouting lips. She was a scrap of life, a mere moment in time and yet she would grow to occupy all their lives, to occupy her own life. The thought was dazzling.

'Oh Mave, she's gorgeous.'

'Isn't she?' said Mavis, without a hint of irony.

'What does it feel like?'

Mavis shrugged, unable to take her eyes off her daughter. 'Not what I expected. It's like my heart's melted or something, like it's made of chocolate.' She ran her finger down her baby's cheek. 'She's so soft and she's so tiny.'

'Have you got a name for her yet?'

Mavis blushed. 'Rose. In fact, I was thinking Rose Dorothy.'

'Really?'

'Of course. You're my best friend, Dot. I do love you, you know. If I'd have told anyone it would have been you.'

They looked at Rose together and Dot wondered if she should ask the obvious question. In the end the words ran through her head so persistently she had to simply to say them out loud: 'Who's the father?'

Mavis looked up and she looked scared. 'Promise you won't tell Dad.' Dot nodded. 'It's Clive.'

And again the world swooped, like an eagle going in for the kill. 'Clive Buzzard?'

'Yes. Dot, please don't hate me. It only happened once. I couldn't tell you, it was all so fucked up and I knew you liked him.'

'But when? How?'

'He asked me to give him maths lessons at the end of lower sixth. Apparently the teachers thought he was going to fail and his dad was freaking out. He was really embarrassed by it all and made me promise not to tell anyone and, I don't know, I guess I was star struck or something because I agreed. And then it went on and on and it seemed like too big a thing to admit.' Mavis swapped Rose into her other arm and coaxed her other breast into the baby's mouth. Dot thought she was sucking with an impressive urgency, her tiny hands fluttering round her face. It seemed obvious that Mavis belonged to her now and the thought made Dot feel small and sad. 'I can't tell you how much I've fucked up, Dot. Or at least, that's what I was thinking. Now I look at Rose and think it was all for the best.'

'I still don't see how you went from maths lessons to sex.'

Mavis reddened. 'It was after that beginning of upper-sixth disco last year, you know, when he drove us home.'

'Oh my God, I knew it. I must have asked you about that night, like, fifty times.' It was the first moment of indignation that Dot had felt, but within it she realised that she didn't care that Mavis had slept with Clive, only that she hadn't felt able to tell her.

'I know. I'm so sorry, Dot. But it wasn't exactly nice. In fact, it was horrid. We went to the common and had sex in the back of his car and it wasn't loving or even caring, it was just fucking, that's all. I even knew he didn't like me that much – he'd probably had a row with Debbie or something. When he dropped me back home I felt so low and shitty, so bloody angry with myself that I put it to the back of my mind and tried to forget it had ever happened.'

'Until you missed your period.'

'Yeah, exactly.'

Dot put her hand over her friend's. 'I still wish you'd told me.'

'I know, so do I.'

145

They both watched Rose suck and then Dot half laughed. 'Debbie's gonna freak.'

Mavis pulled her hand away at this and when Dot looked at her, Mavis's eyes were sparkling and cold. 'No way, Dot. You can't say anything.'

Dot's mind wrapped itself around what Mavis had just said and it felt soft and spongy. 'You are going to tell Clive, aren't you?'

'No fucking way. Absolutely not. He's a wanker, I don't want him anywhere near Rose.'

The world did its flip again, which Dot was almost getting used to. Everything was moving slowly; something important was happening, but she wasn't sure exactly what it was. She saw Mavis's face change and her arm tighten around Rose until it seemed as if a mist had invaded the room.

'Dot,' Mavis was saying, 'Dot, what's wrong?'

Dot put her hand to her cheek, which felt warm and wet; she wondered if she was bleeding but when she looked at her fingers they were simply wet and then she knew she was crying. A knowledge that she didn't understand flapped inside her like a trapped bird. She opened her mouth to speak but nothing came out. Finally she said the first words that formed: 'Give Rose my name, Mave, but please don't give her my life.'

Mavis drew back at this. 'What d'you mean?'

She heard her voice, high-pitched and catchy. 'I've spent all my life wondering who my father is. You know that. It's crap. It's probably why I didn't notice you were pregnant. I can't . . . I can't . . .' Dot clutched at Mavis's sheets to stop herself from falling. 'I feel like I can't move on without knowing who he is. It feels like I'm only half here sometimes.'

Mavis reached out to her with her one free arm. 'Oh my God, Dot, I'm so sorry. I didn't think.'

146

The world was returning slowly to its usual focus. 'It's OK. But you have to tell Clive.'

Mavis nodded, her eyes filling with tears. 'Why don't you ask your mum?'

The door opened and the nurse from before came bustling in, followed by Mavis's mum.

'We're going to move you to the ward now,' she said. 'How's the feeding going?'

'It hurts,' said Mavis, 'but well, I think.'

'She's beautiful, isn't she, Dot?' Sandra Loveridge was saying, pride beaming out of her face as if she was a sun. 'And Mavis was so good, so calm. Has she told you?' Dot nodded, not trusting herself to speak. 'It's so sweet of you to have come so early,' she said. 'Did you get the bus? Gerry could always drive you home. He's got to pick up some clothes for Mavis.'

'Oh no, thanks, Sandra. My mum drove me actually.'

'Your mother?' Sandra stopped fussing over the baby at this and her face softened. 'How is she, your mother?'

The day was weird enough to allow this question. 'She's, um, she's fine, thanks.'

Sandra smiled. 'Give her my love, will you? Say thank you to her for driving you over.'

Dot looked at Mavis to see if she'd heard any of this, but she was being helped into a wheelchair, her hospital gown flowing open, her body looking as if it had been in a war. 'I'd better go.' Dot raised her voice. 'Bye, Mave, I'll come again tomorrow.'

'Oh, she'll be home by tomorrow.' The nurse smiled. 'Later today most likely.'

'Really?'

The nurse laughed at this. 'She's only given birth. Women do it all the time.'

Dot watched them leave, Mavis holding her daughter and waving from the chair, Sandra tripping along beside them, laughing with the nurse – or midwife, as Dot suddenly remembered they were called. She walked back the way she had come, down the sterile corridors, with everything changed.

Dot arrived in the car park to see her mother leaning against their car with a Styrofoam cup in her hand. She was talking to a man who had his back to Dot and for a second she didn't recognise him and wondered who her mother might know here that could make those pink spots bloom on her cheeks and the rash blossom down her neck. The man ran his fingers through his hair and suddenly Dot realised it was Mr Loveridge. Realised that Gerry was talking animatedly to her mother. Dot stopped, looking for somewhere to hide, but even the thought tired her out, made her feel she'd had enough. Gerry turned to go; he put his hand gently on her mother's arm and they smiled at each other. He strode off towards his car, but then he saw Dot and changed direction so that within minutes he was standing in front of her.

'What were you saying to my mum?'

Gerry looked even more haggard in the bright sunlight. 'Nothing. She was getting a coffee when I came downstairs. I was telling her about the birth.'

'OK.' Dot turned to go, but Gerry caught at her arm. She could feel her mother watching them from their car. 'Did Mavis tell you who the father is?'

Dot shook herself free from his grip and looked him in the eyes. 'Yes. But I have no intention of telling you.'

Gerry threw his hands up at this and they slapped down

148

again surprisingly loudly on his thighs. 'For God's sake, Dot, this isn't a game. He's got to pay.'

Dot felt as angry as she ever had. 'What, like you?'

'What?'

'Mavis will tell you the name of Rose's father when she's ready. But you'll probably get away with sleeping with me.'

'What, but I thought . . . I mean . . . I thought you wanted to.'

Dot laughed at this and for the first time she felt the power of sex. 'I only slept with you because I thought you were my father.' Of course she'd said the wrong words again. 'Sorry, that came out wrong. But are you my dad?'

'You don't know who your dad is?' His face softened and his jaw slackened. This day was turning out surprisingly for everyone.

'No.'

'Alice has never told you?'

'Oh God, it's *not* you, is it?' Dot heard the pitch returning to her voice.

'No! Shit, do you think I'd have slept with you if I'd thought there was the remotest possibility?'

Dot wondered what her mother was thinking at this moment as she watched their exchange. 'How can you be sure?'

He almost shouted now. 'Because I've never slept with your mother.'

The power had gone now, evaporated like steam, and Dot felt young and foolish. 'Do you know who my dad was?'

Gerry nodded at this. 'Go home and talk to your mum, Dot.'

Dot turned to go but Gerry stopped her with his hand. 'Christ, Dot, I'm sorry. I didn't realise . . . I mean, what we did . . .'

'It's OK, I'm not planning on saying anything, unless you hassle Mave.'

149

He shrugged. 'Still . . .' He rubbed his fingers hard against his temples. 'Shit, I've got to get Mavis her stuff.'

Dot walked away, aware that both her mother and Gerry were now watching her. She got into the car. She couldn't believe it was only nine. It felt as though she'd lived a whole life since she'd woken up.

'What was that about?' Alice asked immediately.

'He wants to know who the father is.'

'Do you know?'

'Yeah, but I'm not telling him.'

'And you said that?'

Dot nodded, wondering how they were saying these words. 'He's a wanker.'

Alice started the car. 'Yes. He probably is.'

'Sandra asked me to say hi to you. She said thanks for driving me over.'

'Really?'

Dot let her head roll so that she could see her mother, smiling at the news. She was no closer to knowing what had happened. 'Mavis said she was amazing, drove her to the hospital and everything.'

'Good,' said Alice and the word was undeniably heartfelt.

They were on the open road now with fields whipping past as if they didn't really exist. Dot thought America might be nice.

'I know I'm not the best mother, Dot. But you do feel able to tell me things, don't you? I mean, you wouldn't go through something like that alone, would you?'

The question seemed absurd. They never said anything to each other and yet Dot realised she probably would tell her mother if she got pregnant. She might even tell her

150

grandmother. Something important stretched between them, like a spider's web. Ask her! Dot screamed at herself. Do it now, do it now! But the moments sped past as quickly as the fields. They left the past behind and sped into the future, always, always avoiding the present.

'What's she like?' asked Alice. 'The baby.'

'Gorgeous.'

'Has she got a name yet?'

'Rose. Rose Dorothy.'

'Oh Dot, that's lovely.'

Dot rubbed her finger into the worn material of her jeans, soft and giving.

'Things will get back to normal now,' her mother was saying.

'Don't be silly, Mum. Everything will change.'

Alice looked over at this, her expression earnest. 'Well yes, babies do change things. But normally for the better. I meant you'll get the old Mavis back.'

'Did I change things for the better for you?' asked Dot, the effort of speech filling her up.

Her mother laughed. 'Of course you did. What a question.'

'But you were only a couple of years older than Mavis is now when you had me. I must have been a mistake.'

They were on the outskirts of Druith now. 'You weren't a mistake, Dot, more a happy accident and I never regretted it for a single second. You must know that.'

'Yes, but it must have been hard bringing me up alone.'

'It was hard.' Her mother's voice was shaking and Dot could hear how carefully she was choosing her words, as if she was stepping over ice. 'But I wasn't alone, Clarice was around and so were you. So are you.'

It is always impossible to imagine life without ourselves in it and Dot failed to do so at that moment. But she could hear the love in her mother's voice and she felt a sense of – what? – gratitude, luck, good fortune? They were unfamiliar words to apply to herself.

Her mother turned the car into their drive and they both saw Clarice standing looking out of the dining room window, concern wrinkling her features, a smile only appearing as she saw them both in the car.

14 . . . Arrival

Considering how prepared Tony was for the birth, he still felt like he made a fool of himself when it came to it. When Alice woke him with the news that her waters had broken in the depth of a night which would never reach complete darkness, he sat up and said, 'Hang on, I'll get my spanner.' He had no idea what he'd been thinking; he wouldn't be able to fix a leak even if he had a spanner.

She looked young and scared, standing over him, her stomach so absurdly huge in front of her that it seemed impossible a baby could emerge without ripping her in two. He'd made her pack a bag a week before, just as Miriam Stoppard advised, and he was pleased at his forethought, telling her now to get dressed, he'd go and start the car. Except his limbs didn't appear to be connected to his brain any more and simple tasks like turning his trousers the right way took what felt like hours. In the end, though, it was lucky that he hadn't gone on ahead because she needed to lean on him while they went down the stairs, walking as gingerly as if they were on the side of a mountain.

'Should we leave a note for your mum?' Tony asked when they reached the front door, but Alice shook her head and gripped his shoulder more tightly.

The car was surprisingly cold, but Alice was sweating, her hands white as she held on to the sides of her seat. Tony tried to put the seatbelt across her but she pushed him away as if she was burnt and he knew better than to argue.

Cartertown General seemed too far; he could see the route in his mind and knew all the twists and turns of the road, but still willed some of them to have disappeared overnight so they could get there quicker. Alice moaned next to him.

'How far apart are they?'

'I don't know.'

Tony felt a surge of irritation with his wife for not reading one word of all the books on childbirth he'd bought and put on her bedside table; he'd even marked some passages with pieces of paper. He wondered if she really knew what a contraction was.

'Well, when did they start?'

'About an hour before I woke you.'

'You know what's happening, right?'

'Yes. No. Not exactly.'

'Your cervix is opening to let the baby out. You have to get to ten centimetres before the baby can be born. So it's nothing to worry about, the pain.'

Alice didn't reply and Tony wondered if he had overstepped the mark, but it was hard to tell with Alice, she might simply not be interested. The next time she sucked in her breath was at least ten minutes, maybe twelve, by Tony's reckoning. They probably shouldn't be going to the hospital yet, but he couldn't bear the thought of putting her through the journey when they were only five minutes apart.

The hospital was bright and busy, a little oasis in the darkness of his worry. Tony held Alice's bag and handed over her notes and answered all the questions the midwives put to her. They were finally shown into a room which held six beds, two with curtains drawn around them and the rest empty.

'Settle yourself in,' the midwife said, 'I'll be back in a minute to give you an exam.' She drew the curtains neatly round the bed as she left, flicking them into shape.

Alice looked at Tony, desperate and lost. 'Come on,' he said, 'you need to get your nightie back on and lie on the bed. She's going to want to see how many centimetres you are. You know, like we learnt in the antenatal classes.' He wasn't sure that Alice had absorbed any information in the classes he'd dutifully made her attend, even though he'd rather have spent time licking paint off a wall. Towards the end Tony had begun to wonder if the jolly woman was trying to frighten them all, if she enjoyed belabouring them with the inevitability of their reality. At least Alice hadn't wanted to swap numbers with the other smiling couples at the end and, for that at least, he'd felt grateful.

The midwife came back, snapping menacing-looking rubber gloves over her hands. She was reading the notes in her hand. 'So, you're Alice and Tony Marks, right? And you're term plus eleven. Your pregnancy looks like it's been perfectly normal. Is that right?'

'Yes,' said Tony. 'Her contractions are about ten minutes apart.'

'OK. Well, my name's Sally. Now, Alice, could you lie on your back and let your legs drop open. I need to feel how many centimetres you are and then we'll go from there.'

Tony worried that Alice might cry; she seemed too delicate to endure any of this and he held on to her hand, making her

155

look only at him as Sally rooted around in her body as if she was looking for something at the bottom of a bag. Sally's face gave nothing away and with every passing second Tony worried that she'd found something wrong, that any moment an alarm would sound and Alice would be whisked away from him to a doctor with a sharp knife.

Sally stood up, snapping the rubber gloves in the other direction. 'You're between two and three,' she said, dropping the gloves into a bin.

Tony was distracted by the thought of what happened to the gloves. Were they really thrown away after such a short life and if so how many pairs of gloves did that mean the hospital needed – all hospitals needed? He imagined the world drowning in rubber gloves smeared with women's insides.

'If you can I'd go for a walk, get something to eat,' the midwife continued. 'You're in the early stages; I wouldn't have thought your baby will be born in the next ten or so hours.'

She left after that and Tony realised Alice was crying. 'Ten hours?' she repeated. 'I can't do this for ten hours. What does she mean walk about?'

Tony thought it might be a blessing that Alice was clueless. 'Some people think you have to move around to make the labour quicker, it's in Miriam Stoppard's *New Pregnancy and Birth*. And you need to eat to keep up your strength.' Alice whimpered but Tony pulled her up, linking his arm to hers and taking her into the corridor where they took small jagged steps to nowhere. Every so often Alice stopped and leant into the wall, biting her lip and moaning softly, her eyes scrunched shut.

'Breathe through it,' Tony said, 'sharp, shallow breaths.'

But Alice pushed him away and all he could do was watch the sweat gathering on her brow, dropping in tiny rivers down her face. In the end he couldn't bear it any longer and took her back to the bed, which was comforting in the fact that it was, at least, a destination.

'Shall I get you something to eat? Maybe some chocolate?'

Alice nodded. 'And a drink please.'

It was a relief to walk away for a moment, like diving into cool water on a hot day and for a minute the realisation that he could keep on walking swept through Tony. The food kiosk was only just inside the main hospital doors and he watched people swinging easily through them. At the last minute he bought a packet of fags and a tube of mints and went to stand in the sharp night air, which rushed around him after the heat of the hospital. He hadn't smoked in ages, since he'd moved in with Alice really, and the nicotine marauded through his blood, flicking that switch in his brain so that his shoulders relaxed and his breathing deepened. If he never met the baby, he found himself thinking . . . but of course he would never do anything like that. He ground the butt of the cigarette into the tarmac and popped a mint into his mouth before going back inside.

Alice was leaning over the side of the bed, her face red and contorted, her hands grabbing for something that wasn't there. Tony immediately went to her and stroked the hair off her face, whispering nothings into her ear. He put a hand on her stomach and it felt hard and mean.

'You've got to stop fighting them,' he said after the pain had subsided and she was lying breathless, her head flung against the pillow. He handed her pieces of chocolate, which she ate slowly. 'That's what those breathing exercises were all about.

Your body's going to do this whatever and if you tense your muscles it'll hurt more.' Tony wasn't sure that Alice had heard but he didn't repeat himself.

The next round of pain came quickly. Alice grabbed on to Tony's hand and wept. 'Oh God, it hurts so much.' He soothed her and they settled into a pattern. He asked her a few times if she wanted to walk again, but she didn't, so all he could do was hand her sips of drink and tiny squares of chocolate. The clock ticked on but the night remained stubbornly immobile. Tony began looking at the clock and wondering which number would deliver them a baby, which seemed an absurd and unlikely thought. As so many other people rested and slept they were here doing this, something that would change their lives for ever. They had only been in the hospital for three hours, a period of time which could float past him and disappear down a hole most days, but which he had now lived through experiencing every second, aware of every pulse from his heart.

'I'm going to be sick,' Alice said and he stood up, panicked, rushing from the bed to find a nurse who chuckled at his worry and handed him some cardboard bowls.

'Don't you want to check her?' he asked.

'Someone will be in shortly,' she answered. 'Don't worry, it's all perfectly normal.'

It didn't seem normal to hold your wife's head as she retched brown bile into something which, if painted, could pass as a clown's hat. Tony felt annoyed by Miriam and wondered why she hadn't written that he would feel scared and helpless in the 'fathers' story' chapter. There had even been photos of men physically supporting their wives as babies slipped from their bodies. As Alice retched next to him he was sure he remembered reading, just a few nights before, that it was a mystical event. She was writhing again, clutching his hand so hard he thought she might break it, her voice whimpering and far away. 'Tony please,' she was saying, 'I can't do this, please help me.'

He knelt down so that their faces were level and tried to make her look at him, but her eyes flickered away, her face a jangle of pain. He didn't recognise her and it scared him to think of her lost to him, even her strangeness was something and he knew he would miss it. Tony ran into the corridor again and stopped another midwife. 'Please, my wife really is in agony. Can someone come and see her?'

The woman clicked her teeth. 'We're very busy tonight. Childbirth does hurt.'

Her presumption annoyed him. 'I know. I'm not stupid. I have read the books. But her contractions are really close together now.'

The woman sighed, no doubt cursing her luck that she had been walking past at that moment. 'OK,' she said, following Tony back into the room.

Alice was off the bed now, leaning over it and gripping on to the sheets.

'We'll let this one pass then I'll examine her,' said the midwife, snapping on yet more plastic gloves. 'My name's Dora.'

'Tony and Alice,' answered Tony. Alice's body was releasing her for a minute.

'Do you think you could lie back, Alice, so we can see what's going on?' said Dora in a voice that left no room for compromise. Alice only whimpered.

Dora pushed Tony out of the way, her hand strong on Alice's back. 'Now, now. Is it really bad?' Alice moved her head

159

imperceptibly. 'I'm sorry but I do need to examine you.' Dora checked the chart by the bed. 'You were between two and three, three hours ago.' Alice didn't answer; instead her body stiffened and her hands turned white with the pressure of gripping. 'OK, love, breathe through it,' Dora said. 'They're pretty close together. As soon as this one's over I'm going to examine you standing up.'

Tony didn't know how Dora knew the exact moment the contraction had finished, but she was quick and concerned. She stood up and looked at Tony. 'Your wife is just about ready to give birth. We need to move her to a labour room. Get her on to the bed. I'll be back in a second.'

'But how, I mean, that's too quick, isn't it?' said Tony, his mind feeling like a blender, scrapping all the useful information it had ever stored.

Dora laughed. 'Try telling that to the baby. There's no rule book, you know.'

'Are you coming in?' someone was asking him and he looked down and somehow Alice was on the bed and it was being wheeled away from him.

'Yes, of course,' he said, tripping over himself as he followed them down corridors and into another room.

'Is there a pressure in your bottom?' Dora was saying as she pushed Alice's legs into the air. 'Push into that. Well done, that's right.' Another midwife was holding a wet cloth against Alice's forehead, whilst a young girl busied herself on the other side of the room. Tony stood against a wall, his coat draped over his arm, Alice's bag in his hand. He felt as if he was underwater and that he couldn't breathe. 'Push,' women shouted all around him whilst Alice screamed. Shouldn't he get someone? Didn't a doctor need to be present? Hold your wife's hand, Miriam

160

Stoppard advised, tell her she's wonderful, she'll need your support. But Tony was stuck to the wall, fear flattening him like a coward. 'That's it,' Dora said, 'one more now.' Alice made a noise from somewhere deep inside her and then there was an instant of total silence, broken by the screams of a baby. 'Congratulations, Alice,' Dora said, handing her something which Tony understood to be a baby. It lay on her chest, as shocked as the rest of them.

Dora came over to Tony. 'Congratulations,' she said, 'your wife was amazing.' She nudged him in the arm. 'Why don't you put down your stuff and go and meet your baby?'

So Tony did as he was told, and all the while the water was filling his ears and his lungs so that he thought it likely he would faint before he reached the bed. Alice smiled up at him and she looked as if time had travelled across her face and punched her in the eyes. He could see tiny broken veins splattered across her nose and cheeks like freckles and her hair was as wet as if she had been swimming. He remembered their beach and his body tingled.

'Let's weigh her then,' Dora said, taking the tiny being from Alice's chest. The baby cried at the intrusion and Tony followed it with his eyes, only hearing the words seconds after they'd been spoken.

'A girl?'

'That's normally the first question most dads ask.' Dora chuckled. She put the baby on to the scales. 'Seven pounds three. Now I think this baby needs a feed.'

The other midwife helped Alice to sit up and then both women bent over her as the baby, now wrapped in a blanket, was placed into her arms. The air vibrated as the baby nestled into her breast, its tiny eyes shut, its rosebud mouth closing convincingly over the nipple. Alice stared down at her and the midwives started to tidy up, making Tony notice the oceans of blood on the bed and the floor. 'You'll need a few stitches,' Dora was saying, 'I'll get them done now.' Tony sat down heavily in the chair next to the bed which held his wife and daughter and for a second felt unworthy of even breathing the same air as the people who brought life into the world.

Alice rolled her head to the side and smiled at him. 'Are you happy she's a girl?'

'Of course. Are you?'

'I didn't mind,' she answered, which Tony thought was probably true. Secretly he'd hoped for a son, but now the baby was here he could see that it didn't matter. Alice winced as Dora sewed her up.

'I can't believe how amazing you were,' said Tony. 'I lost it when we got in here.'

She laughed. 'Don't worry, I didn't notice.'

'Were you scared? What were you thinking about?'

'I can't remember. Actually I can, but it's so strange. At one point I thought about, you know, how sometimes you see beetles lying on their backs with their legs waggling in the air?' Tony nodded. 'Well, I'm never leaving one like that again.' He laughed. 'And then I thought about my mother. I thought about her doing all this and it seemed impossible.' She shook her head as if ridding herself of the thought.

'I can't believe how' – he searched for the word – 'how violent it was. Did it really hurt?'

Alice nodded. 'D'you want to hold her? I think she's finished.'

Tony looked down at his daughter, so small it was ridiculous.

He stood up and lifted her into his arms and she was so light it was almost as if she didn't exist. Alice shut her eyes and he went to stand by the window, looking down into the car park as the sky over the hills broke into a pinkish dawn. A cacophony of emotions knocked at his heart and it felt dangerous to let them all in. I will be a better man, he promised himself as he held his daughter in his arms. I am a lucky, blessed man. We'll get through this together, I won't let you down.

'So,' Dora said from behind him, 'has baby got a name? I like to know the names of all the babies I deliver.'

Tony looked over at Alice, who opened her eyes. He'd been trying to discuss names with her for weeks, but each time he'd made a suggestion, she'd shrugged him off.

'You've got some ideas, haven't you?' she said and so Dora looked at him.

He ran through his top three girls' names in his head: Holly, Jasmine and Isabella. None of them were right, none of them captured what it meant to be standing here holding this little life.

'Dot,' he said, surprising even himself.

'Dot?' repeated Alice.

He blushed. 'Well, Dorothy, I suppose, but we'll call her Dot.'

'Dot,' Alice said again.

'Obviously only if you like it.'

Alice wrinkled up her nose. 'How did you think of it?'

Tony worried that she was playing for time. He could feel the midwives busying themselves and he felt suddenly self-conscious, so he lied. 'Oh, I had an Aunt Dot. She was lovely and I just thought, you know . . .' Dot, he thought, let her be Dot. Because she is a beginning. A tiny dot of a life that will grow into something wonderful. The need for her to be Dot tugged at his heart.

'Well, I think it's a lovely name,' said Alice, shutting her eyes again.

Tony smiled and looked down at his daughter. At his Dot.

15 ... Recklessness

Alice's heart sank when Sandra called her on the morning of their circus trip to say that she'd been up all night being sick and didn't want to risk going anywhere because of the baby, but that Gerry would take Mavis and drive them all there. It had seemed too rude to balk at this after Sandra had gone to all the trouble of organising the trip and buying the tickets and, besides, Dot was very excited.

So Gerry picked them up at the appointed hour in his battered white Chrysler and the girls giggled in the back while Alice asked him polite questions about his teaching and music as he drove them to Cartertown. Once they got there the girls were so overcome with the bright bodies throwing themselves around the big top and the huge animals within touching distance that Alice only had to smile occasionally at Gerry from behind Dot's bobbing head.

It was getting dark by the time they filed out into the night, a group of excited people who dispersed into a cold evening, all going back to warm homes and cups of tea. The girls pulled on their parents' hands, tired out by the excitement. Alice strapped them both into the back seat and then settled herself into the front. Gerry turned on the heating and put the Police into the tape deck. Both girls were asleep before they'd even left Cartertown.

'How're you feeling now?' Gerry asked as they bumped along a deserted road, so dark that his headlights carved two neat lines out in front of them and nothing seemed real.

Alice had become used to Sandra's openness and only blushed slightly at the question. 'Oh, you know, good days and bad days.'

'San says you haven't heard from him at all.'

'No, still nothing.' Alice turned her head and saw herself reflected back by the window, Gerry glancing at her from over her shoulder.

'Well, he's a bloody fool.'

'Apparently he left with a barmaid called Silver.' Alice didn't know why she was saying this, but the car was like a bubble of life which wouldn't exist when she left it.

'I know. God knows why.'

'You met her?' The link was tenuous but intoxicating.

'Yeah, I drink at the Hare and Hounds sometimes.'

'Did you see them together?'

Gerry shifted. 'Well, not really. I saw him talking to her in there a few times.'

'Oh, right.'

'But she's nothing compared to you. Honestly, he needs his head reading.'

Alice smiled at this; she was learning to take what she could out of small kindnesses, even when it felt like termites were burrowing into her skin. 'Thanks.'

Gerry looked at her and so she looked back and smiled at him, wishing he would keep his eyes on the road. 'No, really, Alice. You're amazing.' The car was slowing and Alice looked forward, trying to see what might be stopping them, but there was nothing, just a hedgerow that flashed past as the car crunched to a stop.

'Is everything OK?' she asked, flicking her eyes back at the sleeping girls.

Gerry leant over and put his hand on her knee, the movement so unexpected that she flinched from his touch. He laughed. 'Come on, Alice. I know you must be lonely. I can read those eyes of yours.'

Alice pulled her skirt down, smoothing it over her legs. 'I'm sorry, what?' Sting's voice pulsated through the steamy car: *Don't stand, don't stand so, don't stand so close to me*. Gerry leant forward, his breath hot and smoky on her neck. Alice pushed him hard on the shoulder and his head jerked back so that it banged on the side of the door.

'What the fuck?' He put his fingers to his head and when he brought them down they were bloody.

'God, I'm sorry, it's just, I mean, what were you doing?'

'I was trying to kiss you.' Gerry found a tissue in his pocket and dabbed at his head.

'Kiss me?'

'Oh come on, don't play dumb. All those little smiles and Lady Di eyes, I know what you want.'

'What I want is to go home.'

'"What I want is to go home."' Gerry mimicked her voice and Alice realised she sounded prim and proper. He started the engine. 'You're nothing but a prick tease.'

Her mouth floundered like a fish until she found the right words. 'But Sandra's my best friend. Your daughter's asleep in the back of the car.'

He laughed at this, turning the music up and lighting a

167

cigarette without opening the window. 'Are you for real? Are you really that naive or is it just part of the act?'

Alice dug her nails into her palms to stop the tears. 'What act?'

'Jesus. I'm starting to see what Tony saw in Silver.'

They drove the rest of the way in silence. If Alice had been alone she would have asked to get out, not caring that they were in the middle of nowhere on a dark night. And she felt sure that Gerry would have obliged. But of course she wasn't on her own any more and Dot was more important than anything that happened to her. When they arrived she lifted Dot out of the car and walked up the path to her home without speaking or looking back – not that it mattered as the car had turned the corner before she'd even opened the front door.

Once inside she carried Dot to her bedroom, managing to take the little girl out of most of her clothes and tuck her into bed without waking her. She kissed her podgy cheeks and smoothed her hair off her face, wishing that she could climb into bed next to her daughter and cuddle up to her tiny body. But it was only half past seven and Alice knew she had to put on a better show than that, so she went downstairs and made herself a cup of tea, which she took into the sitting room where Clarice was reading in front of the fire.

'I've made some soup if you're hungry,' she said, not looking up.

'No, I'm fine with tea, thanks. I'm shattered actually. It was a long day.'

Her mother laid her book on her lap and looked at her over her glasses. 'Was it fun?'

'Yes. Dot loved it.'

'Good.'

Alice thought her mother knew there was more to say, but was glad that she simply picked up her book and started reading again.

The idea of sleep was so much more appealing than the actuality. However tired Alice felt, and most nights she climbed into bed with a bone-aching exhaustion, as soon as she was lying on her back with the light off her mind jumped to attention and sleep ran from her side. By the next morning she had resolved not to say anything to Sandra. Surely she had been mistaken, surely Gerry felt foolish and stupid himself, surely he'd just been swept up in some strange emotion. And what good would come of saying anything? Sandra was due to give birth in four months and Alice didn't want her friend going through the same pain as she had.

She got Dot dressed and took her downstairs where she made her a boiled egg and looked out of the kitchen window at the greyness of Sunday, wondering how they would fill all the hours between now and bedtime. Clarice came in carrying her portable radio blaring out the news which Alice couldn't listen to if she tried. It all just went in a pattern anyway: stories she found interesting stopped being talked about and depression ruled the airwaves. Dot pushed another mouthful away, spraying tiny flecks of yellow and white egg on to the floor which would have to be swept up in a minute.

The phone rang and Alice looked at her mother, who herself had stopped to look at her. The same thought spun in both their minds: how could it be anyone else at ten past nine on a Sunday morning?

'Shall I get it?' her mother asked.

But Alice stood up. The symmetry of Tony ringing this

morning after all that had happened last night was so perfect she felt she could perhaps forgive him.

'Hello.'

'Alice.' It wasn't his voice.

'Sandra? Are you OK?'

'No, I'm bloody not. How could you?' And even though her friend's voice trembled down the phone, still Alice didn't make the connection.

'How could I what?'

'Gerry told me everything when he got in last night. Don't play innocent.'

'What did Gerry tell you?'

'That you made a pass at him on the way home. He had to pull the car over or you might have crashed. I thought you were my friend.'

Alice put her hand to her head, she almost wanted to laugh. 'Come on, Sandra. You believe him?'

'Of course I do.' But Alice could hear the doubt.

'I would never do anything like that to you. I don't even like Gerry. He made the pass at me and I pushed him away.' Silence vibrated down the line. 'I thought about ringing you last night, but I didn't want to upset you. I mean, I'm sure he didn't mean it, and there's the baby and everything.'

'Don't, Alice, for God's sake don't mention the baby.' Sandra's voice was catching on her tears.

'But, Sandra, you're my best friend. You've been so good to me. You know I wouldn't do that. He's got a cut on the back of his head if you don't believe me.'

'What does that prove?'

'That I pushed him away. If he'd pushed me I'd be the one with the cut.'

'Please.' Sandra sounded young and far away.

'Can't we forget this ever happened? It doesn't matter.'

'It might not matter to you, Alice, but this is my life we're talking about.'

'I didn't mean it like that, I just meant—'

'I can't, Alice. Every time I look at you . . .'

Alice realised she was crying as well. 'What are you saying, San?'

'Look, just don't call me again, OK?'

Then the phone went dead and Alice slid down the wall, as if she was too heavy for herself, as if life itself weighed more than she could bear. She raised her head and saw her mother and daughter staring at her, their eyes wide, their mouths open.

Every fibre in Alice's being wanted to go back to bed, but Clarice made her sit at the kitchen table with a cup of tea and tell her what had happened and somehow it made her feel slightly better. There would be more friends like Sandra, her mother told her, and really Alice should count herself lucky not to be in her shoes, not to be stuck with such an awful man. Although being stuck with an awful man, especially if he was Tony, sounded quite appealing to Alice. Her lack of judgement shocked her. Her total inability to read people and understand what they meant. Life raced at her like a storm, whipping away her ability to see or think straight.

Yet Dot was now an urgent presence in her life and by the end of that day Alice knew she wouldn't go back to bed ever again. But she always remembered that she wasn't to be trusted, that her grip on emotions was tenuous and she mustn't let her bad judgement rub off on Dot. That the only way her daughter was ever going to be happy was to learn nothing from her, that it was a hard ask, but that she must make her own way. Alice decided she would give her all she needed to be as complete a person as she could be, but that she would step back where judgements and emotions were concerned. I can do this, she thought to herself as she put Dot back into her bed that night, I can shut myself up and dedicate myself to her. The thought ran through her like cold water as she saw her life stretching into the future and she wondered how many mornings and nights there were to get through before Dot wouldn't need her any more.

The next morning was bright so Alice decided to take Dot to the swings on the green early, to avoid any of the other mothers she'd recently started nodding to on the street. But of course Ellen was already there with Freddie and by then Dot was excited, pulling her along by the hand so she almost tripped over herself. Ellen was the last person, after Sandra, that Alice would have chosen to see, as the two women lived on the same cul-de-sac, their houses opposite each other. As she got closer she saw the strain on Ellen's face and wondered with fresh horror if Sandra was spreading news of Gerry's version of events.

'Have you heard?' Ellen asked, before Alice even had a chance to lift Dot on to the swing.

'No? What?'

Ellen put her hand out and touched Alice lightly on the arm. 'Oh, I'm sorry to have to be the one to tell you. Sandra had an accident yesterday.'

'An accident?' Dot was screeching now and so Alice bent down and lifted her into the bright yellow swing. 'What sort of accident? Is she OK?'

'She's alive. In hospital. A few broken bones, but she lost the baby.'

'Oh my God, what happened?' The weight of responsibility hovered above Alice's head, ready to crush her.

'I don't know exactly. I saw a police car pull up after lunch yesterday and then Gerry came rushing round and asked me to look after Mavis. He didn't say what was going on but I could tell he was beside himself. He came back a few hours later and said Sandra had crashed their car and was in the hospital. I felt so sorry for him: he nearly cried when he told me about the baby dying, Mavis stayed the night in the end. He came to get her early this morning and he looked in a right state – my God, you should have seen him. Can you imagine?'

Alice didn't seem able to stop pushing the swing backwards and forwards.

'They'd obviously had a row,' Ellen was saying. 'I heard some raised voices coming from their house in the morning. He must feel so awful. Do you know what it was about?'

The question didn't seem real. 'No.'

'Because you all went to the circus on Saturday, didn't you?'

'Sandra didn't come actually, she was sick.'

Alice could feel Ellen staring at her, as if the answers to all her questions might be written on her face. 'That's odd. She's too far gone for morning sickness. Or at least, was. God how terrible.'

'It was just a bug, I think. Do you know which hospital she's in?'

'Cartertown General.'

Alice walked back home in a daze. There was no need to put two and two together, what had happened was obvious and rooted in something she'd done, as if she'd gone round and stuck a knife deep into her best friend's belly. Hadn't Gerry called her a prick tease? Maybe she'd said the wrong things to Sandra? Maybe she should have pretended it had been her who had made the pass and saved her from the truth? Or maybe there were words that she would never know that could have made her friend feel better, stopped her rushing off into a terrible disaster? She felt so ragged by the time she got home that she immediately went to find her mother and told her everything without being asked, before asking her to watch Dot while she went to visit Sandra.

Clarice told her to take the car so she drove back along the roads she'd been driven down only the night before last, wondering which bend in the tarmac and which stretch of hedgerow they'd stopped by. And all the way she tried to imagine what Sandra must be going though, how violent it must feel to have a baby taken from you in that way.

She was directed to the maternity ward when she got there, which seemed barbaric to Alice, and made her angry enough to ask a nurse if Sandra really had to be surrounded by women with their stomachs rounding out their bed sheets. But the nurse looked at her as if she was mad and pointed in the direction of a bed with all the curtains drawn around it.

Sandra looked miniscule in the bed, as if her flesh had sunk on to her bones. Her bump was still there like some ghastly reminder of what might have been. At first Alice thought she was ignoring her, but then realised that she wasn't focusing, so she walked forward and brushed her arm. Sandra started when she saw her, but then her face relaxed and the tears fell. Alice sat on the side of the bed.

'God, Sandra, what happened?'

'I killed my baby.' And she said it so bluntly, it made Alice feel dizzy.

'Don't say that. You had a car crash.'

'I was driving too fast. I wasn't taking any care.' Her fingers twitched at the bed sheets.

'I saw Ellen by the swings this morning, she said Mavis

174

stayed there last night.' They sat in silence, questions circling like hungry wolves. 'Ellen said you and Gerry were arguing?'

'Great, so I'm village gossip now, am I?'

'Not at all. She was worried. I'm worried.'

'Of course we were bloody arguing.'

'I'm so sorry.'

'We both know you have nothing to apologise for.'

Alice felt a surge of love for her friend and went to take her hand, but Sandra jerked away.

'Don't get the wrong idea, Alice. I know the truth, but I'm not letting it in.'

'What?'

Sandra looked up at this and her eyes were a steely blue; the blue of madness, Alice found herself thinking. 'I don't know if I'm going to get over this. But I have to retain something for Mavis. I'm not as strong as you. I can't be a single mother.'

Alice was shocked at this unrecognisable version of herself. 'Stop it, San. Of course you'll get over this. I know it doesn't feel like it now, but one day you'll have another baby and—'

'No!' The word ripped through the room. 'I won't ever have another baby.'

'Come on, San, it'll be OK.'

'Stop it, Alice.'

'Please. You're my best friend. What about Dot and Mavis?' Alice felt she was grabbing at thin air, falling down a hole.

'Dot and Mavis can still see each other. It's not like I can't bear to see you, but there's nowhere left for us to go, is there? I mean, everything I say to you, you'll know it's all based on a lie. What will you say to make me feel better when Gerry puts his hand on the next girl's knee?'

Alice was crying as well. 'I wouldn't judge you, San. I'd have done the same with Tony if I'd had the chance. I'd have forgiven him anything. My God, I probably still would now. I understand what you're doing.'

'Alice, go and have a great life. You've got it all: you're kind and funny and beautiful. You just need to wise up a bit. You and Dot should start again, get out of that old house.'

'But you could do the same.'

She shook her head violently. 'It's all over for me. You can't kill your baby and get away with it.'

'You did not kill your baby.'

A nurse put her head round the curtain. 'Visiting time's over. She should be getting some rest now.'

'She should be getting off this ward,' Alice said, fury blazing in her. 'Can't you move her or something?'

'Don't worry,' said Sandra, 'I'm going home tomorrow.'

The nurse jerked the curtains back from around the bed. 'Like I said, visiting time's over.'

Alice stood up. 'I'm always here, Sandra. If you ever change your mind.'

She shook her head so Alice bent to kiss her cheek, but as she did Sandra grabbed on to her arm, pulling her closer so that her mouth was level with Alice's ear. 'It was a boy,' she whispered, 'he was a boy.'

Alice jolted with the awfulness of the knowledge, but Sandra held on tight. 'I didn't give birth to him. Apparently they had to cut him out of me to save my life. Not a particularly good exchange, wouldn't you say? I never even saw him. Nobody told me anything. I had to drag the information out of Gerry. It's like he never existed. Nothing. I won't even be able to get a birth certificate or have a grave.' Her hand slackened so Alice stepped backwards.

'Sandra, listen . . .'

Sandra was crying again and the nurse had returned with some pills in a tiny plastic cup, which she swallowed greedily before lying down and turning her back on Alice.

Alice waited in the corridor for the nurse to finish with the other women and stopped her as she came out. 'What happened to my friend's baby?'

The nurse shook her head. 'It died, I'm afraid.'

'I know. He died. But what happened to his body?'

'She was only twenty-two weeks gone, so we'd have disposed of him.'

'Disposed?'

The nurse shifted her weight on her overworked feet. 'He wasn't viable. It was a horrid accident, but your friend will be fine.'

Alice cried all the way home in the car, her tears blurring her vision so that she kept having to pull over to stop herself from crashing. People's lives seemed to her like a litany of tragedies; they all lurched from one calamity to the next, each obliterating the one before in its awfulness. And every tragedy is personal; your own is so hard to bear because it belongs only to you. Alice understood why Sandra had told her about the baby, because sometimes even one other person sharing in your grief makes it more bearable, makes it less likely that you're going to jump out of the next open window. People cross the road to avoid you when you have been knocked down because they are clinging so desperately to their own fragile all-rightness, which could be shattered at any minute. Really, Alice thought as she pulled up in front of her house, life is a terrifying balancing act. She remembered the tightrope walkers in the circus with their spangly costumes and safety net.

16 . . . Waiting

It was absurd how long it took to do anything with a newborn. Days would go by and Mavis would be pleased if she'd got dressed and brushed her teeth. Her mum was helping her loads because she seemed to have an incessant desire to hold Rose or take her for walks or make Mavis milk-producing meals. But still time had slowed to a near halt whilst also accelerating way beyond the proverbial speed of light. It was not a dilemma Mavis felt she had enough brain power to pursue. For now being was enough. Mavis found simply existing with her baby was like stepping into a new world, that hours could pass just watching Rose sleep or holding her chubby fingers or smoothing her shock of red hair. She'd call her mum in from the kitchen and they'd both wonder at this tiny new life, smiling at each other because they didn't need to speak. Even her dad seemed charmed. He hadn't smoked in the house since Rose had come home and he always washed his hands after every cigarette, which did seem to be lessening in frequency. He would bring in a cup of tea for them all after dinner and they'd sit round the telly and the night before Mavis had even heard her parents laughing after she'd gone up to bed. There was a completeness and a cosiness to it all that made life feel like a rolling moment of warmth and delight.

Nearly a month after her birth, Rose woke Mavis at around seven, hungry and wet, and Mavis spent the next hour or so changing and feeding her daughter, watching her earnest face as she sucked on her distended breast. She tried calling Dot before she went downstairs to wish her luck, but her mobile was off so she left a message. By the time she got into the kitchen the sun was hot and her mother was washing up at the sink, the back doors open on to the garden, in a way they never used to be. Mavis asked if she'd mind holding Rose while she had a bath, knowing that there was nothing her mother liked better than to be alone with her granddaughter. She would even stop cleaning for her and that wasn't something Mavis could ever remember her doing before. In fact, if she remembered anything from her childhood it was her mother telling her that she would come when she'd finished cleaning, except that the cleaning never ended: dust always resettled, plates were used, floors needed hoovering, surfaces wiping. It used to make Mavis furious that her mother couldn't see the futility of what she was doing and in the end she stopped asking for anything.

She ran the bath hot and dripped some lavender oil into it. She had stopped bleeding now but the stitches were still sore and her breasts only felt normal when she confounded gravity by lying in water. She tried to imagine Dot where she was but couldn't place her so far away. Mavis worried as she washed her hair that it had been insensitive to ask her to come to register Rose's birth. She hadn't thought about it until after they'd left the registrar's and seen Dot's white face and asked her what the matter was and she'd simply said, 'I've never seen my birth certificate.' Mavis remembered how she'd felt the atmosphere tense when the registrar had asked her for the father's name and she'd given Clive's and stupidly she'd thought that was because it was Clive, not because it made Dot realise that there was a piece of paper somewhere in the world with her father's name written on it.

Maybe she should have taken Clive; he'd offered, after all, but it had seemed too strange. And when they'd arrived at the town hall and sat in the waiting room with the other cooing couples, she'd been overwhelmingly pleased that it was Dot sitting next to her and not a boy she barely knew. She'd only told him of Rose's existence the week before and of course she'd only done that because Dot had insisted, which meant it was a fact which still hadn't entirely settled in her mind. But it had unequivocally been the right thing to do; he'd been round and met Rose, brought a stupid pink balloon which had made Mavis laugh and spat out the no-doubt well-rehearsed right words about how he'd like to be part of Rose's life and, when he left college and got a job, he'd help out financially. He'd texted her only last night to ask if his parents could come and visit Rose. Mavis hadn't yet replied, the thought of sharing her daughter was still too much.

'Do you reckon we should get married before or after college?' Mavis had asked and he'd paled so quickly she'd been worried he might faint; she'd laughed and hit him on the arm and assured him she was only joking.

'Debbie's taken it hard,' he'd said then. 'I think it's good I'm going away to college in September.'

'If you get maths,' Mavis had joked.

He laughed. 'Yeah.'

'It'll be OK,' Mavis had said kindly and he'd smiled, but she'd got the feeling that he was ready for a change anyway.

'What about you?' he'd asked.

'I doubt I did my best,' she'd replied. 'I can sit them next year and I'm going to ring Manchester. Mr Hughes rang and he said universities have good policies on studying with babies now. So, you never know.'

Dot had rung a few hours after they'd got home from registering the birth and asked Mavis where she thought her mother might have hidden her birth certificate.

'In your house it could be anywhere,' Mavis had answered. 'Why don't you ask her? It's about time.'

'I know,' Dot had said. 'I want to but I can't. I don't know if I'll ever be able to. This might be the only way. I Googled it and there's a place in London you can go to get a copy. Charles House in Kensington it's called.'

'What if his name's not on there?'

'Then I'm no worse off than I am now.'

'Are you thinking of going?'

'I don't see why not. The exams are all over and all I'm doing is waiting around.'

She'd called back a bit later and said she'd arranged it all. She'd found a B and B to stay at on a place called Edgware Road, which was just a short tube ride from Kensington and she'd told her mum that she was going on an open day to Manchester so would be away for a day and a night.

'I wish I could come with you,' Mavis had said, meaning every word.

'So do I, but you've got Rose. Anyway, it's probably one of those things I should do alone.'

'When are you going?'

'Well, it opens at nine and it says on the website to get there early cos they're always so busy, so I've booked into the B and B for this Wednesday night and I'll go along on Thursday.'

'Wow,' Mavis said, 'nothing like striking while the iron's hot.'

'That's what I thought.'

But then Rose had started squalling and Mavis had had to go and somehow forty-eight hours had passed in a second and now Dot was in London and Mavis had only spoken to her by text last night when she'd been on the coach.

Getting dressed was easier now. Mavis still couldn't fit into her jeans or anything, but every day she felt slightly lighter. The midwife had told her that was because she was so young, her skin was still firm and the baby was sucking the fat out of her. Wait till you have your third, she'd laughed, grabbing a roll of fat on her own belly. Her mother was cooing over Rose in the garden, pointing up at trees which Rose had no way of seeing.

'She'll be smiling soon, in the next couple of weeks I imagine,' her mother said as she handed the warm bundle back to Mavis. 'Why don't we go for a walk by the river in Tinmouth later? I'll drive us over. It's such a beautiful day.'

'Yeah, there's that nice café there, we could get some cake,' said Mavis.

'Lovely. I think she's hungry again. Why don't you feed her and I'll bring you in a cup of tea.'

No wonder Rose was hungry, it was nine-twenty and she hadn't eaten for two hours. Mavis settled herself on the sofa in the sitting room, cushions bulked around her to take the weight from her arms. Her breasts were straining, one was leaking against her bra and it felt like a release when Rose started sucking, as if the milk was coming from deep inside her. The TV remote was just out of reach and she tried to pull it towards her with her foot, but her movement was making Rose restless so she lay back and shut her eyes for a minute, wondering when or if she might ever sleep for more than three hours at a time again. Everything about her old life seemed so far away, so unattainable, it sometimes made her heart race. She was completely in love with Rose and already could hardly remember life without her, but still she knew she was giving up a lot. Of course her life wasn't going to stop, but it was undeniable that it was never going to be the same again, that she would never approach another situation with the carefree attitude of a teenager.

Eventually her mother came in with the tea and some biscuits so Mavis asked her to turn on the TV. For a minute neither women could understand what they were seeing. At first Mavis thought they were replaying footage from 9/11; it was the only logical explanation for all the people emerging from smoke, limping and bedragged, covered in blood and soot. But the ambulances looked British, so did the streets, so did the people.

Her mother sat down next to them, reaching out for Rose's foot.

A woman came on to the screen. She was standing on a street somewhere with people dazed around her, sirens blaring and smoke billowing from behind her head. She was fiddling with something in her ear, but suddenly jerked her attention towards the camera. Her voice was shaky and her eyes darted off screen.

'The scenes in London are devastating. It's like something out of a film with injured people everywhere. We're not entirely sure what's happened, we know bombs have gone off and people have been injured, but at the moment that's all I can tell you. All public transport systems have been shut down and the police are advising people to leave central London by foot. We don't know who is responsible, but suspicion has naturally fallen on al-Qaida.'

The picture flicked back to a studio where a harried-looking man was reading a piece of paper, his eyes nervous and darting.

'Thanks, Laura. Information is coming in so fast that it's hard to get a handle on what is going on. To recap: all we know for sure is that bombs have been exploded on our public transport system. We're getting unconfirmed reports of an incident on a tube train leaving Edgware Road. No news on fatalities as yet.'

'What did he say?' asked Mavis.

Her mother looked round, her hand still on Rose's foot. 'What?'

'Did he just say Edgware Road?'

'Sshh, I can't hear.'

'I think he said Edgware Road.' Rose was still sucking, but Mavis stood up anyway, handing her to her mother, so that the baby started to scream.

'What are you doing?' her mother called after her.

'Dot's there,' Mavis shouted over her shoulder as she ran to the computer.

Her mother followed with Rose screeching in her arms. They both leant over the screen as it took much too long to come to life. The news on the Internet was as shaky as on the TV but Mavis still saw the words Edgware Road.

'What do you mean she's there?' Sandra was saying, somewhere over Rose's screaming.

Mavis reached for her phone and dialled Dot's number, but it went straight to voicemail again. 'She went to look at her birth certificate. She said she was staying at a B and B on Edgware Road cos it was an easy tube ride to Kensington, where she had to go.'

184

'It doesn't mean she was on that tube,' said Sandra, a sickness registering in her voice that made Mavis want to howl like her daughter. Her mother was holding Rose tight against her chest. The screaming had become background noise.

'She wanted to get there for nine.'

'Her birth certificate?'

'Yeah.'

'Doesn't Alice have a copy?'

'I expect so. But she's never shown it to Dot.' Sometimes Mavis found there was too much to explain, too many words needed to get you where you wanted to be.

'Are you saying she doesn't know who her father is?'

'I thought you knew that.'

'No, I mean obviously I know she doesn't see him. I presumed she didn't even know where he was. But, my God, are you serious?'

Mavis nodded, trying to work out how it was possible that her mother didn't know something that was so fundamental to the knowledge encased within her own life.

'Does Alice know where she is?'

Mavis started to cry. 'No. She thinks she's at an open day in Manchester.'

'We have to let her know.'

'Oh God, Mum.'

Her mother was already leaving the room so Mavis followed her back into the sitting room, where the television was showing increasingly terrible pictures of ambulances and stretchers and bodies lying on pavements covered by blankets. The television was getting good at this now, practised at rolling over the images of destruction in foreign lands that filled their screens nightly, images which now belonged at home.

Her mother gave Rose back to her. 'Finish feeding her so she stops crying.' She walked over to the phone and Mavis did as she was told, her daughter choking on her first few mouthfuls, whimpering and scrabbling at her breast, her own tiny tragedy coming to an end, making Mavis sure that she would never, ever let anything bad happen to her.

'Alice, it's Sandra.' Mavis wondered absently how her mother knew the number to dial. 'Yes, yes, it's been wonderful. Look, I'm calling with some bad news. Well, not necessarily bad, but – have you seen the news? . . . Mavis has just told me that Dot's there . . . No, she's not in Manchester. Hang on a sec . . .' Sandra held the phone away from her face. 'Mavis, how sure are you that she's really in London?'

'She's there, Mum. It was after she came with me to register Rose's birth and she realised she'd never seen her own birth certificate. She was going to look it up at some place called Charles House.'

'Did you hear that?' Sandra said into the phone. 'Don't say that, that's not true. Alice, do you remember that day in the hospital when you told me I hadn't killed my baby? . . . Well, you were right, it's just taken me all this time to work it out . . . No, of course that hasn't happened. I'm sure she's fine . . . No, Mavis has tried, it's switched off . . . That won't do any good, you won't even be able to get there. It's best that we all stay by our phones and then she'll call us when she can. She'll be fine . . . Call if you hear anything . . . OK, bye.'

Rose had fallen asleep on Mavis's breast and so she lifted her on to her shoulder, her totally trusting body warm and soft. Sandra came and sat heavily down on the sofa.

'I'm going to call Dad and get him to come home to be with you. I think I should go and sit with Alice.'

'What did you mean about the baby and the hospital?'

'It's a long story.'

'I want to know.'

Mavis's mother then told her a story as outlandish as the one enfolding on the screen in front of them. She had met Alice just before Dot's father had left, they'd become good friends and she'd helped her after Dot's dad had walked out without a word. To make her feel better she'd organised a trip to the circus for all of them, but on the day she'd come down with a sick bug so she'd stayed at home. She had been five months pregnant at the time. When Gerry got back on the evening of the trip he'd told her that Alice had tried to kiss him. She'd known it was a lie, something which Alice confirmed, and they'd had a terrible row which had culminated in her driving off too fast and crashing into a tree. She'd lost the baby and damaged her womb so badly that she'd destroyed her chances of ever having any more children, which had felt pretty much the same as destroying herself as all she'd ever wanted was a house filled with children and chaos and noise and life. Alice had come to see her in hospital, but she'd told her they couldn't be friends; she'd pushed away the one person who could have helped her. Over time she'd forgiven Gerry, if you could call it that. They'd slipped into a quiet pattern of strange mutual dependency without any intimacy. Then Rose had come along and it had made her realise that life is for living, that no one was to blame, that to waste the next sixteen years would be to waste a whole life and what was the point of that.

'Oh my God,' was all Mavis could say when she'd finished. 'I wish you'd told me before.'

'I should have done,' her mother replied. 'God, I didn't know Dot was so desperate to know who her father was, although it's completely obvious, of course she would be. I could have told her.'

The words sounded so pathetic, so out of date and pointless that Mavis wondered how it was that none of them had spoken to each other in sixteen years. Why had they all lived in their own worlds, terrified of letting each other in, terrified of being the first to crack?

'We've all been so bloody stupid,' her mother said as if Mavis had spoken out loud. She stood up again. 'And now Dot could be lying on a street in London when any of us could have stopped her.'

'Oh Mum, you don't think that's true, do you?'

'No, don't worry, I'm sure it's not.' But of course Mavis knew that this chance of life or death was a lottery and not something that your mother could influence in any way. A realisation dropped through Mavis's mind: that her mother could not save her from dying, any more than she would be able to save Rose. That we do our best, but that ultimately we are all at the mercy of the little decisions that see you alone on a London street for the first time in your life on exactly the same day as others decide to blow it up.

Sandra left the room after that to get Gerry home and call Alice again and Mavis heard her voice soft and low from the kitchen and felt an amazing surge of pride for her that felt very much like love. The man on the screen was talking about how the police had shut down all the mobile phone networks and it made Mavis feel slightly better, until she saw a woman of Dot's age being helped down the road, her head gashed, her face black, her eyes staring. It wasn't just death that could get you on those streets, Mavis realised, there was also all the pain and fear, not to mention the maiming, the people who would no doubt lose limbs, others who would be psychologically scarred for ever. She wondered how anybody ever had the courage to simply leave their house when they had a baby, when the baby became a child, the child an adult. She wanted to lock Rose and herself into a padded cell, as if that would do any good. For the first time ever she started to understand her mother and Dot's mother, started to see how loving someone so completely can sometimes make you scared, can make it easier not to say the painful things, to hide behind cleaning or silence, to become less of a person yourself to make them more of one. When Dot came back to them Mavis would tell her all of this.

A little later Mavis's dad arrived home, his face grey and his eyes blood-shot. He kissed her mother and then she left; Mavis heard the car driving off. She'd never seen her parents kiss before and it felt odd. Her dad sat on the sofa next to her.

'Any news yet?'

'No, I keep trying her mobile, but it goes straight to voicemail.'

'I heard on the radio they've shut down the mobile networks in case the terrorists use them to set off more bombs.'

'I know.'

The images rolled relentlessly in front of them. Other people's lives ending or being destroyed. But neither of them could look away.

'I wish I'd said something to her,' Mavis's dad finally said.

'You?'

He reddened. 'Well, anyone really.'

'Mum told me all about what happened with Alice and the baby and everything.'

'I know.'

'Anything you want to add?' They both kept their eyes on the screen, on the ridiculousness of the carnage.

'Not really. Everything she said is true. I was a total fool. I haven't been a good husband.'

'No.'

'Maybe I can make it better?' He looked round at Mavis and she was struck by how lost he looked, how childlike. Did anyone ever stop guessing?

'You're lucky you've got that chance,' she said finally, sounding much more grown up than she'd meant.

Thirty-three people were now confirmed dead, the woman on the screen said, but the number was expected to rise.

190

17 . . . Leaving

Tony thought he remembered his mother once saying something like: Where there is a beginning there is also an end. He couldn't remember when or in what context but he wished he could because he felt lost and cast adrift in a world that understood him as little as he understood it. He was twenty-four, living in a topsy-turvy house with a possibly mad wife and her definitely mad mother. He took the bus into Cartertown every day to work at a job which sickened his soul, calling people to sell them something useless. At least ten people a day called him a cunt, twenty told him to fuck off, fifty just put the phone down. Although the worst were the old duffers who probably hadn't spoken to anyone in weeks and would painfully prolong the conversation even though they were never, ever going to buy. Scott, his manager, was ruthless; he told them to cut those calls as quickly as they could because 'time is money', a disgusting epigram which was written in large red letters across a banner at the front of the room. The banner hung next to a bell which you had to get up and ring every time you made a sale over a hundred pounds. It was always the same three people who rang the bell and, after doing it once, Tony had vowed never to ring the bell again. The only,

only part of his life which brought him any joy was his daughter, whom he loved with a passion he had never thought possible.

Recently though it hadn't felt like enough. All through his youth, listening to his dad's Rolling Stones records, Tony had never doubted that he was going to be someone; but now, as he bumped home on the bus staring out of the window, Alphaville and Kirsty MacColl and the Beastie Boys on his Walkman (bands that Alice wouldn't even know existed), he wondered at what he had lost. People from his office sometimes went for drinks after work and he'd gone a couple of times, standing in wine bars feeling totally excluded from their lives. Girls would often talk to him, as they always had, but he was never really able to get into it and would tell them about Dot and Alice as quickly as he could to make them walk away.

Then he noticed the pub in the village, which he had to walk past every night, and he'd taken to stopping in for a pint or two before undertaking the long walk through his front door. People were starting to nod at him when he came in and the night before he'd had a semi-conversation with the butcher. You cannot become this person, he found himself thinking as he left. Of course Alice was always waiting for him at home, dinner cooked and Dot in bed, her mother lurking somewhere in the background like a terrible memory which he couldn't place. Alice never mentioned the fact that he was late or that he smelt of beer and the cigarettes he'd recently reverted to. He would sit sullenly in the kitchen, spooning her often-tasteless food into his mouth, willing her to ask him what he'd been up to, why he was late. But she always talked about Dot and things they'd done in the day, her enthusiasm bubbling out of her so innocently that he sometimes wanted to smash the plate into her face, just to see what she would do. At least Clarice was open in her disdain, which was something after all.

If you had asked Tony in the years between him becoming interested in girls and meeting Alice to name the qualities he was looking for in a woman, he'd probably have described Alice. Most men would in fact probably describe Alice: beautiful, passive, submissive, unmoody, caring, intelligent. But now he had all that, he thought he probably wanted something different – he just didn't know what yet.

Simon, the pub landlord, was full of the news that he had hired a new barmaid; 'A right cracker,' he said to anyone who would listen, 'and she's starting next week,' The air in the pub vibrated as they waited and Tony laughed at the men behind his pint, wondering at the limits of their lives. Maybe we should move, he began to think, try a city? Perhaps if he got Alice away from her mother and out of the house she'd been born in she'd be forced to engage more with life?

He had forgotten that it was the new barmaid's legendary first night when he turned into the pub the following Thursday, but as soon as he saw her standing behind the bar he couldn't help letting a smirk cross his face. She was exactly what he'd expected Simon's definition of a 'cracker' to be: blonde and brassy, slightly plump, too much make-up and a skirt which should have continued for another few inches. Her feet looked uncomfortable squeezed into high heels and her scarlet nails flicked nervously round her throat.

Tony sat at the bar and ordered a pint from Simon, who was as puffed up as a rooster, luxuriating in the wonder of having provided this specimen for the village. His clients were far from disappointed as well, leaning over the bar as they told jokes and asked questions. Tony thought of his own real cracker at home and felt like a heavy duvet had been wrapped around his head.

Alice had cooked an indeterminable stew and he ran upstairs to kiss Dot before eating. His daughter was lying on her back, her arms flung above her head, her head turned lazily to the side, her lips a perfect pout and her ginger hair fluffed against her pillow. She stirred when he kissed her fat cheek and for a moment he willed her to wake up so he could hold her in his arms.

'I met a really nice woman today, on the swings on the green,' Alice said as they started to eat. Clarice was watching TV in the sitting room and the sound of condensed voices drifted through. 'She's got a daughter called Mavis who's the same age as Dot. She runs some playgroup or something at the village hall and she asked me to go.'

The gravy was pallid and weak and making Tony feel sick. 'Are you going to?'

'Yes, I think so.'

He felt annoyed at this. 'I've been telling you to do something like that for ages.'

'I know.'

'It'd do you good to get out and meet a few other mothers.'

'Yes.' Alice was still eating; she never seemed to taste what she cooked. Tony wondered how she would appear to a group of mothers. He stabbed a piece of meat. When you got down to it, she had no real idea what life was about.

Donna from work tried to persuade him to go to a bar in town with them all, but he couldn't see the point and got on to the bus like a good husband. The Hare and Hound twinkled welcomingly as he rounded the corner. If you were going to be the sort of man who went to the pub then it seemed crazy not to go on a Friday night. It was warm and noisy inside, busier than usual, which Tony presumed must be the new barmaid. He raised his hand in greeting to a few people and sat at what was becoming his usual stool at the bar, opening up his copy of *The Times* to see if he could finish the crossword.

'What can I get you?'

Tony looked up and saw the new barmaid. 'Pint of Guinness, please.'

He watched her pull it badly, the white head too big and spilling over the side. Her hand was shaking as she put it down and Simon bumped into her as he reached up for the nuts, making her trip, and the pint flowed over the bar on to Tony's legs.

'Oh shit, I'm so sorry,' she said.

Tony caught her eye and saw tears sprinkled at the corners. 'It's fine, don't be silly.' He dabbed at the beer and his trousers with a bar towel. 'I don't think anyone else saw anyway.'

She smiled. 'Thanks. I'll get you another.'

The second was as bad as the first, but she didn't spill it this time. 'We haven't been introduced yet,' said Tony, holding out his hand over the bar, 'you were pretty monopolised last night. Anyway, I'm Tony.' Her hand was soft.

'Silver.'

'Silver?'

'Yeah, I know, stupid, right?'

'I wouldn't say stupid, just unusual.'

'Well, if you ever met my mother you'd understand why.'

'You should be on stage with a name like that. What's your surname?'

She laughed. 'Sharpe.'

195

'Christ.' He laughed as well. 'I can definitely see that on a poster: Silver Sharpe.'

She tucked her hair behind her ears. 'No posters for me, thanks.'

Tony watched her work her way round the bar, her nervousness evident with each customer. There was something unlikely about her which didn't fit the way she looked, as if she was inhabiting the wrong skin or maybe just uneasy in it.

He spent the weekend at home, playing with Dot, chatting to Alice, being polite to Clarice. It was all fine unless he was on his own, when he would sometimes be overtaken by the sensation that the ground was swaying beneath him and his life was falling down a hole. He found it almost impossible to be present in anything more than body, watching himself interacting with this beautiful woman and child, marvelling over the colour of a leaf or running across the grass. This is amazing, he said to himself over and over, look at the life you have, what's wrong with you, you stupid bastard. At night he lay awake next to Alice's heavy breathing, staring into the blackness, trying to make out things he wasn't even sure existed.

Tony avoided the pub on Monday and Tuesday and Alice seemed so pleased when he walked through the door on time and sober that he resolved never to go again. But then just before he left work on Wednesday he got a crying woman who railed at him because he wasn't her daughter and Scott shouted out from the front of the room that he had the lowest bell-ringing tally and eleven people called him a cunt in the two hours before he left, which was a new record. He wasn't going to go into the pub until he saw it – or maybe he was, maybe that's where he'd always been heading.

Silver smiled when she saw him and he felt his shoulders loosen, felt the sickness lift from his chest and the band unwind round his head. He understood why he'd been avoiding the place. He went back on Thursday and Friday nights as well and Alice looked as if she was going to cry each time he came home late, making him hate himself. He stayed at home again over the weekend, but felt angry and restless, picking fights with Alice and failing to listen to Dot properly. On Sunday when he was pushing Dot on the swings on the green he saw Silver going into the Co-op and emerging with two filled plastic bags. He watched her walk down the road in her cheap plastic heels and imagined her in her own space, wondering what she ate, what music she listened to, what TV she watched, whom she spoke to, where she lived. He was struck by the knowledge that life is lived in so many different ways by all of us, that Silver no doubt had worlds of which he was unaware, and the thought knocked him off balance.

She wasn't there on Monday night and Tony longed to ask Simon what had happened to her, but knew he couldn't. He went home early and dreamt about her fucking a faceless man next to him in his bed. Alice told him he looked tired the next morning and he said he wasn't feeling great.

He held back until Thursday evening, only to find Silver talking to some bloke he thought was called Gerry when he arrived and Tony had an insane urge to pull the man off his stool and pummel his fists into his smug face. The man's laugh seemed to boom around the pub, his confidence rippling through the atmosphere. Simon served Tony his pint which he drank much too quickly so he ordered another. Finally Gerry got up and left and Silver saw him.

'Hi, there,' she said, 'you OK?'

'Fine.' Tony couldn't keep the gruffness out of his voice. It was ridiculous.

'You don't sound it. What's up?'

'Shit day. Take no notice of me.'

'Right,' she said, moving on down the bar, 'I've had enough of those.'

Tony took his pint and went to sit in a corner. He was hungry and remembered he hadn't eaten any lunch. The beer mixed with his gastric juices, rushing through his body. He ordered another pint from Simon, taking it back to his table without speaking to Silver, marvelling at his own stupidity but unable to stop himself. It was past ten now and he thought he'd rather sleep on the green than go home to Alice. He didn't have anything to say to her.

Half an hour later his head was fuzzy and so he stumbled into the fresh air and sat on the bench on the green opposite the pub. He checked his watch a few times and didn't admit to himself what he was doing. But eventually the last stragglers left and he could see Simon and Silver clearing the glasses and wiping down tables through the lighted windows. He was pleased to notice they did it almost in silence, exchanging a quick goodbye before the lights went off and Silver emerged, her coat done up to her chin and her stride purposeful. Tony stood up without knowing exactly what his plan was and followed her down the road. In the end there was very little option but to quicken his stride and come up behind her. He touched her lightly on the arm and she jumped away from him, letting out a little scream.

'No, sorry, Silver, it's just me, Tony.'

She peered up at him. 'What the fuck are you doing creeping up behind me like that?'

'Sorry.'

'Bloody hell, don't do that to me. You might live in a tiny little village, but where I come from you don't want men coming up behind you in the dark.'

'Sorry. I don't come from here anyway. I've only lived here two years.'

Silver shifted her weight on to her hip. 'Is that what you've stopped me to say at eleven-thirty at night?'

'No.' Tony looked at the sky and felt as if he was falling upwards through the stars. 'I don't really know why I stopped you. Truth is I can't stop thinking about you.'

She spluttered at this. 'Please.'

'I know that sounds crap, but it's true.'

Silver sighed. 'When I was younger I used to think I was quite a good judge of character, but the last few years have shown me how far off the mark I am there and you've just proved it to me.'

'What?'

'I thought you were nice, Tony. I've seen you round the village with your wife and your daughter and then you come in the pub and you're friendly without seeming like you want anything and now this.'

There was such a gap between what Tony meant and what he'd said, he pulled at his hair, not confident that he would ever get her to understand. 'I know it looks shit. Christ, it is shit. But this isn't me. Look, I'm not going to lie. I've got a great wife, but a shit marriage. And a daughter who I love more than anything else in the world. And I haven't done anything like this before. But I can't stop thinking about you.'

Her face was set hard, even in the dark. 'And what do you think you'll achieve by telling me that?'

He felt desperate enough to cry. 'I don't know.'

She turned away. 'Go home to your family, Tony.'

He grabbed at her arm again. 'No, please.' It was only a second's glance but their eyes met and Tony saw all he needed. 'My God,' he said.

'No.'

'Silver, please.'

'Please what? I'm not that type of woman.'

'I know. I'm not that type of man. Just meet me for coffee or something. Away from Druith. Please, just once.'

Silver wasn't that type of woman, in fact she wasn't like any woman that Tony had ever met before. She was only two years older than him but she seemed to have lived fifty lives already and cynicism ran through her veins. Her father had been an alcoholic like his own and her mother had been blasé about her existence. She'd married an unsuitable man too young who'd hit her twice and after the second time she'd packed a bag and got on a train and ended up in Cardiff. But it had been scary on her own there and so she'd started looking for jobs in the country and ended up in a hotel, where she'd met Simon and agreed to come and work for him in Druith, which seemed like exactly the sort of no-place she needed.

They became lovers quickly, making love on Silver's creaky single bed in her studio flat on the edge of Druith in which they were as desperate as each other. When he was with her, Tony felt he could touch the stars. He liked to lie on her stomach, breathing her musty odour, tasting her at the back of his throat. And she would stroke his hair and laugh at the things he said.

'I'm going to organise a party for Dot's second birthday,' Alice said one Sunday as they walked along the river.

Tony kicked a stone into the water. Ironically they'd got along much better since he'd met Silver. For one thing he didn't go to the pub much any more, but also he found it easier to be kinder. 'Really?'

'I've met so many nice women at the playgroup. And Dot seems to enjoy playing with their children. I just thought tea or something.'

'Sounds great.' Dot ran across the grass in front of him and Tony felt a tightness in his chest, a sudden realisation that things could not continue in this way. He wanted to watch a child he had created with Silver. He wanted to take her home to meet the parents he hadn't spoken to in years.

Tony said all of this to Silver when he next saw her. She didn't want to take him away from Dot, but sometimes you don't have a choice in these matters. They agreed to leave in the weeks after Dot's birthday. Tony would start looking for a flat in Cartertown and Silver for a job. He'd explain everything to Alice and, although it would be hard and ugly for a while, ultimately she'd meet someone much better suited to her. He imagined a time when they'd all be friends. When he'd go to pick up Dot for the weekend and have a nice chat with Alice's new husband and they'd look back on this time and maybe not laugh, but at least think they had been brave and right.

Alice was filled up with her plans for Dot's party for the next two weeks, so much so that she didn't notice when Tony spent more time than usual with Silver. Even Clarice seemed to have entered into the spirit of things and one evening Tony came home to find the two women huddled over a book, discussing recipes. Maybe they weren't mad, he found himself thinking, just different and so removed from his own experience that he found it easier to let himself think that they were unhinged.

'D'you want me to give Dot her bath?' he asked.

'Oh, would you?' said Alice, turning her smile on him, which was still capable of taking his breath away.

Tony scooped his daughter into his arms, bounding up the wooden stairs as relatives who would never belong to him watched their every move. He ran the bath higher than Alice did and filled it with bubbles, shutting the door so that the steam filled the room. Tony hung his jacket over a chair, rolled up his sleeves, took off his tie and shoes and helped his podgy daughter out of her clothes. Her arms and legs were like pillows and her skin mottled as he placed her into the bath. She splashed at the water, clutching at the bubbles which dissolved in her hands, her fiery hair sticking to her scalp as it got wetter and wetter.

Tony knelt on the floor, resting his arms on the side of the bath and staring so intently at his daughter that he stopped seeing her; he started to doubt her reality. The thought rushed through him that his actions were going to affect her, that how he managed the next few weeks, months, years would determine the person she would one day become and the responsibility seemed awesome.

'I love you, Dot,' he said.

She looked up and smiled. 'I love you, Daddy.' She reached over to him, chasing the tears he was crying down his cheeks with her fingers.

'We'll get a nice flat, Silver and I, and you'll have a beautiful pink bedroom and I'll fill it with toys and dolls and you can stay whenever you want.'

'Dolls,' she squealed.

'Whatever you want, angel. We'll all be happier this way, I promise.' But the words sounded hollow and tasted stale and a sickness rose in him that made him retch over the toilet until he was hot and trembling.

Dot woke them on the morning of her birthday as she did most mornings, her warm body between them from some indeterminable point in the night when she'd cried and Alice had left the room and reappeared with her. The day was bright and the sun poured over his wife and daughter, so that they looked unearthly. He'd made love to Alice the night before and the memory shamed him. He'd kissed those perfect lips, run his hands over her blemish-free flesh, held her tightly, moaned into her neck. And, worse than all of that, he'd meant it. As Dot tore at her presents he knew that his mind only had a few more hours left in it, that the route he was travelling only led one sure way and that was madness. He knew that better – or maybe worse – men than him could split themselves, but it was tearing at his soul. He decided to call Silver that night and say he was going to talk to Alice tomorrow and that they should leave on Monday. Silver had a job lined up at a pub in Cartertown and they could stay in a B and B until they got a flat sorted.

The day dragged him towards it. Everywhere he turned he felt as though he was at a ghastly fairground in a hall of mirrors showing him what could have been. Dot was amazing, bounding around in her delight like a puppy. He heard Clarice laugh; he marvelled at the plates of food Alice produced. Even the house felt warm and friendly as balloons brightened dark corners and music pierced the silence.

After lunch Tony took Dot into the garden and spun her round by holding her hands so that she shrieked with joy. They fell into the grass together and Tony noticed how the roses in the border were the same colour as her hair. Pieces of his daughter fell all around him, shredding his heart and mangling his brain. He lay on the lawn with Dot resting on his stomach and looked back at the tall house with its dark windows and magical turret and realised that he no longer knew right from wrong. He felt sure that the right thing to do would be to walk away from Silver and yet even the thought was impossible. He tried to imagine his future without her as he stroked his daughter's hair and it felt as empty as death. He had maybe minutes to save himself. He now knew that if he stayed and witnessed his daughter become two he would never leave. Tony stared into the electric blue sky and understood what had eluded him for so long: he loved Dot more than anyone but in order to stay alive he had to take care of himself and Silver was as integral to his staying alive as oxygen.

Tony got up off the grass and took Dot back into the house. His head felt large and full, as if he'd had a skinful the night before and was still wobbly on his feet. The kitchen smelt like a bakery, like a place he'd have enjoyed growing up in. Alice was standing by the table, squeezing pink icing out of a white tube on to miniature cakes. She smiled, pushing her hair out of her eyes with the back on her hand, leaving a trace of pink on her forehead.

'I'm just going to nip out and get some more balloons,' Tony said.

Her expression changed at this. 'But we've got loads.'

'Oh well, I just thought we could do with some more.'

Alice glanced at the clock above the door. 'The party starts in an hour.'

'It'll only take me five minutes.'

'OK.'

He hesitated at his moment of freedom, unable to turn and take his exit. Instead he walked over to where his wife and daughter were standing. The next time he saw them everything would be different and they would no longer belong to each other. He picked Dot up, kissing her red cheeks. 'You do know you're an amazing mother, don't you Alice,' he said. She laughed nervously. 'No, I mean, look at all this. Look at Dot. You're incredible.' It wasn't enough, he wanted to say more but nothing formed in his mind.

She blushed. 'Don't be silly.'

Tony put Dot back down next to her mother and turned and left the kitchen. He pulled his jacket from the cupboard in the hall that Clarice insisted they use and shut the front door quietly behind him. He still didn't know exactly what he was doing, but as he walked down the road and felt Clarice watching him from the sitting room windows he knew he wasn't going back.

The only person who could save him now was Silver and Tony wished he had one of those phones he'd read about in some of the papers recently. Phones that posh businessmen kept in their briefcases and were able to use standing on street corners. The report he'd read said there were satellites in the sky which transmitted their conversations to each other, that one day we'd all have one in our own pockets which we could use to call people on the other side of the world. But he didn't care about the rest of the world, only Silver. Tony walked to the Hare and Hounds and went straight in without stopping. Silver was pulling a pint for Charles Wheeler but when she saw Tony she stopped. He turned and left and she followed him.

'What are you doing?' she asked as they stood on the green with so many pairs of eyes watching them. 'I thought it was Dot's party.'

'I can't do it, Silver.'

She put her hand on his arm and it was the first time that day that his heart slowed to anything like a normal pace. 'Calm down. You're white as a sheet. What's happened?'

'We have to go now.'

'Have you told Alice?'

He shook his head and tears spilt out of his eyes without warning. 'I can't do it any more, being there and thinking of you all the time. It's wrong. And Dot – shit, Silver, what am I doing?'

'We don't have to. You can walk away from me now and there won't be any hard feelings. I'll go to Cartertown; you won't ever have to see me again.'

'But I love you.'

She was crying as well. 'I love you too. But sometimes—'

'No, I went through all that in my head this morning. It has to be you, Silver. It's always been you.'

'You've got to speak to Alice. You can't just leave.'

'I can't go back and I can't tell her now. Dot's party is about to start.'

'Then we can wait for tomorrow.'

'No.' Tony heard his own desperation, as pathetic as a drowned kitten. 'Don't make me go back there, I can't.'

'But Dot—'

'She won't even notice. I'll call Alice tomorrow or next week. We'll get a flat and Dot can come and stay.' Tony grabbed on to Silver's hands. They were cold.

'Of course she'll come and stay,' she said, using the back of her hand to wipe the tears from his cheeks just as his mother had done when he was small.

If you say something enough it becomes true, doesn't it? Tony shut his eyes and believed this with all his heart. Silver didn't need any more convincing; Tony knew that she understood him better than anyone else when she turned and they walked away from the pub, back to her flat where they packed all her things, got into her rusty Renault 5 and drove out of the village. By that evening they were clinging to each other in a double bed in a dingy B and B in Cartertown, as Dot's party finished and Alice went to bed, not thirty miles away, although they might as well have been in different universes.

18 . . . Tragedy

Gerry had twenty minutes tops to make a decision about what to say to Sandra. What a prick! He replayed the drive home in his head and his stomach twitched with embarrassment so that he groaned like a dying man. He hadn't planned it because what sort of fool would plan to make a pass at his wife's best friend? Of course he'd noticed how absolutely gorgeous Alice was, you'd have to be a woofter not to, but he'd never considered anything happening between them. He'd never even wanted anything to happen between them, which was why what he'd done was so unfathomable, even to himself. Gerry liked to keep his dalliances totally separate from his life because that's what they were. Stupid young girls, as he liked to think of them, with short skirts and red lips who made him feel better for a few hours and then disappeared from his life like a passing fog so that he could often pretend they had never existed. And he hadn't even done anything like that for coming up to two years now anyway, not since Mavis had been born. He drew up outside his house and saw a light on in their bedroom. Mavis was still asleep so he allowed himself a cigarette as the car cooled down and the engine ticked over. He banged his hands hard on the steering wheel. He had to think fast because

208

Alice might already be on the phone to Sandra, and the real, ugly truth of it all was that he couldn't imagine his life without his wife, the woman he'd loved from the first time he'd knocked those books out of her arms outside the library in Kelsey.

Gerry got out of the car and flicked his cigarette into the bushes, zipping up his bomber jacket to keep out the cold. The air was prickling and he could feel in his nostrils that it would be icy by morning. He lifted Mavis out of the back seat and hurried her into the house. The atmosphere inside was calm and still and he could hear the murmur of the radio from their bedroom. Sandra had not received any bad news yet, that much was clear. He took his daughter up to her bedroom, easing her little limbs out of her clothes. Her cheeks were sticky and she should of course brush her teeth but there was no way he was going to wake her now. He left her vest and pants on and tucked her under the pink duvet, kissing the side of her head and smelling the sugar and excitement still lingering on her. Her bright hair glowed in the light trickling in from the landing and he felt a surge of ownership for Mavis, a sense that she belonged to him. A life without her and the baby in Sandra's stomach would be worthless, he realised, perhaps two hours too late.

Gerry stayed by her bed for a minute, trying to organise his whirling thoughts. There was a chance that Alice might not mention it to Sandra but it was a slim chance and if he didn't get in there first there wasn't a hope in hell of her believing him. There'd only been one other time that he'd come this close to being caught, when a student had got a bit too interested and started sending him letters to his house, which he'd had to intercept on an almost daily basis for a few weeks. It was all so stupid anyway. He couldn't understand why Sandra would care about these girls, who meant nothing to him. He wasn't like that prick Tony who'd gone and fallen in love with Silver and had now run off; he had no intention of ever even liking them. What he did with those girls was no different to an evening spent in the Hare and Hounds with his mates on a Thursday. They were just a distraction, a way of passing the time, and they had absolutely no bearing on his feelings for Sandra.

She was a little prick tease, that Alice, anyway. Come on, no one was really that innocent unless they were stupid. Gerry replayed the afternoon on fast forward in his mind and knew he hadn't been imagining it, those big eyes and Lady Di smiles and infectious giggles. Come on. She'd just got cold feet and then gone all hoity-toity and made him feel like a complete dickhead. Some women were like that; they wanted to know that you wanted them so they could feel better about themselves and then make you feel like a total bell end. Maybe she was a lesbian? Yes, maybe that's why Tony had left?

By the time Gerry crossed the hall to his bedroom he felt much better about what he was about to do, much more in control of the situation. Sandra was in bed, sitting propped up by pillows, her stomach rounding out the sheets and her eyes closed.

'Hi, love,' he said. 'You feeling any better?'

She shook her head. 'I've lost count of the times I've been sick.'

'D'you want anything? Cup of tea?'

'Ooh, yeah, that'd be lovely.' Gerry turned to go but she called him back. 'Was it good? Did the girls enjoy themselves?'

'It was fab. Mavis and Dot loved it. She's flat out, I put her straight to bed.'

'Did you make her do a wee?'

'Yes,' he lied. 'I'll get you that tea.'

Gerry had another cigarette standing by the back door as he waited for the kettle to boil. The breakfast things were still in the sink and he reminded himself to come down and wash them before Sandra got up in the morning. Not that she'd care, but because he wanted to be nice to her. Sandra had told him that Alice and Clarice had a cleaner and the memory made him hate her even more.

He left his bomber jacket hanging over a chair in the kitchen and his trainers kicked off by the back door, and then carried the tea tray to the bedroom. He half lay on the edge of their bed and poured out the tea, which Sandra sipped at gratefully.

'Try having a biscuit,' he said, holding out the plate, 'you probably need some sugar.'

Sandra took one but each bite looked as if it was causing her pain. 'It must be a bug. D'you think it'll harm the baby?'

'No. But I'll ring the doctors in the morning if you aren't any better.'

'I've been thinking today. We really need to decorate this room.'

Gerry looked around at the swirling brown carpet and sad floral wallpaper. 'Guess we do.'

'Don't you remember we said we'd do it when we moved in, but that was four years ago now.'

'Time flies.'

'But seriously, Gerry, it's awful. D'you think we could do it before the baby comes?'

'I don't see why not.'

They smiled at each other and Gerry knew he was losing the moment. In a few more rounds of the clock what he was about to say would sound ridiculous. 'Listen, San, I've got something to tell you. I nearly didn't, but I don't want to keep it from you.' She sat forward at this and she looked white and tired so that guilt trickled down his spine for a minute. 'Something really odd happened after the circus.'

'Odd?'

'I think Alice made a pass at me.'

'You what?' Anxiety rippled through Sandra's voice but Gerry kept hold of her eyes. He saw sweat break out above her top lip.

'I had to pull the car over. I didn't know what to do.'

Sandra put her cup on to the bedside table and he saw her hands were shaking. 'What are you talking about? Tell me exactly what happened.'

Gerry had rehearsed this bit in the kitchen and he pulled the lines from his brain as his body drowned. 'We had a great time at the circus; the girls loved it, like I said, but Alice was quite giggly. I've never seen her like that before and it felt like she was flirting with me, but I thought I must be wrong because she's your friend and everything. Anyway, we got in the car to come home and the girls fell asleep and it was really dark on the roads so I was concentrating on driving, but she turned on the radio and found this station that was playing slow songs and then she started talking about Tony and how he'd left and how lonely she felt. And I was saying nice things back, which I probably shouldn't have, but I felt sorry for her. Then I felt her hand on my leg and I was so shocked I didn't do anything at first, but then she squeezed my leg and started moving it upwards, towards my dick, so I pulled the car over and as soon as we were stopped she sort of lunged at me and I had to push her back and explain that I wasn't interested.'

Sandra had won the staring competition. Gerry felt her eyes fixed on to him like a hawk: one slip and he was dead. Her voice was spookily calm. 'What happened then?'

'She apologised and said she must have read the signs wrong. If it hadn't been for Dot in the back I'd have told her to get out and walk but I couldn't turf a little girl out on a country lane. So I asked her how she could do that to you.'

'And what did she say?'

'Just more claptrap about being lonely. Then she started crying so I drove her home and when we got to hers she got out the car, got Dot and went inside. She didn't even say bye.'

Gerry's whole body was pulsating with heat. He forced himself to look at Sandra and the situation was so ridiculous he almost laughed. The words he'd said sounded absurd: they laughed at him from where he'd spewed them on to their bed.

'Are you telling me the truth?'

'What the fuck? Why would I lie about that?' The anger he felt at himself was easy to translate to Sandra.

'Because you've always been a dog, Gerry, and Alice is a very beautiful woman.'

He spluttered at this in what he thought was quite a convincing way. 'Come on, San. I'd have to be mad to make a pass at her. She's your best friend. Anyway, I love you; you're pregnant with our baby. Give me some credit.'

The air settled slightly over this and Gerry let himself look at his wife's stomach; she would want to believe him, he had that on his side.

'Alice would never do something like that.'

He came and sat next to her, putting his arms round her shoulders, ready to deliver his best line, the one thought up with the help of the second cigarette. 'You haven't known her

213

that long when you think about it, San. And she's probably going a bit mad, what with Tony walking out like that.'

Sandra nodded and he saw tears on her cheeks. 'But still, she's meant to be my friend. I really liked her.'

Gerry pulled his wife into his chest. 'I'm sorry. Maybe there's more to Tony leaving than we know.'

'What d'you mean?'

'Well, it is pretty bizarre, to walk out on your wife and kid like that and not to even let them know where you are. Maybe there's something about Alice that's, I don't know, strange or something.' Which, when you thought about, was probably true, Gerry reasoned.

Then Sandra had to be sick again and Gerry was able to hold her hair and stroke her back, before putting her back to bed. He went downstairs and did the washing up and put Mavis's toys back in the box under the window. He drew the curtains and plumped a few cushions. Then he got himself a tinny from the fridge and sat on the sofa to watch *Match of the Day*. A tiny part of him felt like a massive shit, but most of him felt as though he'd won a small war.

When Mavis came into their bedroom at six the next morning, soaked in her own wee, Gerry was able to get her cleaned and dressed and the sheets in the wash without waking Sandra. She'd only been sick once more in the night and she'd slept deeply so Gerry hoped she was on the mend. The day seemed fresh to him, as though they'd dealt with something and now they could focus on the things that mattered. As Gerry poured cereal out for Mavis he felt he'd learnt an important lesson, as if someone had stripped him to the bone and showed him what mattered. He was sure he wouldn't let Sandra down again.

She came downstairs a bit before nine, as Gerry and Mavis were reassembling a jigsaw for the fifth time on the sitting room floor, his daughter's delight actually increasing with each repetition. He felt a surge of joy at the sight of his wife in her nightie and dressing gown, a bit of colour returned to her cheeks.

'Hey, beautiful,' he said, 'you look better.'

Sandra lingered in the doorway. 'Could you keep her occupied for a minute longer? I'm going to make a phone call.'

The bottom dropped out of Gerry. 'Who to?'

'You know who to.' Her voice was scratchy, like a cat's claws on the furniture.

Gerry stood up at this and Mavis shouted, 'Daddy. Come back.'

'Do you think that's a good idea?' he tried.

'I'm not going to leave it if that's what you're suggesting.'

'Come on, love. I don't want you upsetting yourself, not with the baby and everything.'

'I'm not going to upset myself. I'm going to upset her.'

'I don't see what you'll achieve.'

'You sound like you don't want me to speak to her.'

Their eyes locked and Gerry knew he'd been stupid to underestimate his wife, that all he loved about her was bound up in this response. He let Mavis pull him back towards the floor and watched Sandra shut the door. Gerry heard Sandra's voice rise and fall as he fitted together an innocent picture of a little girl pulling a duck on a string next to a river. The simplicity of an action that required no more than the ability to locate the right piece which would then reward you by slotting into place seemed revolutionary.

Sandra burst back into the room. She walked over to where he was sitting on the floor and touched the congealed blood

215

that had formed over the cut on the back of his head. 'You fucking shit.'

He stood up. 'What?'

Mavis started to cry.

'I knew you were lying last night.' Sandra's eyes were red and bulging.

'San, sit down. What are you talking about? What did she say?'

She jabbed her finger at him. 'I bloody knew it. I knew it.'

Mavis tugged on his jeans so Gerry picked her up. 'For God's sake, you're scaring your daughter.'

'She said you made the pass at her, you shit.'

'She's lying.'

Sandra looked at him; they knew each other too well for this. 'I hate you.'

'Sandra, please.'

'Please nothing. I should have fucking known. Everyone told me not to marry you.'

'But I love you. I've always loved you.' His words sounded pathetic, even to himself.

The tears were cascading out of her eyes now. 'You do not love me. Don't say that. Don't you dare.'

'San, please, sit down. Come on, think of the baby.'

'Think of the baby!' Sandra spat the words into his face.

Mavis howled.

'Hasn't it entered your mind that she might be lying?' he shouted back, trying to match her anger. But in the open air the words didn't sound as he'd meant them to, they fell into a black hole and were lost to themselves. Sandra calmed at this and looked into him; Gerry felt as if she was rooting through his bone marrow, dissecting his soul.

216

Finally she turned round and he heard her going upstairs. He kissed the top of Mavis's head and tried to think of something useful, but his brain felt blinded. She came back a few minutes later, dressed. 'You're pathetic,' she said as she started to put on her coat.

Gerry followed her into the hall. 'San, please. Come back in. You haven't eaten anything and you've been sick. Let me at least make you a cup of tea.'

Sandra picked up the car keys from the hall table and shut the door without looking back. Moments later he heard her driving away.

There was nothing to be done after that apart from get on with the day. Gerry felt tired and stale, ridiculous in his little box as the day unfurled relentlessly around them. And Mavis needed things like lunch and wees and playing with and so things beyond his control pulled him forward. At half past two there was a knock at the door and he foolishly answered it thinking it might be Sandra even though she had her keys. Two policemen were standing on his doorstep and for a moment he thought they'd come to arrest him for being a terrible husband.

'Mr Loveridge?' asked one.

Mavis hung off his leg. 'Yes.'

'I'm afraid your wife's had an accident.'

Fear crashed into the house, exploding the walls with its hugeness. 'Oh my God, is she OK?'

'She's alive. They've taken her to Cartertown General. She was very lucky, she was going double the speed limit.'

'Oh shit.' Gerry felt his knees buckle but knew that they couldn't.

'Do you know where she was going?'

He shook his head, knowing and not caring what he looked like. 'Was anyone else hurt?'

'No, she went into a tree.'

'What about the baby? She's pregnant.'

'I'm sorry, Mr Loveridge, we don't have that information. But we can drive you to the hospital.'

He grabbed his and Mavis's coat but the policeman put his hand out. 'Isn't there a neighbour or someone you could leave her with? She might not want to see her mother in, well, in a state.'

'Really?' Gerry's mind spun on to paths where Sandra was disfigured or maimed – or maybe they were lying and she was already dead? He ran to the house opposite even though he couldn't remember the name of the woman who lived there. He knew that she had a daughter Mavis's age and that she and Sandra often had coffee. He stumbled over his words, knowing that he wasn't making any sense, but the woman seemed nice and reliable and told him not to worry, Mavis could stay as long as he needed and to give Sandra her love. He nearly laughed.

The drive to the hospital was much too slow. Time wound itself around their car, dragging them backwards, creasing the road. A heavy rain was falling, slicking the tarmac and making driving dangerous. Except this was now and that was then, when a bright winter sun had shone out of a pale blue sky.

The policemen dropped him at the front entrance and he had to search his mind to remember his and then his wife's name at the reception desk so that the young girl looked at him as though he was mad and hovered her finger over the security button. Eventually she gave him directions which he felt unable to follow, tripping over himself as he ran down corridors, trying to focus his eyes so that his mind could process the words on the signs above his head. He wondered at one point if he was dreaming, or if maybe he was dead and this was hell, an endless succession of hospital corridors with your wife in an unknown state at the end of one of them.

Finally he found the right ward but he wished it was wrong. As he opened the doors he could feel the sickness heavy in the air, hear it in the silence which clung all over the space. Gerry whispered Sandra's name to the nurse behind the desk and she told him to wait in the room next to her desk, she'd fetch the doctor. The room was as blank and terrifying as anywhere in which you are about to receive bad news. Gerry stood by the window, looking down into the car park where people came and went and laughed and smoked, as if nothing was wrong. Eventually a tired-looking young man in a long white coat came in, shutting the door behind him.

'Please sit down, Mr Loveridge,' he said, indicating one of the chairs. He sank into another one, as if he hadn't sat for days.

But Gerry stayed standing; his body was alive with nerves and he didn't think he'd be able to sit. 'Is she OK?'

'She's sedated at the moment, just coming round. She'll be OK, but she's had a nasty accident.'

'I don't understand. What happened?'

'According to witnesses she was driving too fast and she lost control on a corner and went straight into a tree. Even though she was wearing a seat belt the force of the crash threw her into the steering wheel and the windscreen.'

'Where was she?'

The doctor looked at his notes. 'Kelsey.'

'Kelsey?'

'Had you had an argument?'

Gerry nodded. 'But also, she's been sick for the past twenty-four hours and she left without eating or drinking anything. And she's pregnant, of course.'

'Mr Loveridge, please sit down.'

Gerry did as he was told this time; the air was being sucked out of the room, lights flashing before his eyes.

'I'm very sorry, Mr Loveridge, but the baby didn't survive.'

Gerry felt his eyes twitch.

'We had to operate as soon as she arrived. She was bleeding internally. The baby was already dead. He'd been killed by the force of the crash.'

'He?'

The doctor blushed at this. 'Sorry, yes, it was a boy.'

'Oh God.'

'She would have died if we hadn't operated.'

Gerry stood up, the need to finish this conversation as pressing as anything had yet been in his life. 'Yes. Thank you. Can I see her now?'

'Mr Loveridge, there's more, I'm afraid. Your wife's injuries were extensive and severe. Because of the pregnancy her bleeding was hard to contain and the baby had damaged some of her internal organs. I'm very sorry but we had to remove part of her womb.'

Gerry felt he was missing something; a memory flickered in his brain. 'Her womb?'

'What I'm trying to say is that she won't be able to get pregnant again.'

'But . . .' The implications of what he'd done rushed through Gerry. 'But she has to. I mean . . . she'll want to. She'll need to.'

'I know it's a lot to take in, Mr Loveridge, but she has no chance of conceiving again. I'm very sorry. We do have counsellors available in the hospital to help you come to terms with this.'

Gerry steadied himself by leaning against the wall. 'Does she know?'

'Not yet. I'm going to make my rounds in about an hour. I was going to tell her then. But obviously you can do it, if you think that would be better.'

'Yes, I'll tell her.'

The doctor put his hand on the door handle. 'Was she pregnant with your first baby?'

'No, no. We have a daughter, Mavis, she's two.'

'Well, hang on to that then,' he said as he opened the door. 'Her bed is the last on the right. And please let us know if we can help at all.'

Gerry shook the doctor's hand, feeling the skin and bone which had saved Sandra's life and killed her hope. He realised that he would choose his wife over any baby, but that she would choose any baby over any life. Part of her would have wanted to die with the baby; part of her probably would die. He walked down the middle of the room, all the beds cocooned behind their own curtains of grief, knowing that his life had changed beyond recognition, knowing that his one stupid action had been the catalyst, knowing that he was nothing more than the dog shit which sticks in the groove of your shoes.

Sandra was lying on her back, her eyes open and her hand on her stomach. She started crying when she saw Gerry. He went to sit in the chair next to her bed and kissed her cheek.

'San, I'm so sorry.'

221

'I didn't mean to crash,' she said and Gerry realised that he had already been wondering.

'What were you doing? They said you were in Kelsey.'

'I don't know why I went there. We were happy there, I just wanted to . . .' She trailed off, overcome by sobs. 'Where's Mavis?'

'I took her across the road. She's fine.'

'To Ellen's?'

Tony nodded, supposing that was where she was.

'I must have scared her.'

'Don't think about it. She'll have forgotten already.'

'I've asked the nurse if I can see the doctor. I want to go home but nobody's telling me anything.'

'I've just seen the doctor. You won't be able to go home for a few days, San.'

'What's happened to me? I can't remember anything.'

'You crashed into a tree, but you're going to be fine.'

She was crying again, soaking the bed sheets. 'I can't feel the baby move.' Her hands scrambled on the covers. 'My stomach aches so much. What's going on, Gerry?'

Nothing that Gerry had ever said before had really mattered, he realised as he prepared to jump off the cliff. He took Sandra's hand in a way that would have made him scoff if he'd watched it in a bad made-for-TV movie, but which he now understood. 'The baby died, San.'

Her face dissolved but he thought she had probably worked it out already. 'Oh my God, no. I killed our baby.'

He covered her face with his own at this, the awfulness of what she was saying needing to be blocked out. 'No, San. Don't say that. If anyone killed our baby it was me. But neither of us did; it was an accident.'

222

Her face was crumpled, like nothing more than a piece of paper. 'Have you spoken to the doctor? Are you sure?'

'Yes. I'm so sorry.'

'Oh God, no.' Her hands twisted round the sheets. 'Oh God, Gerry, please tell me this isn't true.'

He smoothed her hair off her face. 'Ssh, darling. It'll be OK.'

'I was five months. Did the doctor tell you what it was?'

Gerry shook his head but ultimately there'd been enough lies. 'It was a boy.'

Sandra choked on this information, as if there were too many tears to leave her body. Gerry knew he had to tell her the rest, knew this was his punishment for being a terrible person. 'San, listen, the doctor told me something else. I'm going to tell you and we're going to get through it, do you hear?' She said nothing, her eyes opening wider than he'd ever seen them. 'You were badly hurt when they got you in here, bleeding internally. If they hadn't operated, you'd have died. What they did, they did to save your life. And your life is precious. If you'd died you'd never have seen Mavis again. Do you understand?' She nodded. 'But the damage was bad. They had to cut out some of your womb. We won't be able to have any more children.'

Gerry had expected screaming and hysterics but the calm silence with which Sandra took the news was worse. He reached out for her hands, but she snatched them away. 'San, we'll be OK. We've got Mavis. Some people can't ever have children.' She turned her face away from him. 'Please talk to me, San. I love you. We'll be OK, I promise.'

Sandra rolled on to her side, her face only inches from the wall, and curled her body tightly into itself. Gerry stood up and leant over the bed, watching silent tears fall down her cheeks. 'San, please. I'll make it OK.'

'You can't,' she said. 'Please leave.'

'Don't be silly, San. I'm not going to leave you like this.'

She shut her eyes. 'If you don't leave I will scream and I won't stop until they make you go.'

Gerry put his hand out to touch his wife's shoulder but she was already too far away. 'I'm sorry,' he said, 'I love you. It'll be OK.'

'No it won't,' she said and there was more tragedy in those words than he knew how to deal with. 'Go away. Now.'

Gerry knew his wife well enough to leave.

19 . . . Despair

Death comes to us all. Isn't that the saying? But I do not want to see another person I love die. I feel as though I have been watching that all my life. Dealing and watching and keeping my upper lip stiff. When you are young death seems like the worst tragedy that can befall you, but as you get older and you lose more and more people it stops being so fearsome. Up until this I felt quite sanguine about it, sometimes I even looked forward to the release, but now the person I love more than anyone else is in danger and once again death has taken on its old mantle and I quake in its presence.

She cannot be dead or even hurt. And I know there are lots of people dying behind the cameras showing us those images on the television right now, but one of them cannot be Dot. Do you hear me, whoever you are who sees fit to constantly drag destruction across my life? If anything happens to my granddaughter I will hunt you down, so help me God, and I will sacrifice my soul to make you pay. I recognise our world less and less. It seems desolate.

I was in the garden when Alice got the call from Sandra. I heard the phone ringing from where I was standing admiring the agapanthus which seemed to have sprouted forth overnight.

I was thinking what a majestic plant it is, how it looks fierce and beautiful at the same time, when Alice practically fell out of the house. It was obvious that something was very wrong, but I didn't expect to hear the words which poured out of her. I brought her inside and sat her on the sofa and we turned on the telly and now we are stuck, bound by the endless loop of news telling us nothing, making no sense. Every five minutes or so Alice calls Dot's mobile, but it never connects. At least it's not ringing; I think that would be worse.

'Sandra said she'd gone to look at her birth certificate,' Alice says finally, her eyes never leaving the screen.

'Let's not think about that now,' I answer.

She turns to look at me. 'No, Clarice, let's think about it.'

'Have you not got a copy?'

'Of course I have.'

There is nothing to say to that; it's too obvious.

But my daughter continues, 'I've ruined everything. Tony, Dot. I thought I was doing OK. I always meant to tell her about him, but it always felt like the wrong moment. I never knew which words to use.' She looks over at me and her beauty is so fragile it seems fake, so exactly like my mother's that I have to look away. 'It made it too real. Does that make sense?' I nod, but she's not looking for reassurance. 'I thought she'd blame me for being too unlovable to keep her father around. I thought she'd feel sorry for me, see me as some pathetic woman with no life.' Her voice catches. 'But she's got eyes. She can see me for who I am without me telling her.'

'Come on, Alice,' I try.

She's angry now. 'All of that is about me. Me! I wasn't thinking about what's best for her. I'm a total idiot.'

I feel angry as well now, but not with Alice. 'Alice, you have

226

done your best. Do you hear me? You were so young when you had Dot and then Tony left without a word. You've coped brilliantly. You've been a brilliant mother.'

She looks at me as if I'm mad, her huge eyes swimming. 'We just spin through life, don't we? Your mother was right. There's no one looking out for us or protecting us. And we grab on to anything that gives us that sense of stillness. That's why I've clung to Tony for so long, even though he's been gone for years. But you know what, right now he doesn't seem so bloody scary. I could have told Dot all of this years ago and the sky wouldn't have fallen in. What did I think was going to happen, Clarice? Something worse than this?'

'You were scared, Alice. Life can be terrifying.' I grab at things to make it better for my daughter who, I see, is as lost as her own daughter. 'I used to watch you in the garden with Dot and I'd feel so proud of you, how capable you were of giving love. Alice, I doubt I'd have done any better. In fact, I didn't do any better. I'm the one who should be apologising to both of you, probably.' We are on uncertain ground and I feel my heart fluttering with what I want to say, but now is surely the time to be brave. 'In fact, maybe my mother should apologise to all of us. Or maybe it's her mother's fault, or her mother's. Or maybe our fathers. Why do they all get away scot free?'

Alice is crying in deep, heaving sobs. 'What's happened to us?'

'I don't know, but I'm sick of it. Alice, we've kept on going, we've stuck in there. And by God we've probably got a lot of things wrong, but we're still here. My mother, Tony, Howie: they all opted out one way or another. But we didn't, we're still here.'

'If something's happened to her I'll die.'

'Stop it. Nothing's happened to her.' I stand up and go to sit next to her on the sofa. I put my arm around Alice and I've forgotten how good it feels to touch warm flesh. She sinks into my shoulder and I feel her tears on my neck so I rest my face against the top of her head. It's been maybe twenty-five years since I held another human being but my body remembers how to do it as if it was yesterday. All this wasted time: what were we thinking?

'Oh Mum,' she says. 'It hurts so much.' I kiss the top of her head and whole chambers unlock inside me. Words do mean something, I remember, it is always within our power.

There is a knock at the front door and we both jump to our feet. The possibility of redemption is too sweet to imagine. Sandra is standing on our doorstep and I am rushed backwards through time, sucked down a rabbit hole of remembrance.

'Can I come in?' she asks and we both stand back, and then all go into the sitting room.

'Is Mavis OK?' Alice asks.

'Yeah, I got Gerry to come home and sit with her and Rose. Obviously they'll call if they hear anything.'

'Do you want some tea?' I ask.

'No.' Sandra sits on my chair by the fire and so we both sit back on the sofa. For a while we listen to the numbers and details on the telly. The people emerging from the smoking holes seem to have an incessant need to tell their stories, but all the stories are different and there is nothing concrete to grab hold of.

'I hope you don't mind me being here,' Sandra says finally.

'No, it's good,' says Alice.

'It's just I know what you're like,' Sandra says and then blushes.

'I know how easy it is to blame yourself for things that happen to your children. But it's not helpful, thinking like that.'

Alice starts to cry at this and so I take her hand. 'I'm only thinking what is true,' Alice says.

Sandra sits forward at this. 'Alice, you were the only person who spoke any sense to me after my accident and I so wish I'd listened to you.'

'I can't even remember what I said.'

'You told me that it wasn't my fault.' Sandra stands up at this and goes to stand by the window, her hand tapping against her thigh. I feel as though I'm watching a play. 'But I didn't listen. I've spent the past sixteen years cleaning away my sins, repeating actions that stop me falling apart in the middle of the day. Then Rose was born and it was like someone slapping me. I stood in that hospital where I felt everything had ended for me and watched my daughter give birth. My God, it was . . .' She reaches out and touches the window as if looking for the right word in our garden. 'It was so bloody real. And I thought: What am I doing torturing myself about something that happened because of lots of different reasons, lots of different moments, split-second decisions?'

'That's different. Dot wouldn't be in London now if I had told her about her father.'

'It's not different. I wouldn't have driven my car into a tree if I'd trusted my instincts when Gerry lied to me about you and him after the circus. Not that any of that matters. We are where we are. You have to just keep moving forward, that's all there is.'

'What if I have no forward, San? Dot is my forward.'

Sandra comes over to the sofa at this and squeezes in next to us. She's always been emotionally brave and I wonder what it's been like for her, these past sixteen years, entombing herself like a mummy. 'Dot is going to be fine. She's too special.'

It is a ridiculous and preposterous thing to say because as we sit here I realise that everyone is special. That people will die today who are special. That the men who blew themselves up for an ethereal idea are special. That we all have our own reasons for being where we are at any moment, but that in the end you simply cannot let any of that count. In the end we are all only in control of ourselves and we have to make our actions count. We have to find our own peace because there are no answers out there. There is no right or wrong; there is no correct way of living. Who was it who said we come from nothing and we return to nothing? I can't remember. I just know that in my moment of return I want to know that despite all my mistakes I did my best. That I was loved and that I loved back.

Sandra and I cocoon Alice on the sofa as we all go on watching the pictures of jagged cars, blackened faces, fires and turmoil, holes gouged out of the ground and men and women rushing into and out of the devastation in a desperate attempt to save or be saved.

This is worse than my mother or even Howie. There are points in your life which seem desperate, but you should never think that it is the worst it can get. Life can always get darker and when you realise that the world becomes a very scary place. We all occupy tragedy; what differentiates us is how we respond to it.

20 . . . Writing

3b, Colliers Court,
Tredwell Street,
Cartertown, CR4 2TZ

6th August 1990

*Alice, so it's been a year and Dot is 3 today. I
hope you're having a party or something for her.
I hope it's a better party than last year. I'm so
sorry I haven't been in touch before now. You'll
know I left with Silver. I'm sorry for this as well.
I'm sorry I didn't tell you, I'm sorry I just walked
out, I'm sorry we couldn't make it work. I can't
explain my actions. I felt so trapped by you and
your mother and I knew Silver was the person I
should have been with as soon as I met her. I know
that probably sounds harsh to you, but I also think
you're going to (or maybe you already have) meet
someone so much better suited to you than me. I
know you thought you loved me, but it wasn't real.
You can't love someone when they are so different*

231

from you. We weren't right for each other and I
hope you know that as well as I do.

You are so hard to reach, Alice. I tried talking to
you, but sometimes it felt like I was banging my head
against a brick wall and in the end I gave up. It's like
you don't need anyone or anything. You didn't even
seem to get annoyed by Clarice, who is odd, let me
tell you. If you dropped her into Manchester town
centre I think they'd lock her up. Either that or rob
her blind.

I miss Dot like crazy. Please write back to me so
we can sort out me coming to see her or something.

I hope you're well.

Tony

14th September 1991

Dearest Dot,

Silver had a baby boy last night. We're going to call
him Adam. He is 8 lb 3 oz. You were 7 lb 3 oz. You
were very, very beautiful when you were born and
Alice was amazing. Silver was amazing as well. One
day you might have a baby and understand all this.

I was in the room when you were born. I doubt
your mother has ever told you that. Of course she
hasn't, you're much too young to understand things
like that. I held you when you were only a few
minutes old and you felt so tiny I was scared. I got
the same feeling when I held Adam last night. You
both felt so light, you could almost forget you were

232

holding a person. I imagined dropping him or squeezing him too tight, or throwing him against the wall. That sounds so wrong but it's what my arms itched to do last night. Not because I wanted to hurt him, of course, but I think maybe because it was possible and would ruin my life. It doesn't seem real, it doesn't seem possible that this scrap of life will turn into a person and it's up to you to get them there. Not that I've been there for you these last two years.

I probably won't send this letter, not least because you won't be able to read yet, but in a few weeks I will ring your mother and arrange to see you again and you can meet your brother and we can forget the last two years.

I looked out of the hospital window last night with Adam in my arms and I thought that you could be looking at the same stars. I hope you were. I hope you are.

I love you, Dot.
Your Dad x

6th August 1993

Happy Birthday Dot.
Did you know your birthday is the anniversary of Hiroshima?

When you were born you exploded an atomic bomb inside me that's been detonating ever since.

Silver is pregnant again, round and bloated and

233

*happy. I should feel the same way, but I don't. I feel
thin and weak and miserable.*

*Adam is nearly two. He has almost reached the
moment when I last saw you and now every day is
torture as I wonder if you are the same as him.*

*If Silver has a girl this time I might jump off a
bridge.*

5, Drovers Place,
Kelsey KT2 6RJ

6th August 1996

Dear Dot,

*I wanted to write and say Happy Birthday. I think
of you all the time, especially at this time of year and
I look at little girls of your age when I'm on the bus
and wonder if you are the same. 9 years old, I can't
believe it. I have two sons now with Silver and we
live only an hour and a half from you in Kelsey.
They're your half-brothers, Adam who's nearly 5 and
Jake who's 3. I've put my address at the top of this
letter and I would so love you to write back to me.*

*I can't explain properly why I left and didn't
contact you. I didn't plan it and I never thought I'd be
the sort of person who would behave like that. In fact,
I'm not that sort of person. If you met me now you
wouldn't think I was capable of anything like that.
My partner Silver goes out to work and I keep the
house. I've got a little part-time job, but really I look*

after everyone and do all the cooking and cleaning. I think I'm what's known as a 'new man'. My friends from home take the mick a bit, but I hardly ever see them and, anyway, I don't care what anyone else thinks.

I hope your life is going well and I hope your mother and grandmother are well.

Please show this letter to your mother and then write to me and I could come and see you.

Love Dad xx

5, Drovers Place,
Kelsey KT2 6RJ

31st December 1999

Dear Dot,

I am going to contact you this year. I am going to send this letter and fulfil the only New Year's resolution I've ever made. I can't believe that you are 12 and I haven't seen you for 10 years. Although that's not entirely true, I do sometimes sit outside your school and watch you come and go. It was hard to do that unnoticed when you were at Druith Primary, but now you're at Cartertown Secondary it's easy. I was waiting there after your first day in September last year and I couldn't see you in that sea of uniformed bodies and my heart felt like it had dropped out of my body. I sat there shaking and sweating, imagining that Clarice had got her way and sent you to some posh private school, maybe even a boarding school, and I wouldn't have any way of seeing you again. But I waited again the next day and there you were, hard to miss with your bright hair, which I am so glad to see hasn't faded over the years. Please don't ever dye it, Dot.

You have two half-brothers, Adam who is 8 and Jake who is 6. They both go to the local primary in Kelsey. Adam loves it, but Jake can't see the point. Sometimes I can't see the point. It feels unbearably cruel to make him go in there every day when all he wants is to come home with me and potter about at home. I end up telling him that I'll get into trouble if he doesn't go in, which sounds so pathetic, and he still has far too many days on the sofa with a stomach ache. Do you like school? Have you always or did you go through a time when it made you unhappy? And if you did who kissed you better and held your hand? I hope Alice has been a good mother. She is a kind and loving person, but I always found her very closed off, as if she lived behind a brick wall. Sometimes I used to imagine that she was Sleeping Beauty, trapped behind all that overgrown ivy and all I had to do was fight really hard to find a way in. But maybe I didn't try hard enough or maybe she was still asleep, I don't know.

I know she'll have told you about Silver; we're still together and I love her very much. But that doesn't mean I'm proud of what I did or wish I hadn't handled things better. I think about what I did to you all the time; on most days it crowds *everything else out of my brain so that I find it hard to concentrate on the small daily tasks that face me.*

I'm so sorry, Dot. So, so sorry. I hope that is enough. Please write to me or call me (07700 900961) anytime and perhaps we could arrange to meet?

Happy New Millennium.

Love, your Dad xxx

> 5, Drovers Place,
> Kelsey KT2 6RJ
>
> 6th August 2000

Dear Dot,

I am a coward and I probably won't send this letter. I have just sat in my car at the end of your road for two hours, waiting for you to come out. I was the man in the red Volvo talking on his phone as you walked past. Although you probably don't remember seeing me and even if you knew who I was you probably wouldn't speak to me and who could blame you.

You looked amazing today. It's not the first time I've sat in a car and watched you, by the way. Sometimes I wait outside your school and see you with your friend, the girl with the ginger hair. I don't think either of you realise how striking you look, with your flaming hair and determined expressions. The boys probably ignore you a bit

237

now as boys are very obvious at your age and are scared of anything different. But don't change for anyone.

I am trying to find the right words to say I am sorry but I don't think I possess them. I don't think they've been invented. If I knew why I left like I did I'd explain it to myself. I am still with Silver and we have two sons, Adam who's coming up for 9 and Jake who's 7. God, I'd love you to meet them. I'd love to be able to tell them about you. And you'd love Silver. I know your mother has probably told you lots of things about her and she has every right to do so. But Silver is the woman I was always meant to be with. She is kind and warm and generous and wants me to be in contact with you almost as much as I do myself. She wanted me to tell Alice before we left and she spent the first year badgering me to let her know where we were. I don't know why I didn't. I can't explain it.

You look happy and well. I hope Alice and Clarice are as well.

Please write or call (07700 900961).

With much love, Dad x

5th June 2002

Dear Alice,

I know it will be a shock to hear from me and I cannot begin to say sorry enough for what I did all those years ago. Not a day has gone by when I haven't thought about Dot and longed to make it better, but something has always stopped me. My leaving had less to do with you than me; I hope you know that. I hope you recognise me for the angry, stupid young man that I was. I hope that time is nothing more than a bad memory for you now and that your life is full and happy.

I am still with Silver and we have two sons, Adam who'll be 11 this year and Jake 9. We live in Kelsey, which is only an hour and a half from where you are. The reason I am writing is that we are moving house tomorrow and I wanted to send you my new contact details. I know how stupid that must sound considering you didn't know where I was living before. But it's time we sorted all this out. I want to be a father to Dot, if you'll let me. I would love to get to know her again and for her to be part of our lives. She should know her half-brothers, apart from anything else. I'd also like to start contributing financially. I know you don't need my money, but it seems immoral somehow not to be paying in some part for my daughter's life. I have been putting money aside for her each month, which of course she can have, but I'd like to do more. Really, I'd like to get to know her again.

I really hope you and Clarice are well. Please write or ring or email and we can set up a meeting.

23 Downland Avenue, Kelsey, KT1 2GH, 07700 900961, tmarks66@bthubs.com.

Hope to hear from you soon,

Love, Tony

Dear Dot,

   *I read today in the paper about a girl who was
murdered on her way home from school. She got off a
train near her home and walked down a busy road,
taking the same route that she always did. But she
never arrived. Her parents probably went mad, calling
everyone they knew, trying to persuade the police
that it was out of character, calling her mobile incessantly. She was exactly the same age as you and she
stared out of the newspaper at me today with her
sweet smile and eager look in her eyes and I realised
that if anything ever happened to you I would have to
read about it in a newspaper. And then I realised that
I would only read about it if it was newsworthy and
actually a million things could happen which I'd
simply never know about. I could be sitting here
thinking about you and you could not exist any more.
And then I thought, What's the difference anyway?
How do you exist for me? Or how do I exist for you?
Just because you are there is not the same as knowing
anything about you. And surely you have to know
about someone for them to be real. Are you not just
the same as someone I've never met on the other side
of the world? Why do I feel like we are connected just
because we share some genes? The whole thing makes
no sense. Everything I've ever thought is wrong.
Which is no great news really as I am the man who
walked out of his daughter's second birthday party
and never came back, never sent a letter, never picked*

up the phone. I play the part of the family man with
Silver and our two sons, but really I am not that man.
I don't even know the person I am. I wouldn't
recognise him if he punched me in the face right now.
Men fly planes into buildings, countries flood, people
sleep on the streets every night, parents abuse their
children in their homes, wealth is unfair, society is
diseased. And I sit here and think I am any different.
Nothing is real. It's all a joke. We're all a joke. And a
bad one at that.

23 Downland Avenue,
Kelsey, KT1 2GH
07700 900961, tmarks66@bthubs.com

8th July 2005

Dear Dot,
  This letter will come as a surprise to you, but I
have, in some senses, been writing it for sixteen years.
It is 4 a.m. right now, a time I've become well
acquainted with over the years. I spent most of
yesterday and last night watching the news, as I'm
sure you did, as I'm sure most people in Britain did.
It sounds stupid to say that it made me think of you,
but it did. As I watched other people's lives fall apart
on streets a few hours' drive from us, I wondered why
I was ruining my own life. It seemed almost rude to
all those people who were losing their children or
parents or sisters or whatever yesterday. I've spent all

*these years feeling scared of contacting you in case
you hate me and it suddenly seemed so pointless and
such a waste of time.*

*I'll start with the easy bit and tell you something
about myself. I'm sure your mother has filled you in
on the whys and wherefores. Everyone in the village
must have known that I left with Silver, who was the
barmaid at the village pub (it was the Hare and
Hounds back then, but now it's the White Crow). I
know that she will have told you about that and
I know how awful it must sound. All I can say is
that I knew I was meant to be with Silver from the
first moment I spoke to her. I don't know if it will
make you feel any better to learn that we are still
together and we have two sons, Adam who is coming
up for 14 and Jake who is nearly 12, who are
obviously your half-brothers. I did love your mother,
but we were very young and totally wrong for each
other, which is not a good combination. I always
hoped that she would meet someone who could make
her happy. I have sat outside your house quite regu-
larly over the years; it's only a ninety-minute drive
from our home and in my darkest moments it's
calmed me to see you. In a sense I've watched you
grow up. You look like a lovely young woman. I'm so
pleased that your hair has stayed as bright as it ever
was and I love the way you dress, so different from all
those tiny skirts and Ugg boots and skinny jeans that
every other girl of your age seems to wear as a
uniform. In all my watchings I've never seen anyone
else, apart from Alice and Clarice of course, and a*

nice-looking girl of your age who also has ginger hair and who I presume is your friend. It makes me think that your mother hasn't met anyone else; she certainly still has that far-off look in her eyes and this has brought me much sadness. I am often consumed with the thought that I ruined her life and that you will hate me for that. Often I hate myself.

I work in a shop that fixes things. It's a really old-fashioned shop, owned by a lovely man called Ron, who has become like a second father to me, or maybe more like a first father. I've spoken to him about you so much over the years I probably should be paying him, rather than the other way round. He's always told me to contact you, just like Silver, and I've always known that they're both right. I tried lots of jobs before I found this one, but I've been with him for ten years now and I doubt I'll ever leave. All those jobs in call centres and banks and insurance companies chilled my soul. I know that sounds melodramatic, but that's what it felt like. I would walk into those offices and it was like someone had put an icy hand into my stomach and twisted my guts. I would sit at my desk and watch people out of my window and it would seem like a waste to be shuffling numbers and papers which in the end amounted to nothing. After Jake was born Silver and I swapped and I stayed at home and looked after him and Adam and she went to work in a builders' merchants. She runs it now and has just opened their second shop in Cartertown. I'm not ashamed to say that it's because of her that we have a roof over our heads. I

started working for Ron when Jake was 2, just
part-time at first, but as soon as the boys were both
at school full-time I've gone in every day. Ron lets me
leave at 3 and I used to walk down the road and pick
the boys up and take them home for tea or to scouts
or karate or whatever it is they do. Now I go home
and cook supper and wait for them to return.
Somehow this life makes sense to me. I mend broken
things, I look after my sons, I have dinner on the
table when Silver gets home and I go to bed most
nights tired in my bones rather than my mind, which
is so much the best way round. Never let anyone tell
you any different, Dot. We all find our bone-tiredness
in different places but I am sure there is little
meaning in money beyond the obvious and chasing it
is a fool's paradise. What matters to me is us sitting
down to supper together as a family every night,
welcoming Silver home at five and shutting the door
on the world.

I think you have coloured my life to such an extent
that this is the only way I can live. For so many years
I was a stranger to myself, unable to believe that I
could have left you and then never called. My mind
would tell me to pick up the phone, but my fingers
simply refused to punch in the numbers. I was scared
of myself and all the things I could be capable of,
frozen in terror at any action. Silver, the boys and
Ron are the only reason that I am still breathing
today. What I have with them has given me a purpose
and yet I still have this great hole in my soul that
only you can fill.

Are you still reading or have you screwed up this letter in disgust? I know I sound pathetic and I am not trying to justify what I have done. What you want is an explanation and if I had one I would give it to you. Christ, I'd give it to myself.

Silver says I remind her of a very fat woman who stares incessantly at pictures of models in magazines whilst eating cakes and saying that she'll start the diet tomorrow. I torture myself with memories and imaginings of you, always telling myself that I will contact you tomorrow. Yet tomorrow never comes, which I know it a terrible cliché, but sometimes clichés are the only words that make sense. I don't know how Silver has put up with me over the years. There have been two periods over the past sixteen years in which my despair at myself has been so great that I've only functioned with the help of those horrid white pills which the doctors like to dole out. I haven't gone down that route for a while though now; I take my vitamins, exercise well, play football with Adam and Jake, chat to Ron, listen to Silver and life moves on.

I'm not asking you to feel sorry for me, by the way, I just want you to understand as much as I can explain. When I met your mother I was an angry young man. I had left home a few years earlier and I hadn't spoken to my parents since then. I remembered them as mean and unloving, which was true to some extent; my father certainly drank too much but I don't think he was the alcoholic of my memory. He had four young boys, a wife who had to take in other people's ironing and a job in a mine that was shutting down and sometimes he had to choose between food and heating. Show me a man who wouldn't fall apart in that situation? Silver made me contact them again after Adam was born. My dad had stopped drinking by then and my mum and brothers were so pleased to see me, it made me feel ashamed. My mum would adore you, by the way. All of her boys have had boys and I know really she's always wanted a girl. I think she only had me because she thought she was due a daughter. I've never told them about you. But I would so love to take you to meet them. And I know you might be thinking: How come he was able to contact them again but not me? The answer is simple. I could have accepted their rejection, but I have so much (possibly everything) to lose if I hear that you have no interest in seeing me.

Seeing them again made me realise the importance of family and how we only really know ourselves when we know where we've come from. But still I didn't contact you. God, I wanted to. Every night Silver would ask me if I'd done it and I'd shake my head and feel like the world's biggest loser.

You see, by then I didn't know how I was expected to love people and be loved back when I'd let you down so badly. I constantly doubted myself. I would worry that I would find myself walking out on Silver and the boys as if what I had done to you was some sort of sickness. Then I would wonder what the point of contacting you was, considering what a terrible person I was. And then of course time, in this instance, does the opposite of healing; it solidifies like cold porridge, it drags across your mind and laughs at you.

You'll see that I've enclosed a post office book with this letter. I've been putting money in an account for you since I left, not much, as you'll see, and also not nearly enough, but it might help in some way, especially if you're thinking of going on with your studies. I am hesitating about putting it into the envelope because I don't want you to feel like I'm buying you off or that I think money in any way compensates for what I've done. I know it's no substitute for all the bedtime stories I've missed or the dinners I've never cooked you or the kisses I've never given you. All it's meant to be is proof that you've never left my mind, not once, in all the years I've been away. You are going to be 18 very soon and what I would really like would be to know you well enough to buy you a present that would make you smile. I would love to buy you a present.

I'm also going to put in the other letters I've written you and Alice over the years. I never posted any of them, so don't think that your mother didn't show them to you. I've really deliberated over showing you these. You might get the impression from reading them that I'm unstable, and in some senses you'd be right, but I'm not that person now, I'm the person on this page. In the end I think you need to know as much as I can show you and so I'm going to put them into the envelope.

I wish things were different. Sometimes I can't believe that time is real. We fix a lot of clocks in Ron's shop and when all the pieces are lying in front of me waiting to be reassembled I think: We invented that, why do we live by its rules? In the spring and autumn we make it go backwards and forwards and yet it is still our master. And we all know the feeling when it speeds up or slows down. In fact, that first year with Silver was the fastest year of my life and perhaps has some bearing on why I never contacted you (not that I think that's an adequate excuse). I imagine rearranging time by putting the pieces together differently and going back to the day I left. I would have still made a life with Silver, but I would have been braver. I would have stayed for your birthday party and then told Alice properly and now you'd be coming to stay every other weekend and I'd know things about you. I never planned to walk out like I did. But (and I've never told anyone this, not even Silver), I suddenly realised that if I stayed and witnessed you becoming two I would never leave and if that happened I was going to die or become so bitter that I would have been a horrid father and husband. By which I don't mean that Alice or Clarice are bad people, but they were too different from me, so far removed from anything I understood that I felt completely lost in that life. Even the house terrified me with all its blind turns and false doors. I used to feel like it was laughing at me, like it knew I was no match for it and nothing but an interloper.

I don't know if she's ever told you, but Alice never wanted us to live there when she found out she was pregnant. I used to get so annoyed with her when she was carrying you, as she'd go on about how we could live on love and cheese on toast on the Cartertown *estate and I used to think: You don't know what you're talking about. But maybe she was right and I was the one who didn't know what I was talking about. Because I was very narrow in my thinking back then and there isn't ever only one way to travel, you know, Dot.*

But maybe we are the people we are only because of the things that have happened to us? Maybe everything has a meaning? I'm not sure; I wonder what the people lying in hospital now after having been blown up on their way to work would say to that. I long to know what sort of person you are. Are you going to university? How did you do in your A Levels? What music do you like? What's your favourite food? God, and that's only scratching the surface. I can tell what Jake and Adam are thinking by the turn of their mouths and yet I don't know the most basic things about you. And yet I love you just as much as I love them. How is that possible? How can I love you when all I have of you is the imprint of that last hug, the smell of the top of your head from that last moment, the sight of your eyes as I walked away?

Dot, I have laid all my cards on the table. I deserve nothing but contempt from you. I know that. But I am asking for your forgiveness. One of the things that I learnt when I took Adam to see my parents when he was first born was that being a parent does not give you some mystical inner knowledge. We have more training when we start a new job than when we have a baby and yet it is the most important, scary and difficult thing we'll ever do in our lives.

As I watched my mother hold my son I realised that she was nothing more than a guessing, fallible human. That she had made mistakes because that is what humans do. I made a huge, grotesque mistake which I have been repeating every day of my life for sixteen years. I've paid a large personal price for this and so, no doubt, have you. I am truly sorry and, whatever else comes from this, I hope you will always remember that. My leaving had nothing to do with you. You were, and I am sure are, an amazing, special and beautiful young lady. I have this dream that you will come and visit and we will sit round our kitchen table: you, me, Silver, Adam and Jake. That I will cook us dinner and we will all laugh at something and for a brief second it will feel normal. Although maybe the beauty of it will be in the fact that it isn't normal, that our family will have been hard won. I am here waiting for you, we are all here waiting for you, and I hang on to this image so hard it sometimes feels like it has been branded onto my brain.

Enough. It is now 4:49 a.m. and I am going to get into my car and drive this letter to your house and post it through your front door. I have just been upstairs and told Silver this and she hugged me and told me she was proud. I peeked in on Adam and Jake, sleeping peacefully, and hope they will know their sister soon.

Dot, I love you. What happens now is up to you.

Dad xxx

21 . . . Kindness

Dot woke into a suspension. She momentarily forgot where she was and panicked at the sparse surroundings of the B and B, but then she remembered her journey the night before and the reason why she was there. She reached out for her phone but it had turned itself off. She pressed the green button and it sang itself awake like a mechanical bird. It was 10.05 a.m. which meant she'd slept through her alarm – if it had even gone off – and now she'd probably have to queue for hours at Charles House. She dialled Mavis's number in an attempt to quell her rising anxiety, but even after three attempts she couldn't make the connection. She got out of bed and showered quickly in the tiny cubicle in the corner of her room and then dressed hurriedly. Something was wrong. Dot stood still for a moment, trying to work out what, but no answers came. There seemed to be a silence, as though time had trapped her in a bubble and she no longer existed.

The front desk was empty when she got downstairs and the front door open. She could see the lady who had checked her in the evening before standing on the steps, slippers on her feet and a gaggle of people around her. They were smoking cigarettes and pointing up the road. Dot hoisted her bag further up her shoulder and stepped into the sunshine.

'Excuse me,' she said to the lady, who turned to reveal a tear-stained face. 'Oh, I'm sorry, I just wanted to pay my bill.' The others turned round as well at this and Dot saw they were all crying, their faces grey, so that Dot wondered what reality she'd landed in.

The woman waved her away. 'Don't worry.'

'But I stayed here last night.'

'It's all over anyway. Doubt I'll have a business this time next week. Doubt any of us will.'

Dot tried to make sense of what she was hearing, but the group of people closed around her landlady again, leaving Dot to wonder if she actually existed. She looked down the road and saw five police cars parked across it at right angles and a crowd of people jostling to see over them. There were more women weeping on the pavements and children seemed to have vanished from the world. A shoe and a briefcase were pathetically discarded in the middle of the road. Then the noise exploded into her ears: the sirens peeling through the air, cutting and shattering normality. And the smell: acrid smoke and a choking sickness.

Dot left the crying group and walked towards the cars. Halfway there she saw a girl and boy of about her age.

'Don't go no further,' shouted the girl, so Dot crossed the road to speak to them, pleased at least that someone had noticed her.

'What's happened?'

'Are you tripping?'

'No, I just woke up.'

'Man.' She whistled through her teeth.

'What's happened?'

'Al-Qaida, innit,' said the boy. 'Has to be. It's all over, man.'

'What d'you mean?' Dot could hear her own desperation.

'Like, bombs everywhere. The police say there's more. They could be anywhere.'

'Are the tubes shut?' she asked, now wanting only to be at home.

The boy laughed at this. 'Of course they're shut.'

'D'you have a phone I could borrow?' Dot tried. 'I need to call home and mine's not working.'

'No one's is working,' he answered and as he spoke Dot saw the gold in his teeth. 'Like I said, it's all over. Civilisation as we know it and all that shit.'

'Anyway, don't call,' said the girl. 'It'd be bad luck. I walk there every day.' She held her hand up to her face. 'I was only late this morning cos my mum was freaking cos I forgot to get her script last night.'

Nothing was making any sense to Dot. All she knew for certain was that somewhere out there was a coach which could take her home. 'Can I walk to Victoria from here?'

'Are you mad, sister?' asked the boy.

'But I need to get to the coach station. I need to get home.'

The girl sighed at this. 'You got a pen and paper?'

Dot rooted through her bag until she found one and the girl rewarded her with a basic map. Her boyfriend nudged her. 'Something's happening,' he said. 'My cousin told me something big was gonna go down. He's psychic, you know.' Excitement rippled through his voice, jangling the words he was saying, which Dot could see he barely understood.

Dot took the girl's rudimentary map. 'Anyway, thanks for that.'

'You take care,' said the girl, her eyes already back up the street.

Dot walked away from them and it felt lonely. The walk looked doable. She noticed that halfway along the girl had drawn an arch and on it a lady in a chariot. Next to it she'd written: 'Some warrior woman, can't remember her name, but you'll know it when you see it.' It was oddly well drawn and Dot was touched by the attention to detail. She wondered what the girl did, where she went every morning, why her mum needed a prescription.

There were policemen everywhere, but still fear marched along the streets next to them all. Dot recognised the fear as she walked. She realised that she had been frightened all her life: of sitting in the wrong chair, of upsetting her mother, of not doing well enough at school, of being laughed at by her peers, of never meeting her father. But this fear was different. This fear was visceral, it swept through her blood, confusing her mind, blocking her ears, drying her throat, heating her body.

Dot's country had been at war for over half her life in places that seemed as far away as they were on the map. Language that she didn't understand was shouted out of screens, politics she didn't listen to spouted by men in suits. She had marched against wars; she had spoken the right words. But in the end she was a child of conflict and that conflict had finally tracked her down, just as it did, on a daily basis, to the people of those hot, desert lands.

The streets were thronged and most people were on their own, but still everyone kept their eyes down because who could you trust if people were prepared to stand next to you and blow themselves and you to nothing? Often roads were closed and the police wearily directed them down another street, into which they filed like proverbial sheep. She heard people talking as she passed them: hundreds were dead, no, thousands, more bombs were imminent, the skies had been closed, the government had already been evacuated. It was impossible to tell what was real and what wasn't, but Dot believed everything she heard because in the end it seemed better than not believing anything.

Dot stopped after a while and tried to buy some water and chocolate but the man behind the counter waved her money away, as her landlady had done, his eyes glued to the TV above the counter.

'Thanks,' said Dot, but he didn't hear.

She ate as she walked and the sugar filled her blood with enough energy to stop her from crying. More than anything she wanted to call home. There was no doubt that Mavis would have let her mum and gran know where she was by now. It occurred to her that she could have used the phone at the B and B, but she never thought of landlines any more. Her mobile was still dead.

Everyone was going home. That's where they were all heading. Lots of men and women in suits, some with backpacks, a few briefcases, designer handbags, plastic bags. Dot thought this must be what the end of the world would be like: everyone reduced to the same moment, walking the same streets, desperately looking for home.

She didn't need to shut her eyes to see her home as if it was on a screen in front of her. The heavy brown velvet curtains in the sitting room which were fraying at the ends because they had been closed on generations of nights. The polished dark floorboards and the oriental rug with its reds and browns and patterns she might never understand. The huge mirror covered in age spots which hung just inside the front door and

255

blurred your own image. The black marble fireplace, heavy with photographs, and the clock which always lost time. Her grandmother's blue velvet chair by the fire; the sofa with the indentations of lives on its seat. China which mattered to her grandmother on all the surfaces; the outdated kitchen in which her mother cooked bad food. The huge staircase which led to bedrooms; the tower which fooled anyone who came calling. The cupboard in the study which opened on to a flight of stairs leading into a huge stone cellar.

Of course none of these were the real reasons why she wanted to go home so much. The real reasons were the two women who lived with her in the house. She heard her grandmother admonishing her in her mind, saw them laughing at a film together on a dark night. 'Choke up, chicken,' her grandmother would say whenever she coughed. She felt her mother's hand on her hot forehead as she lay in bed, watched Alice's face as she recounted her days at school, listened as she read her a bedtime story. Towels had always been wrapped around her body after warm baths, Christmas trees stood bedecked every year, school concerts were never missed, kisses often given, laughter sometimes heard, dreams recounted, radiators turned on or windows opened, fresh flowers in vases, mown lawns, hot tea.

As Dot walked the bleak streets the colour of thunderclouds, strewn with rubbish and disaster, she realised the absurdity of where she found herself. What was she doing looking for the name of a man who had barely existed, who had left without looking back? She had two people in her life who loved her more than most people deserved. She had a good friend and a hopeful future. And yet she'd risked it all on a man who didn't care.

She lost her way many times and everyone she asked for directions told her not to bother going to Victoria. But where else was there to go? Her purse held a scrap of paper which was quite literally her ticket home. A long ride on a warm coach to the place she wanted to be. It was four-thirty by the time she reached the coach station and her feet felt swollen and her limbs ached. The place was seething with people. All the departure boards were blank and loudspeaker announcements told everyone to please be patient, they would try to resume some kind of service as soon as possible. Dot sat on a bench and let herself cry. Of course it had been stupid to imagine that the men who drove the coaches wouldn't want to rush back to their own families. Maybe London had been cut off. She didn't know anything any more.

The woman next to her was somewhere between her mother and grandmother's age and Dot could feel her gazing at her.

'Are you all right?' she asked in the end.

Dot looked at her and saw that she was round and bright, with a mass of blond curls shining incongruously on top of her head. 'Not really. I want to go home.'

'Where's home?'

'Well, I need to get to Cardiff, then it's a couple of hours from there.'

'I need to get to Oxford.' The blonde woman held out a tissue, which Dot took. 'They'll get us on to coaches as soon as they can, you know. There's nothing we can do but be patient.'

'I know. It's just I walked so far.'

'And you're so looking forward to getting home?' Dot nodded. 'We're all looking forward to getting home today.'

'I know.'

'Who's at home?'

'My mum and gran. They'll be worried sick.'

'I just got hold of my daughter,' said the woman. 'Apparently they've turned the signals back on.'

'Really?' Dot took her phone from the front of her bag and dialled her number. It rang and in seconds it was answered. 'Mum.'

The words which gushed out of her mother were simply an expression of relief. 'Dot! Dot, oh my God, Dot. Are you OK?'

Dot could only cry down the phone. 'I'm fine.'

Her mother was shouting off-stage, 'Mum, Dot's OK,' and it took Dot a minute to compute that her mother's mum was her grandmother. 'Where are you?'

'Victoria coach station. There're no coaches but I'm going to wait here until there is one.'

'Oh God, we thought . . . What happened?'

'I don't know, I think I slept through it. Then it's taken me all this time to get here and the phones weren't working.'

'I'm so sorry that you're there.'

'It's OK, Mum. Listen, I'll call you as soon as I know when I'll be in.'

'And we'll come and get you.'

'OK.'

'I love you, Dot.'

'Love you too. And Gran.'

'Dot, I want to explain. I want to tell you about him.'

'I know, Mum. They'll be time.'

'But I should have . . . I'm sorry . . . I . . .'

'Mum,' Dot could only think of one thing to say. 'I found a photo of him under your bed, years ago. But then I thought it wasn't him because of the hair.'

258

'The hair?'

'This man had dark hair and so do you.'

'Your dad had brown hair.'

'But, how come, I mean why is my hair red?'

Her mother sighed. 'That's from Grandad. There are so many photos of him, I mean, I didn't know you didn't know that.'

Dot saw their mantelpiece, she searched the photos. There they were, the young man bouncing her mother as a baby, marrying her grandmother, smiling on a boat. 'They're black and white,' she said finally. 'They're black and white.'

'Oh, Dot.' said her mother.

'It's OK, Mum,' Dot replied.

The woman was smiling when Dot got off the phone. 'They've called my coach,' she said, getting up. 'You know, it'll be OK.'

Dot looked at her. 'What will?'

'They want us to think that the world is bad, the people who did this. But it isn't, you know. Most people are kind and most things are wonderful.' She touched Dot's hand as she spoke and her fingers were icy cold. 'Keep calm. You'll be home soon.'

The woman disappeared into the crowd and only after she'd gone did Dot wish she'd asked her how she knew any of that to be true – how anyone could know that? –and whether or not life was wonderful or if that lady had simply had a wonderful life. Ultimately, it had been nothing more than a small act of kindness, one person's attempt to make her feel better. And yet it had worked. Sometimes small acts were all you needed.

The first two coaches to Cardiff were filled up before Dot could get on, so it wasn't until midnight that she was able to take a seat on the vehicle that would transport her home. She'd spoken to her mother five times by then and Mavis once. Mavis told her that her own mother had gone to sit with Alice while they were waiting for news. That she had come home and wept on her father's shoulder and he'd held on to her as though he'd meant it. 'There's so much I have to tell you, Dot,' she'd said, 'so much we didn't know.' And Dot had laughed at that and said, 'No shit, Mave.'

Dot sat in her seat and let the heating warm her tired toes, shutting her eyes against the brutality of the day. Her head felt unbearably heavy on her neck, and as her eyes relaxed against the lights on the motorway her body took her down while her mind pulled her back up. She occupied that moment between sleeping and waking more than any metaphysical poet on that journey and in those moments she forgot who she was. The wheels on the coach turned, propelling them over the concrete beneath their feet, each revolution taking them further away from the chaos and closer to home. You couldn't worry for all those left behind that night, you could only be thankful that you were saved, that you had a chance to start again.

Dot woke to the light of dawn, which she saw out of the window of the coach as it rushed along the motorway. Up ahead the hugeness of the Severn Bridge loomed like a child's drawing. The traffic pulled them along, on to the heavy metal structure held together by gigantic bolts and titanic feats of engineering. The houses on the hillsides were like white building blocks, a few miles distancing them from the English ones they'd passed only minutes before. The towns beckoned and receded, held together by a seam of industry which spewed smoke, but today made Dot feel as though she was coming home.

Everything still seemed unreal; even the fact that she had

been in London was beginning to fade. Eventually the coach took the turning to Cardiff and she saw the fields and open spaces turn into the greys of buildings and factories. Traffic lights now slowed their progress and her skin itched with the anticipation of arrival. The clock read 6:24 a.m. as they pulled into the coach station.

Dot's mother and grandmother stood on the sand-coloured concourse waiting for her, along with all the other families having loved ones returned to them on this new day. She stepped off the coach and felt herself running before she could check herself, rushing into the arms of the two people she could have stayed at home to see. And as she stood there Dot knew that she would forget so much about the previous day, so many memories would become blurred with half-truths and things she heard, but that she must not forget this moment. She felt as if she had been on a strange circular dance, turning in ever-decreasing circles, spinning like a top with no resolution. But in the moment of seeing her odd little family, of being held by them and holding on to them, she stopped. She knew she might forget the kind woman and even the frightened faces, but that she would remember this. There was a way to stand still. And anyway, Dot thought from the midst of her strange triangular hug, aren't we all just guessing? It could even be true to say that when her father left he probably wasn't entirely sure he was doing the right thing.

'Anthony George Marks,' her mother said finally. 'Your dad's name is Tony. He left on your second birthday and I haven't heard from him since. But he was here. He was here and he loved you very much.'

'It doesn't matter, Mum,' said Dot. 'Really, it doesn't matter any more.'

'Come on,' said her grandmother. 'Let's get you home.'

The drive back was uneventful. Dot felt her tiredness deep in her limbs and she couldn't do much more than doze in the back. No one spoke and they left the radio silent but the silence was beautiful. By the time they pulled up in front of their home it was bright and warm, the day promising perfect summer conditions, because of course that particular wheel simply turned, unaware of the tragedies which befell those brave enough to live.

Dot's mother unlocked their front door and they crossed the threshold, stepping over a bulging letter which had been pushed through their letterbox only a few hours earlier, at exactly the same time as Alice and Clarice had arrived in Cardiff to pick up Dot. None of them would ever know about that particular coincidence and none of them even noticed the letter at that moment, so eager were they to bathe and feed and enclose Dot. But they would notice it in the coming hours. They would open it and read it. They would cry over it and Dot would want to burn it. But, in the second small act of kindness shown to Dot in less than twenty-four hours, Alice would stop her. With her mother standing behind her Alice would tell her daughter to ring the number. She would tell her that we are all capable of mistakes, but that the important thing to remember is that we are all also just as capable of forgiveness.

'It is only when you stop forgiving that you stop living,' Alice said as Dot wiped away her tears. She looked out of the window at the new day and realised that, as she said the words, so they became true.

Acknowledgements

Firstly, massive thanks to everyone at HarperCollins, who are consistently patient and helpful and bursting with amazing ideas. Especially my editor, Lousia Joyner, who is insightful and kind and a complete pleasure to work with. Thanks also to Carol MacArthur who is always on the other end of the phone and knows the answers to everything I ask.

Also, as ever, thanks to the people who have to put up with me on a daily basis, my husband Jamie and our children Oscar, Violet and Edith. (Feel free to read it now, Jamie!)

This book has been rattling around in my head for a long time and, as a result, a few people have read it in various incarnations over the years. I have received lots of encouragement and advice from many people, but most especially my friends Polly, Amy, Craig and Richard, my sisters Posy and Ernestina and my mother, Lindy.

The biggest champion of this book has however been my father, David, who has read *Dot* in every version, not just with encouragement, but also with constructive advice. Which is not a surprise, as he is the reason why I love reading and writing as much as I do. I was lucky enough to grow up in a house filled with books, with a father who guided my reading and was never too busy to talk to me about it. If I have learnt anything from my parents it is that the things that matter in life are not what we would expect and certainly not material, which is a lesson I hope to pass on to my own children.

So, whilst Dot's parents are somewhat absent, mine have been ever present, something for which I am truly grateful.

A Q&A with Araminta Hall

What inspired you to write _Dot_?

No one thing inspired me, I have just always been very interested in our relationships with our families and how myths and mistakes can seep through generations. I wanted to explore how we are often most secretive with the people we are closest to and how small actions can have huge consequences that reverberate down the generations. I'm also very intrigued by the idea of story-telling itself and, for me, _Dot_ is as much a story about stories as anything else. All of our history, both public and personal, is only a succession of stories and each time they are told the person telling them brings their own experience to bear. So, as such, nothing that we know can ever be called completely real. I wanted to write about people trapped in their own stories but unable to tell their way out of them, not even really aware that they are trapped. The events of the book, however, evolved. I completely re-wrote this novel four times over ten years, writing another novel in between and sometimes not going back to it for years at a time. As a result the finished book is very different from anything which could have inspired me in the beginning.

You mention in your Acknowledgements that _Dot_ is a book which 'has been rattling around in my head for a long time'. Can you expand a little on this and on your own creative process?

Yes, this book has had a very long gestation. I've always wanted to be a novelist, since I was a little girl and _Dot_ has in some ways been my first real attempt at a book. I'm not sure that I will ever write another book in the same way that I wrote _Dot_. Certainly my first published novel, _Everything and Nothing_, was a very different process and the one I am working on now is following a more straight-forward pattern. As a rule however, writing for me is always based in character. I like to know my characters inside out and often they do things I am not expecting, which sounds bizarre, but is true. As yet I have never planned the events of a novel, but find that they evolve because that is how my characters would behave. Which is not to say that plot is not fundamental to a good book. I am very aware that you cannot just write about people and relationships, but that you need to ground it within a believable and good story. I am a great believer in sitting down and writing and not caring about how good I think it is as I know I will change it so many times. I re-wrote _Dot_ so many times simply because I knew it wasn't working as a story and of course with every re-writing your characters and plot get tighter and hopefully your writing gets better. In a nutshell my creative process involves copious reading and writing and re-writing.

Much of the book focuses on different female relationships, often as a source of conflict but also great intimacy and protection. How important would you say the role of female relationships is throughout a woman's life?

For me women are absolutely integral to my happiness and wellbeing. I am lucky to be married to a lovely man and have a fantastic son, but without the women in my life I would flounder. From your mother to your sisters to your daughters to your friends, women support each other. It is women who I turn to when I have a problem or feel low because women are so great at honesty. There is a chapter in *Dot* when Alice meets Sandra and feels enclosed by their friendship, which is what women do for each other. We break down society's myths and reassure each other that we are not alone, that what we are feeling is normal. Because women still operate primarily in the domestic arena and that is a solitary and lonely place. My best advice to any of my friends who get pregnant is always to find themselves a network of women as quickly as possible.

Would you say these relationships change and evolve over a woman's life, especially after having children?

Absolutely. The first relationship that changes is the one with your mother as you suddenly need her help in a way you haven't done since you were a child. You also of course see her differently, suddenly understanding the reasons

269

why she said and did the things that annoyed you in your own childhood. Then of course you develop relationships with other women who are sleep deprived and feeling like they're going mad, you drink tea and laugh at the fact that you haven't even brushed your teeth in a week and everyone feels better. My children are all at school now, but I still have a network of friends who I don't need to explain anything to and we still help and support each other constantly. And then of course life comes full circle. I have just watched my mother help my grandmother through the last years of her life, where the roles were reversed and it was often like watching my mother deal with another child. I think women are always like the central pin in the wheel, with an eye on all the moving parts and only other women really understand this.

Are any of the characters and relationships in *Dot* based on people you know or knew?

Clarice is very like my grandmother. All Clarice's strange beliefs are hers and the not being allowed to sit many of the chairs round the dining room table comes straight from her house. Like Clarice though my grandmother was very intuitive and caring if you got beyond her hard exterior. She was worth listening to, something I only realised quite late in her life. The other characters however are totally made up and nothing like anyone I know.

Much of the novel is centred on Dot's search for her father, with Chapter 20 being wholly comprised of letters from him to Dot. How important, would you say, is the presence of a strong parental figure in one's life and to what extent does it impact a child's identity?

I think it is totally essential to know where you come from. Which is a different thing from saying that we all need to be part of a nuclear family. We live in a modern world in which the idea of family has blurred and evolved. Dot's problem is not that her father is absent, but that she has no idea who he is, or if he even existed. I know families of every shape and size, with almost every permutation of relevant adults as you can imagine and what makes their children secure is a knowledge of where they came from and that they were wanted. On the cusp of adulthood Dot needs this information before she can move on with her life.

Are there any authors who influenced *Dot*, or who have influenced your work in general?

I don't know whether any writers have influenced my work, although I think it is sometimes hard not to find your writing marked by a very good book. It is probably however no coincidence that my favourite writers are ones who deal with families and our relationship to the world, like Anne Tyler, Alice Munro, Margaret Atwood, John Irving and Charlotte Brontë (to name but a few!).

On p. 26, Alice concludes that her mother Clarice 'saw the world as a place of threat and violence and manners and rules. It was obvious now to Alice that she had simply never been in love.' Is love presented as a source of liberation in this book?

I wish I could answer yes to that and I wish life was that simple; that love can save us. Of course love can do this, but no emotion is one-dimensional and the flip side of love is fear, paranoia and heartbreak. I sometimes think that loving someone is one of the bravest things we do as humans. When I had my first child fourteen years ago I felt proper fear for the first time and spent the first two years of his life in a pretty constant state of anxiety. We love in so many different ways, as children, parents, partners and friends and each brings its own perils and joys. A life without love would be miserable and I think that many of the characters in this book are unhappy because they are holding back what they feel for each other. I'm not trying to say that learning how to love will bring them unbridled happiness, but it seems like a good place to start. Learning to let go in love is an important lesson that we all need to learn at some point. We are not in control of either who we love or who loves us and this is why loving is so often an act of bravery. Perhaps it is fair to say that expressing their love for each other brings the characters in *Dot* a sense of self-liberation, which might make their lives that bit easier.

To what extent do Clarice and Alice's differences reflect the changing attitudes and expectations of women? Is Clarice a product of her generation, more than anything else?

I'm not sure that Clarice and Alice are that different actually. Of course the way they interact with the world is skewed by the times they live in, but in fact I think they have a similar attitude to life, if only they would speak to each other and break out of their own head spaces. Clarice is certainly a product of a generation who believed in manners and rules, but I think Alice is wrong to think that she has never been in love or that she fails to love now. Dot is as much a product of her generation as Clarice is and in fact, all three women are more a product of their experiences than anything else. All three of them have been abandoned in one way or another; Clarice by her mother and Howie, Alice by Tony and Dot by her father. They share this fundamental marker and yet none of them have ever spoken to each other about it; they are very similar characters, how they deal with it is, however, influenced by the times they occupy.

What would you like the reader to take away from this novel?

Whatever they want. For me that is absolutely the joy of reading, occupying a world that is your own for the time it takes to be there. It is very rare that you ever talk about a book with someone and find yourself in complete agreement (something which book groups across the land could no doubt testify to). I have spoken to strangers about my first book and heard them say things which I had not consciously meant anyone to take from my writing, but which I realise is there. I hope that people find *Dot* uplifting, but really as long as people enjoy reading it, I am happy for them to take from it what they will.

Do you have a favourite book?

I have been asked that question a lot since my first novel was published and of course the answer is no as there are so many books which I have loved. When pressed to pick one I do however find myself answering *A Prayer for Owen Meany* by John Irving. For me this is a pretty perfect book filled with pathos and love, families, struggles and meaning. It is one of the few books I have re-read more than twice and each time it leaves me breathless.

Many writers say that finding a particular place to write a novel is essential to their writing routine and helps with creativity. Do you have any personal habits that help you when you're writing?

No, I have three children and a husband who commutes so I handle the majority of our domestic life. Our youngest started school last year which has made life a bit easier, but I think creative routines and places are the luxury of male writers! I write whenever and wherever, my only constant being a cup of tea. I'm not very good at leaving mess and so I tend to drop the kids at school, walk the dog, rush round the house and then hopefully sit down for an hour or two before the kids need picking up. Although, realistically I'm lucky to do that more than three days a week. Maybe in ten years I'll only be able to write when wearing a yellow jumper drinking my tea out of a special mug, but for now I can't afford to be picky or I'd write about two words a week.